The Known Stranger

The Known Stranger

V. Krishnamoorthy

MP
MAHAVEER PUBLISHERS

Published by
MAHAVEER PUBLISHERS
4764/2A, 23-Ansari Road, Daryaganj
New Delhi – 110002
Ph. : 011 – 66629669–79–89
e-mail : mahaveerpublishers@gmail.com

First Edition: February 2012

The Known Stranger
ISBN(10) : 8183520979
ISBN(13) : 9788183520973

This novel is entirely a work of fiction. The names, characters and incidents portrayed in it are the work of the author's imagination. Any resemblance to actual persons, living or dead, events or localities is entirely coincidental.

Distributed in India by
VAIBHAV BOOK SERVICE
e-mail : vaibhavbookservice@gmail.com

Distributed in Nepal by
BAJRANGBALI BOOK ENTERPRISES PVT. LTD.
Jyatha Mushyabahal, Ward No. 27, Kathmandu, Nepal
e-mail : bajrangbalibooks@gmail.com

Printed by Jaico Printers, New Delhi

Dedication

To my father

Acknowledgement

I wish to thank my family. This novel would not have been written without for the support I received from my family. They dispensed love that I never deserved.

I also wish to thank Stanley Paul Memury, for countless number of things.

I wish to thank the entire team of Mahaveer Publishers, for making my dream come true. Any one, who is capable of writing, wishes to see his book, one day, in print and I am not an exception. I am indebted to their invaluable contribution. If lapses, or mistakes, remain in the narration, the blame rests squarely on me.

And finally, thanks sai and Narendiran for being there.

"As flies to wanton boys
Are we to the gods
They kill us for their sport..."
- King Lear, Act IV

Prologue

Five months after my father died, I had to go to the railway station to receive Bhaskar. He was not keeping well either, and he could not make it to Bombay for the funeral. He came now to pay his last respects to his departed friend and meet my mother. The five months had been hectic – followed by the funeral, the notorious rites, the endless well-wishers and Neelam's operation. The doctors were called immediately as he had agreed to donate his kidney. My daughter was finally told about her congenital flaw and the magnanimity of my father's gesture. Her recovery from the operation was still not complete. Why did Bhaskar have to come now and remind everything that the family was trying to forget?

Bhaskar broke down when he saw my mother and what I feared, had happened. Healing wounds were ripped open and the amount of crying must have led my neighbour to believe that someone else had died again.

I started tidying up my father's desk, just to avoid spending time with Bhaskar. Words were still filtering in. Bhaskar finished the task of rekindling all the forgotten memories in my mother and turned his attention to Maria.

"Do you know that it was Anand's idea to approach your parents without exposing the lover angle? He wanted me to do the talking just to lend more credibility to the proposal. He always had this high thinking," exhaled Bhaskar dramatically.

I was surprised. I would never have credited my father with such inventiveness. Even now what was the guarantee that Bhaskar was not making it up? Were we not all brought up to respect the dead?

I spotted the bag containing the last instalment of the medicines. As I was getting ready to dispose it, I remembered that I had not stood in the medical shop for the last four months. I was smiling.

Something did not feel right with the bag. I opened it and saw that the last batch of medicines, I bought, was almost intact. I say almost, because all the sixty tablets of Inderal were missing. I fumbled around in the desk, on the table, and in all the possible places even as my heart was racing. Suddenly I knew what had happened, and my search grew more desperate, in order to prove my fears wrong.

"Be careful about any overdose, particularly with Inderal. While these medicines are necessary to keep the degeneration at a check, Inderal is known for its notorious side effects. An overdose of Inderal could well be lethal."

Things were becoming increasingly clear to me, as I frantically searched the room for the missing tablets, steadily realising that I would not be able to find them, while the above warning, that our doctor uttered regarding the tablets, to Maria, was playing in my mind.

The withdrawal inwards; the silence; the phone calls; the bank accounts; and the final "Goodnight" – I started crying silently at first and then with complete abandon.

Bhaskar, my mother, and Maria were not sure, why I was crying, now, five months after my father died.................

CONTENTS

1

The Birth of Another Son

Mullaikudi is smaller than a village – the English language may not have an adjective to describe a place so small. If all the homes in the place had removed the walls in between and lived under one roof, it would have qualified as a fairly large mansion. That's how small the place was. Forget finding the place on a map, even the bus driver plying on that trip could not tell where exactly it was. If you wanted to go to Mullaikudi, you had to take a bus from Tanjavur to Thrukattupalli and get down near a banyan tree, some 12 kilometres before the last stop. From there it was a 4 kilometre walk through lush green fields that only a village can offer. If you are wealthy, it could be possible to cover that distance in one-tenth of the time you took on your own bullock cart. The place had not become commercialised enough in the early 20th century to conceive about running a bullock cart as a business enterprise. Either you were wealthy and rode in your own cart or you walked.

The priest walked. His walk was weary. Not because of his age. He was weighed down with the thought of the imminent arrival of another child in the family. His wife, his second, was very advanced with their next child. The midwife was certain the child could be born any day now. In the characteristic way that defined the male mentality of that period, he was cursing his wife for this predicament as if he had no role in the situation. This would be his seventh child. Actually it was the eighth if you chose to count the one through his first wife; eleventh, if you took into account the two that were stillborn and one that died in its third year. The cause of death was never known. Not surprising considering the fact the medicine for any ailment was either the holy ash from the Shiv Mandir or the vermilion from the Kaliamman temple. The priest juggled the two with consummate ease and developed his own system of complete randomness that was impossible to duplicate. His one fear was that if the wailing village folk with an unconscious child draped over their shoulder could judge beforehand if it was going to be the ash or vermilion, then he could lose his unique monopolistic position of the priest and the doctor rolled into one. Most of the children in the village were actually healthy and needed no treatment. The few that really needed treatment died after a week of ash or vermilion. The death was usually an act of God. Every family in the village usually had about eight or nine children and the death of any one, however sad, was not inconsolable. The priest used to ride in his own bullock cart, but that was before he married off his three daughters. He had two more daughters left. He was resigned to the fact that by the time those two get married, his land and house also would go away. His son through his first marriage was already married and settled in Madras. He only had some vague recollections of his son growing up as his growth was punctuated usually with the birth of the other children through his second wife. This boy was surprisingly intelligent for someone in this surrounding and to the surprise of many, not in the least like his father. He had completed his schooling, all 11 years of it. That you needed to walk 6 miles a day and survive on food that was available, never that was liked, helped tide over the occasional fever with ash/vermilion making it a Herculean task. The priest had no distinct recollection of his journey to Madras or the son settling down with a job and a family of his own. All he remembered was the dowry he collected, 70 per cent of which went towards his third daughter's marriage. He was successful because he gambled away the remaining 30 per cent and convinced his wife that he had fallen in debt because he had to spend more than what he had inherited through his son's wedding. The wife, ever the believer in Indian society, mortgaged her mangalsutra and gave him the money, which he promptly went and lost in another night of cards. The priest was doing some mental calculations. After certainly losing his remaining wealth in the marriage of the remaining two daughters, he was now left with one son. That would have meant an additional dowry after a clean slate. If the impending child was to be a daughter, it would have meant going back to zero. If it was a son again, then bingo! Though still strong in his libido and not afflicted with any life threatening ailments, he decided that this would be his last child. The combinations of the incoming dowry and outgoing expenditure eased his mind to a sense of drugged stupor. So it is with an absolutely carefree mind the priest reached his home to be told that he was now the proud father of another son.

2

Anand

Naming the son proved to be tricky. In the time tested tradition of that period, the names of grandfathers, grandmothers and more popular gods had already been used up in naming his predecessors. The priest had enough time. You named your child on the eleventh day after his birth. So the priest decided on a very different name – Anand, meaning 'happiness'. Little did he know then that the child would grow up to see more than its share of misery too.

Anand's childhood was far from spectacular. He grew up with the usual near misses. There was on many occasions a very thin line between his continuation on Mother Earth and a swift goodbye. Though he had two sisters in the house yet to be married off when he was born and who still remained spinsters by the time he reached his obligatory school-going days, he developed a strong bonding only with his elder brother, Gopal. Though events in his later life made him responsible for the lives of most of his sisters, his love and loyalty to his brother Gopal remained steadfast, much to the surprise of many in the family and often to even himself.

One fine sunny morning in June 1936, he set out for his first day at school. Accompanying him on this mission was his mentor, big brother Gopal. "I will tell you something about school that you do not know," said Gopal.

"What?" asked Anand with an air of expectation and abject submission that only a younger sibling is capable of.

"There is nothing to learn here. We are sent only because our mother and sisters can do the work at home uninterrupted while father can play cards with his friends without setting a bad example in front of us. The teachers are better off without us. They will make you feel that right away from day one. For them we are a responsibility that they do not want. We are the same for our parents back at home. The compromise between our unwilling parents and an underpaid teacher was the starting point of his joining a school."

This was too much for Anand. He did not understand it fully. He was too scared to ask his brother to repeat it. The general scheme of things as understood and explained by Gopal became clear. They are expected to spend the day at school and the nights at home, both places where they were not wanted. The evenings were one grey area. No one told you what you should do. By implication no one told you what you *should not* do either. The evenings were the best time of Anand's childhood. Even as he grew up, he always was in his best frame of mind..

The budding philosopher Gopal stopped attending school from the third year. Anand had just completed one year in school then. Gopal's decision was sudden and whimsical, as most of his actions were which Anand learnt to understand. Anand did not find school as loathsome as Gopal made it out to be. Then it was easy to please Anand even as a small child. His needs were meagre. There was no specific reason for Gopal to stop going to school. The family was busy with the marriage of the last but one daughter which, as predicted, made the priest bereft of his land. This time he could not hoodwink his wife with another story of misappropriations of funds. The family was anyway busy with either one of the forty-five festivals or with any of the married daughters coming for delivering another offspring to strengthen the family tree. Those were not the days of having to handle a situation of a delivery of an *unmarried* daughter. Amidst all this, the Lady could not care whether the two boys actually went to school when they left home. It was enough if they remained absent from home in the hours they were expected to be.

The Lady was the title of the priest's wife. No one ever remembered her actual name. She was the Bismarck of Mullaikudi. Of course no one in Mullaikudi knew about any Bismarck, leave alone *the* Bismarck. A lady of iron will and a great believer in dispensing absolute justice, she was what the family of this priest needed. The priest did not deserve her. Though the reason mentioned in the matrimony was that a mother was needed to take care of the young boy from his deceased first wife, the actual reason was that the priest was a spineless man who shunned responsibility at every junction. She was a boon he never expected, nor deserved. She was brought up in a culture which imbibed that a woman in the house is just above the furniture in hierarchy of things and she was too honest and simple to question that. In a period when step-motherly treatment was the norm, she was an exception. So considerate she was that the only son from the first marriage came to know that the Lady was his stepmother only when he was nine-years old. This knowledge was also a result of an unsuccessful attempt by a few of the relatives with vested interests. As the attempt was unsuccessful, no one ever came to know what the vested interests were.

3
The Scheming Gods

"Why are you not coming to school and what do you do during the day?" asked Anand.

"Why should I come to school?" shot back Gopal.

This technique of replying to a question with another question to the contrary was a technique mastered by Gopal and with excellent results in his later years. This technique was as powerful as its simplicity.

Anand could not think of an answer to this. He knew it was not correct and beyond that, nothing. He could not argue and prove why it was wrong. He thought may be Gopal was right. But his thoughts were not enough motivation to follow Gopal. Seeing that Anand had no answer, Gopal smiled widely and said, "See, you really do not know. May be I should be asking you as to why are you *going* to school? Anyway I will tell you. I find the lessons meaningless and the teachers lifeless. The mangoes and the tamarinds in the neighbouring orchard are delicious. The shepherd there can tell me more about the world. There is also a workshop where they service cars and buses. I find that more interesting than writing the same alphabets every day. I am certain that if you write the alphabets once in the beginning of the year and never wipe your slate, the master would not know any difference."

This was way too high for Anand. He saw a weird logic in what his brother said but an inbuilt resistance to being a rebel did not allow him to follow his brother.

His brother was bulkier and more vociferous. Without ever directly threatening him, he had made it clear that Anand would keep the adventures out of the home front.

So it was that while Anand memorised the alphabets and became an expert in arriving that two plus two was always four, Gopal became one with Nature. Climbing trees, scraping knees, milking cows and goats, knowing different types of lubricants used in automobiles – all became passions for Gopal.

Though the ever vigilant eyes of the Lady spotted that Gopal was growing stronger and bigger than expected of his ration, she attributed it to the ever-convenient genes, the single explanation to all that was inexplicable. She could not have factored in the additional fruits, milk and the stuff he managed at the garage. Her feelings were symbolic with that of every housewife of that time – if a child could grow up with little demand and virtually no attention, you did not disturb that equilibrium with unwanted curiosity. Anyway, she had one more daughter to be married off and she knew that her days in their home were numbered. The priest was becoming sullen day by day. Whether it was due to mounting debts from his gambling, or the certainty of becoming a non-entity post the last daughter's wedding, the absence of carnal pleasure or a combination of all was purely speculative. The Lady decided to ignore it for the time being and was finally thankful to the unexpected break in the amorous activities of the virile priest. In the first three months after the birth of her last child, the absence of nocturnal advances was normal. When it continued after the self-proclaimed grace period, she grew suspicious. Not of his faithfulness. That she was certain. Her husband was faithful, although the reason was an absence of opportunities. She was suspicious that he might be suffering from some ailment and not disclosing the same. When it continued, her mounting suspicion became a relaxed vigil and finally attained a complete state of relief. She no longer needed to cover her breasts after feeding the child, as the mere sight of the mammary glands in the past was known to convert a docile sleepy man into an uncontrollable beast. Sex, then, was more a utilitarian act than the art it evolved. The beginning of the first move to the exhausted collapse of the male organ of course (that women were capable of orgasm was not known) usually lasted four minutes. The Lady considered herself lucky if it was short, as it usually was. The average time of copulation, if one ever timed all the occasions, must have been about 160 seconds. This sudden relief from her husband and the fact that she had only one more daughter left to be married off, coupled with her last two sons spending the designated time out of the house (though unknown to her, one of them was spending that time *out of the school* also) lulled her into a state of an almost bovine equanimity. She was for the first time in her almost constant state of pregnancy since the marriage – relaxed. She thanked all the forty-two gods that mutely hung on the wall of the main hall.

Little did she know of the plans that the most powerful of those forty-two gods was hatching.

4

The Passing of the Priest

The next few years of schoolgoing for Anand was punctuated with tragic events at alarming regularity. The Lady who was thanking the gods, all forty-two of them, did not know which of these gods conspired against her. In retrospect that the writer is blessed with, it could be said that the Lady's most peaceful and comfortable years lasted between the birth of Anand and till the completion of his seventh year. Calamities started to befall her as if with a renewed vengeance. First of the series of unfortunate events unfolded when Anand was just completing his second year in school. The priest died suddenly. Of course, people die suddenly most of the times. Death is not in the ninth month after conception, like birth is. There is a lot of predictability about birth. Death on the other hand is almost always sudden. The poorer you are, the more sudden and untimely the death is. The fear of death interestingly is exactly the reverse. The wealthier you become, the more paranoid you become about dying. The priest did not give any indication about anything abnormal other than the loss of his sexual appetite. He also did not suffer for any period of time which would have necessitated administering his own panacea of ash/vermilion. He coughed for one day almost non-stop. This made the Lady produce a watery soup of pepper. The next day he hiccupped for an alarming period of time. He drank water, pinched the fleshy portion between his thumb and the index finger till his eyes watered, held his breath for a surprisingly long time and exhaled slowly through one nostril. The water did not work. The pinching, as had been chronicled, brought tears to his eyes but the hiccoughs stayed. The hiccups remained below the surface during the breathing circus but resumed the moment the exhaling was about to be completed. The Lady, or for that matter no one else in the household, had heard of scaring a person as a remedy. This knowledge, had it been known, would have been redundant as no one could have dared to scare him; no one knew and hence this was not put to use. That night the Lady became aware of the fact that someone could actually hiccup while sleeping. Whether the priest slept at all that night was also pure speculation as he was not alive when it could have been confirmed. The hiccups stopped towards the morning, along with his breathing. The metronomic hiccup was in fact so soporific that it lulled the Lady to sleep, as if listening to a lullaby. The absence of the sound woke her wide awake and her prodding enquiry to ascertain that all was well resulted in her realising that she had just been widowed.

Crying and lamenting is a privilege that many can afford and our Lady was not one of them. She had to marshal all her resources and inform everyone about the event. The first son, the official holder of the funeral rites, was away in Madras and it fell on the tender shoulders of Gopal to carry out the last rites. The last rites are a problem in any religion, but no other religion takes a more sadistic pleasure out of the remaining survivors like the Hindu religion. It pummels you non-stop for thirteen days from the day of the death, with no time for either physical or mental rejuvenation. Gopal went through most of them almost in a semi-comatose stage. The rituals never allow you to forget that you have had a death in the family. They keep reminding you of the horrid event through a well-orchestrated string of events. Over this period the near ones, the not so near ones, the far ones, those who matter, those who do not, relatives who are hitherto known only by names but never seen in person and virtual enemies, all descend on the household with an alacrity that would put a circling eagle above a visibly dead rat to shame. The Lady had no official time to even mourn. She was wedded to the kitchen with an unending task of preparing food and refreshments for over seventy people three times a day for thirteen days.

The house was suddenly full of kids. The absurd procreating capacity of the menfolk of that period was highlighted by the strange sight of Anand playing with someone just elder than him and who was the first son of the first daughter of the priest and the Lady. Later, much later, would he realise how crazy it would have been for *both mother and daughter to be pregnant at the same time.* All he realised then was that he had had a haircut ahead of schedule and all he later recalled of those thirteen days was how fondly he glided his hand over his tonsured pate.

5

The Return of the Second Daughter

The Lady was surprised that life actually moved on without the priest. The differences were in the loss of her lustrous black hair and one less portion of food prepared. With no steady income to speak of, life became one prolonged misery. Mortgaging the house was out of question as a decent boy had been found to wed the last of the daughters, once the mourning period was over. The house needed to be sold to take care of the wedding. The Lady was not capable of thinking on long-term basis and honestly, she never thought what she would do with two sons and no property. Even if she had spent some time on thinking, it would have been a wasted effort as no solution would have emerged. She was the most practical one, deciding to cross a bridge after covering half the bridge.

Her culinary skills came to her rescue in times of this monumental crisis created by the quick and untimely departure of her husband. She started making papads and pickles, not for her consumption, but towards a living. The enterprise was steady, the income meagre but it sustained their life and pride. If there was one thing that she had not lost till then, and not in the years to come, it was pride. She had accidentally discovered that Gopal has stopped going to school. After administering, what appeared to be the correct amount of parental reprimand, she did not persuade much in sending him back to school, but converted him into her first salesman. This suited Gopal also as he could do what he did all those days, but now, officially. He had the gift of the gab. This alone would make him into a very successful man of stature in his later years. His salesmanship was a spectacle to behold. He could convince the meanest miser that the best his (miser's) money could buy was right under his nose, that is in his (Gopal's) bag. He lied, exaggerated, pleaded, threatened, cajoled, convinced, joked, cried and even raised the names of gods, where he deemed fit, all in the process of selling his wares. Many couples saw this quality of unfettered childhood and buckled under his charm.

Anand was at the receiving end of the other side of Gopal, which was not charm personified but vicious. Gopal blamed, without proof, Anand for the Lady coming into the knowledge of his abstinence from school. All Anand did was to accept the truth when confronted by the towering Lady who already possessed the information. If there was one thing that Anand could not do well was to tell a lie. What came so easily to so many kids of his age always deserted him. He knew he was not good at that and never practiced hard. Gopal thrashed him hard, holding him accountable and further threatened that if the Lady were to know it was Gopal who had beaten him blue, then….? The incomplete threat was more intimidating than it would have been, had it been spelt out. So the Lady found it a surprise that Anand, not-ever the physically active guy, returned one day evening after a scuffle and fall from a game of throwball. She had pickles to make, papads to roll and dinner to make, so the superficial bruises of Anand were soon displaced from her scheme of more important things.

Blood is thicker than water or so the saying goes. With the new found freedom putting wind into his sail, Gopal soon forgot the imagined treachery of Anand and extended the olive leaf. Anand, the forever accommodating chap, grabbed it with both hands and unadulterated glee. Life more or less looked set to sail in these calm waters. After the wedding and only after the actual loss of the last property they possessed was there any need to make plans. Or so they thought. John Lennon said "Life is what happens to you when you are busy making other plans." The next instalment of tragedy in their life fell into their lap three months after the death of the priest. The Lady's second daughter reported one day with four kids, a trunk containing few clothes and no money.

And no husband.

Amidst sobs that soaked only the Lady's shoulder, as she had become immune to further pain, the daughter narrated the shame of her husband running away to the Himalayas. He had run away as he had no steady job. He could not support the family. He did not have the resolution of Lady Bismarck. The parents-in-law blamed the daughter-in-law for being the harbinger of all the bad luck and packed her off, and washed their hands off.

6

Marriage of One and Water from the Well

"Why are my sister and the four kids staying with us now?" asked Anand from his mother. She wanted to ask the same question from someone, but she could not and hence did not encourage Anand on this line of questioning. The actual reasons would have been way over the head for Anand. The Lady pondered over the question for a while with her hand aimlessly drawing patterns in the bowl of curd rice. Ever since the additional mouths to be fed made their presence felt and later became permanent, the Lady switched over from individual plates to a common bowl. She mixed rice with curd in that big bowl and distributed it to all the seven children in the house. This ritual can be understood only by one who has actually undergone a similar experience.

The matriarch prepared the entire dinner in one bowl. The children sat in a semi circle like a crescent of a moon facing her, with their arms outstretched. The Lady would make a small sphere of the mixed portion and leave it on the palm of the first outstretched hand. The process was repeated from one end to another end till the bowl was complete. The bowl was always tilted away from the eyes of the children so that they would not know which round would be the last round. The dexterity of the woman lay in keeping the size of the sphere to such an optimum size that the children felt they had spent a long time in eating their dinner. It was only when the woman stood up after putting the last portion on the last child's palm that the remaining children and the last one realised that the dinner was over. The six other outstretched arms were shyly withdrawn, and any remnants shamelessly licked clean. The children had no idea when or whether the Lady and her second daughter had their dinner.

The Lady mulled over the question of Anand for a considerable time and replied, "Because God wishes so." This answer disappointed Anand. He was expecting something less metaphysical. This answer drew a snigger from Gopal. Anand could not snigger even in his dreams. Though the answer did not satisfy him, it was phrased so cleverly as to discourage further probing. Not that Anand resented them; he was simply curious, as on previous occasions they had not stayed beyond a month. Soon the obligatory mourning year passed and on the first auspicious day the last of the Lady's daughters was married off. She left for her husband's place. The house was sold and there was hardly anything left to call their own, except their skin. The Lady moved to a hut on the edge of the village and took root. This hut became a beehive of activity. From early in the morning to fairly late in the evening, the factory churned out papads and pickles. As to the actual cooking, this was kept very simple. Quantity overrode variety; even the term quantity is significant only against the absence of variety. On its own, it was not worth speaking about. It was easy to keep the house clean as there was no furniture. The children all slept in the open, outside the hut, at night. Only the Lady and her second daughter slept inside. Even they would have preferred the outside cool air but something called decorum forbade that luxury. On the few weeks that it rained, all crawled into the hut. Like piglets each crawling unerringly to its own teat of the swine, the children had their own nook and corner of the house without any proper allocation and tussle.

The children went to school from this hut. Gopal continued with his salesman's job. He was also becoming an expert car mechanic unknown to the Lady. This was a Herculean task as hardly anything escaped the Lady's eyes. May be it was the pressure of running the show called 'life' while the easiest solution was to jump into the neighbouring well. The temptation was there every time she drew water from the well. When she thought that she would not be able to resist the temptation in the face of the mounting misery, she offloaded the job to her second daughter, now the unofficial maidservant of the house. This was one of the very few miscalculations on the lady's part. The young woman was not very strong in mind and could not resist a quicker solution. One night, after putting all the children to sleep and after ensuring that the Lady was fast asleep, she touched her feet with reverence and after planting small pecks of affection on all her four children and her two brothers, went out and jumped into the well. The well was very small but the water was very deep and she did know how to swim.

Her absence was felt the first thing in the morning as it was her duty to draw water from the well. The Lady spotted her *in the well*, instead of near it. She went about the remaining acts as if on automode. She had no time to grieve. She had jobs to do, mouths to feed. One day spent not making the papads and pickles translated brutally into loss of revenue. That she could not afford. Between grieving the dead and nurturing the living, she chose the latter. The four kids, thanks to the virility of the man who ran to the Himalayas, were each separated by one year and the eldest was not even full five. The hut came back to normalcy surprisingly fast. The children were too young to understand and cry. The brothers were confused and blindly followed the Lady and appeared stoic. The Lady, she kept on, now more than determined to face whatever the gods decided to throw at her.

7

One Arrival and One Departure

Anand had company now and also was nursing some secret worries. The eldest of the four children started accompanying him to school. His worries concerned Gopal. Never the one to treat Anand as his equal and always a little blunt and brusque (this grossly misrepresented Gopal as calculative and heartless whereas he was actually neither. He just was not the type to put his affections on his lapel. He was selective in dispensing his affections and selfish no doubt), the recent mood swings of Gopal were the main cause of concern for Anand. Gopal was snappy most of the times. He was also into a new habit of talking to himself. His eyes were distant. His attention span, which at the best of the times was miniscule, started growing lesser, if that were possible. Routine questions made him bark. He was polite only with the Lady; no one dared to be any different. As the other four kids were of course kids, the recipient of all his mood swings was Anand. After a few days, Anand realised that it was wiser to keep the interaction and the dialogues to the barest minimum.

The Lady looked forward to her nocturnal return to the comfort of her dreamless sleep of seven odd hours from the moment she woke up. Nothing else mattered to her. The last daughter was settling down well. She had already mothered two children of her own and seemed, at least for the time being, not intent on adding to the existing miseries. Absence of any complaints from her parents-in-law was equivalent to a compliment. Compliments in these matters were never explicit. One had to deduce. The Lady often used to muse over the death of her daughter, who decided to jump into the well. It was not any maternal instinct. She had crossed the stage of feeling human reactions. She badly needed help in her chores. A boy, however small, was never expected to partake or assist in activities even remotely related to the kitchen. She never questioned this wisdom. Nor was she an iconoclast to go and turn the world upside down. The children were too young to volunteer help.

Gopal was almost a man now, with what he being the eldest coupled with his salesmanship, he never ventured any help. Anand was moved to tears often at the sight of the inhuman labour that his mother was dispensing, but was not sure whether it was the right thing to offer help. He wanted to help his mother though he never understood the process behind the perfectly circular papads and the tangy pickles. He had never seen any other boy in the village do such a work. He could never be the one to set a new trend. He was a stickler for routine and followed instructions. Taking the initiative had never been his hallmark nor would it ever be. Sundays meant trouble for him as he was not certain about what should be done away from the school hours. He needed to be told. He was torn between his indecision and the sight of his mother's backbreaking labour. He need not have bothered. Even if he had offered to help, the Lady would have said 'no'.

The task of pickle was easy. After the cutting, grinding and mixing, it was time, the great magician, who took care of the whole thing. The papads were killing her. Making of those 200 papads a day consumed the better part of her day and her energy, not to say anything about her health. It was literally a backbreaking work. Take a glob of the finely mixed flour, flatten it with a rolling pin into a fairly correct circular shape, flip it over, repeat the rolling, and flick it with a swift action of wrist to a distance to allow it to dry. Every flattening process required the whole upper torso to move forward and backward at least five times, transferring the force from the shoulders to the rolling pin. The flicking process required straightening up to her sitting position. This whole cycle was repeated 200 times a day. When she finally stood up, her back and her cramped legs cried for a pause from this quotidian abuse. She was deaf to such cries. She once even contemplated switching over from making this health-sapping papad to something easier. But the papads were already gaining repute and an acceptance in the highly critical Brahmin community. It was a foolish thought to kill a successful brand and she had no choice but to continue and suffer. She even became known as Papadam Mami in the vicinity.

Time was flying past and the Papadam Mami started thinking about Gopal's marriage in a very vague sense. She was not very certain about his specific age, but he looked old enough to marry. She was actually looking forward to a help at home rather than a spouse for her son. Gopal in the meantime had other plans, of his own. The garage-owner had taught Gopal the trade well. Taking up a career in and around a garage would not meet with the approval of his mother and this was something that he was aware of. A Brahmin can starve but not stain his hands with oil and grease. Mechanical things were menial jobs. A Brahmin was expected to become a priest or a government employee or at the least an accountant to a blood-sucking landlord. No other profession was considered appropriate. The first two options were ruled out and in the last choice, Gopal would have preferred to be the landlord and not the servant. The choice of the profession Gopal had in his mind was doomed to fail at the first whiff. This was the main reason for his sullenness. He had no clear plans of what was to be done. Of one thing he was certain. He was not going to sell papads for the rest of his life.

People get enlightened in many ways and at many places. It was said that Buddha got his wisdom under a tree; Arjun in the battlefield. Gopal got his in a touring theatre. He was watching a movie. He was never able to recall later the name or the actor of the movie. All he remembered was one scene in which the protagonist broke the cash-box, took all the money and boarded a train in the middle of the night to a distant city. There was no cash-box in the Lady's hut. So Gopal did not break any. There was no money to steal. So he stole nothing. There was no midnight train from where he was residing, so he hitched a ride and set off even he knew not where. All he knew was that he would go somewhere, drive a car, maintain other cars and never touch a papad again in his life.

It took almost a week for the Lady to accept that her son had gone. Whether he was dead or gone to some place was not clear. Ever the optimist, she assumed the better of the alternatives. When all the relatives ended up replying in the negative about his whereabouts, she gave up any hope of getting her salesman back. Anand was not capable of a salesman's job. She was in fact afraid that with his bumbling ways he might damage the market that had been so arduously built. Her eyes turned to the younger batch of the four grandsons who were easy to mould and who carried the emotional advantage of being children. She was not aware that she was indulging in child labour and was actually exploiting them. She had more pressing needs to address than being politically correct.

It was then that those gods, who were in favour of playing pranks on her, sent the third daughter and her three kids (sons again) to her doorstep. This time there was no Himalayas. The husband and her father-in-law (the mother-in-law was already dead) were washed away in a freak flash flood while taking bath in a canal where water never swelled above the ankle. The statisticians called this event as a one-in-three-million chance after a lot of calculations. The Lady did not know about this as she was not capable of reading. Even if she had come to know about this, it would have made no difference. All she knew was that certainly she now had the additional help she was longing for, but four additional mouths to feed.

8

Anand goes Places

Anand had lost the one company that he cherished. The exit of Gopal was too much for him. He knew there was a wild streak in Gopal. He was not prepared for the wildness to manifest itself in such concrete action and so soon. Anand would have been equally devastated even if Gopal had run away at the age of seventy-five. He was easily dependent on others and emotional attachments were a second skin to him. For a boy, he cried surprisingly too often and too long. The Lady was at a loss to understand that two sons from her womb could be so disparate. The Lady was not great in arithmetic, but she increased her papads to 350 per day to cater to the additional members of the family. Anand was becoming big and was in his last year in school. The next year was to be the issue of decision making. Anand needed to decide what he would do. This was inconceivable even to the limited worldliness of the Lady. She had to decide for him.

Of course, Anand would follow meekly like a lamb. She took her first favour in her life at this juncture. She labelled it a favour though it was her due by any standard. She wrote to the first son, who had settled in Madras, to find a job and help settle Anand. She was nervous and had butterflies, maybe pigeons, in her stomach while waiting for an answer. When I say she "wrote", it cannot be taken literally as she was not capable of such an act. She used the services of a woman in exchange for 20 papads. The woman was indignant at being offered the papads in exchange for what the least that one could do for the other. She raved about how the whole world was becoming materialistic and that there were no places left for pure emotions and friendships. While returning home, after the letter was posted, the Lady could not be sure of what had transpired and its real implications as the woman took the papads any way and did not offer to pay for the same. This was the Lady's first encounter of "lip sympathy". She was subjected to this so many times later she could smell one before the fourth word left the speaker's mouth. The son was not an ingrate. He said 'yes'. He also offered to take care of Anand till the boy settled down with a decent job. Thus it was that Anand left for Madras after his last day in school and after the results were announced.

If one expected that Anand would retain most of his boyhood charms they were to be proved wrong. Anand was shameless in telling his first lie to the Lady and this was only the first, and the list of lies and web of conceit that he drew around the Lady continued till the death of his mother. As he was convinced himself, often the lies were in good intent and only prevented a sense of bad taste in her mouth, or so he believed. The first lie was that he passed his school-leaving exam while the truth was that he failed in five subjects. There were only five subjects. This news came as a shock to the elder brother as he was counting on getting a government job for his brother with his impeccable credentials. The result ruled out the option and he started exploring private enterprises.

The crying that came so naturally to Anand prevented the elder brother from passing on the bad news to the Lady. The elder brother also did not see any merit in passing on the information other than having a clear conscience. He was a very pious man and on that very day he bribed Lord Murugan with four annas for this breach. Bribing gods was a contradiction in terms but was practiced virtually in every household. This practice continues today also.

Anand was a problem. He did not have the strength to do any manual labour that could be exacting; he did not have the gift of the gab that Gopal possessed; he was garrulous but only among close family members and his tongue turned to lead in the presence of strangers; and, he had no initiative. The elder brother was more in the mould of Lady Bismarck and using all his influence, finally landed him a job of an assistant to a lawyer. He told him that the job would be easy. Those were not the days of reading a job description on the first day of your appointment. The elder brother explained to Anand that the demands of the lawyer would be moderate and if he showed a little bit of industriousness, he could go far. Life could now take a turn for the good, he told his younger sibling. "Welcome to heaven," he said dramatically, something he was not comfortable with.

It was hell. The assistant to the lawyer was a very loose term of employment. He was expected to prepare the briefs, carry the files, pour coffee from the thermos, wait in his chamber (if a chair and table with three-and-a-half leg could be called a chamber) and get snuff powder from the corner shop when the supplies ran out. He was horrified that one could be addicted to a habit that was so filthy. The lawyer's nostrils were rimmed with permanent ochre, and frequent wiping had left its indelible marks on his shirt sleeves and the smell was nothing short of foul. It was inconceivable that a woman would go to bed with someone with such a filthy habit. That his wife probably did was evident from the three brats they had. In addition to the jobs entrusted to him in the office. he also ran errands at the lawyer's house. He bought ration, bargained with the hawker of vegetables, brought the eldest kid back from school, shouted for them to return home at dusk and other jobs that occurred to the lawyer's wife from time to time. This happened every day for six days a week. The timings were from eight in the morning to late in the night.

Anand lost all his sense of time and direction. He was on autopilot. He was not sure why he was doing this job and where it would take him in future. If he had to become a lawyer, then he needed an additional qualification. He was not sure what it was, but knew that he did not have it, nor would he have, even if he tried hard enough. His elder brother tried to convince him to appear for the exams again and clear the same as it would make job hunting a little easier. Anand was convinced that his years of studying were over. The lawyer in question was not a successful one either and Anand was in a state of confusion as to where the money came from, for he had not seen a client in three months. In a way, the lawyer going to office and the kids going to school, seemed to serve the same purpose. The lawyer was expected to be *out of the house* for a definite period during the day. Anand knew he could not continue forever.

One Monday morning, when he did not leave the house, it became evident that Anand was out of his first job. Later would the elder brother know that Anand replaced chilly powder in the box of snuff and told the lawyer's wife that her husband had received no clients for over 100 days, before saying goodbye to them. The elder brother was exhausted, but not yet frustrated. The cumulative effect of Anand's acts did not cross the threshold of gratitude he owed to the Lady. He went about finding another job for this boy with no talent, no education and no patience.

After few weeks the elder brother asked Anand whether he would work as a cashier at a petrol pump in a town called Salem, in interior Madras state. Not that Anand had much choice. He was also willing to relocate to a location away from the prying eyes of his elder brother, who was the male version of his mother.

Meanwhile the Lady in the village was cautiously coming to an opinion that her days of misery might be coming to an end as Anand had sent home forty rupees from Madras after staying there for only five months. Now she knew that her son was transferred to another job in a place called Salem. It was time for her to renew the friendships of the forty-two gods, for they travelled wherever she went, without exception till her death.

9

The First Two Vices

Salem was perfect for Anand. It was not claustrophobically small like Mullaikudi, nor was it suffocating and big like Madras. He fell in love with the place. The job was also more to his understanding, if not liking. He stayed the whole day at the pump. The term 'cashier' was another misleading misnomer like the earlier 'assistant' was. He was to be there when the office was opened, clean the place, light perfumed sticks and place them in front of the altar, where there were only three gods – all connected to managing money, unlike the forty-two he was familiar with. The Hindu religion had gods for virtually everything. It was more like going through a cabinet of ministers governing a vast country. Business establishments always were partial to Lakshmi, the goddess of wealth, Ganesha, the remover of obstacles and Balaji, a God to be trusted for making a profit. While the choice of the first two was obvious, the choice of the last was always an aberration. As per the holy books, Don't use Mr. before God's name. Balaji was the first official loan-taker from a loan shark by the name of Kuber, the original money-God, to whom he was still paying the interest. Legends have it that he had not paid back the capital so far. The loan was apparently taken towards his wedding expenses. The formula used by Kuber is not known though ICICI would love to have such a scheme for its customer. Imagine paying off only the interest forever. If I had a choice, I would have recommended Kuber for the third spot but the wisdom of many successful industries stand testimony to the original choice.

Later he was to fill petrol or diesel in the customers' vehicles and collect money after referring to a readymade cross-index chart. The owner was smart enough not to trust the arithmetical skills of his employees. He also had a helper, who would run across the road and get tea when the owner arrived close to noon, to make his presence felt in the establishment. Anand treated the helper in the same way the lawyer's wife treated him: with disdain. And he also exploited him shamelessly.

In the afternoons, the helper actually filled the cars when Anand was sheltered in the relatively cooler environment, away from the scorching sun. Salem was as hot as Madras and on some days even hotter, thanks to the treeless hills that surrounded the city and reflected the sun mercilessly on the hapless populace. The name 'Salem' itself was an etymological derivative of an earlier word which meant "surrounded by hills." The petrol station closed business at eight at night and Anand had a shack behind the station, that he could call his home. A bachelor living alone in a strange city usually draws a typical assortment of people who become friends from mere acquaintances. Wiser ones normally sift through them carefully and remove weeds from the plants. Wisdom had never been one of Anand's strengths. He befriended the easy ones. He and his bunch of good-for-nothing youth soon became a group of friends. The nights after the work were spent in talking endlessly till sleep overtook them and with frequent trips to the nearby theatre for a late-night show. The make-believe world of cinema was like a drug. Anand found it easy to forget the Lady, his widowed sister and seven hungry children, in the company of his friends and in the make-believe world of cinema. He thought the money he sent every month was what was expected of him to complete his obligation.

One night, Anand was exceptionally sullen as the owner of the petrol pump threatened to deduct ten rupees from his salary as there was an error in the accounting. The money collected and the petrol dispensed did not match. Anand would never know it was his helper who stole half a litre of petrol. He had complete faith in him. This was another trait of Anand – to believe someone easily and lose money and continue to believe the same person. The proprietor was a good man. He threatened Anand to make him realise his responsibilities. He did not recover the money at the end of the month. Anand failed to notice this and unfairly carried a grudge against the owner. One of his friends spotted the usually gay Anand with a sullen look and set about enquiring. "That greedy owner wants to become rich by robbing ten rupees from me," is how Anand put it to him.

"Be precise and more clear," instructed his friend.

When Anand narrated the whole incident with a complete bias to his role in the episode, his friend commiserated with him. A good friend would have seen the whole picture and corrected him. Anand's another drawback in his later life would turn out to be the number of useless acquaintances he gathered. Not that he did not have any good friends. He did, but that was more by exception than the rule. The friend's commiseration was not restricted to consoling words. Like most people with habits that they are addicted to, this fellow was also quick in transferring the habit to the unsuspecting with astounding alacrity.

"Here, take a drag! Everything will be alright." With this, the philosopher extended his hand in which was a burning beedi.

Years of the Lady's presence had left a permanent mark on Anand. He flinched at the very idea. Though he had not read much, he knew he had not read about the medicinal or psychological remedying powers of a beedi. He knew it was wrong but a vague sense of moral righteousness evaporated. He drew on the beedi instinctively and allowed the smoke to stay in his mouth with an acrid taste and blew it out. He did not understand what the whole racket was about. It did nothing to him and he was sure he would have to wash his mouth. The puzzled look brought a healthy laughter from his friend who imparted more wisdom.

"Fool! You are supposed to take the smoke into your lungs. Here, let me show you." He took the beedi back and with a flourish took a longer than usual pull to inhale the cloud of smoke with his eyes half closed, more for special effects. After a decent lapse of few seconds, he exhaled it simultaneously through his nostrils and his mouth. Anand was stunned. All these days he had never realised that people were actually taking the smoke into their lungs. He somehow thought it resided only in the mouth.

With an instructor with not only the knowhow, but also the show how keeping a keen vigil, Anand stepped onto a road, from which there was no coming back. In later years, he was to graduate from beedis to cigarettes and on one occasion, even spend close to a thousand rupees on a cigar from Havana. The smoke did magic. Experts in de-addiction centres maintain that addiction to cigarette is psychological and not physical like drugs. Anand felt a physical relief. Like following the path of a tracer, he could feel the smoke going to all the sad corners of his self, apply the balm of relief and carry the sadness out of him through his nostrils. He felt a sudden lightheadedness and felt obliged to the friend who had just accelerated his dying process.

The months passed. Like it was said earlier, Anand did not notice the non-execution of the owner's threat. He carried the grudge and had already decided to move on to better prospects. The friend who introduced him to smoke was now to play a decisive role in the career of Anand. Another friend, though this one did not mix relationships with money, opened a window of opportunity that was tempting. The way was paved with danger also. For a sum, he promised to forge his school certificate and get him a job in a governmental agency. One had to appear for an exam. That was to be a mere formality and could be *taken care of.* After landing with the job, Anand was to be on his own. If he lost his job due to his stupidity, the agent would wash his hands off. The agent had nothing to worry about. Such deals were not legally recorded anywhere. The payment was to be made *before* even forging of the certificate started. The sum quoted was significant but reasonable. It was a sum that Anand could never accumulate over his stint at the petrol pump. An additional job was ruled out as hardly anyone worked at night in those days. So near yet so far. He was losing sleep. The broker had kept the offer fairly open ended, but no specific action unless the money was paid upfront. His group of friends came to the rescue again. Not with any monetary help. His friends were not such type. They were ready to introduce him to a way of making money. They agreed to take him, only if he consented. Anand was desperate. He was not certain what avenues could exist that could make 'making money' a reality. He proudly told his friends that he would do nothing illegal or immoral. It was a futile attempt in restoring one's conscience.

Incidentally both the terms he used were very subjective and could be interpreted to convenience. The day of the reckoning arrived. Anand with his friends went to a bungalow on the outskirts of the town, where four people sat around a table, smoking and playing cards. The bottle of hooch was kept hidden and Anand did not notice it. Anyway he was confused; playing was not on his mind. And he did not know anything about playing cards. His friends told him to sit and watch while they joined the group. Anand was not able to follow anything. The group became six, or sometimes five, and cards were distributed face down. The guy who picked it up, fanned them in his hand with an amazing dexterity and held them close to him, at a place somewhere between his nose and chest and about five inches away from the body. There were activities like picking, discarding, drawing from the discarded, drawing from the pile left on the table and when nothing was making sense, one would suddenly dump all the cards face up with a flourish. What was the point in hiding it from the other's view for so long? There were murmurs, inspection and a return to the start of shuffling. Anand understood nothing and he knew that he would never be able to follow or play this game. What he did notice was the pile of notes that were growing or diminishing in front of the individuals, and even someone as dull as Anand could not miss the fact they were playing for money. His eyes bulged wider when the winner for the day stuffed an obscene amount of money in his shirt pocket when the game was called off.

Anand left the place, convinced that he would never be a part of this gang.

But, he started playing a month after he had first watched the spectacle transfixed and decided that he would never be able to do the same. There must have been something in the 'genes' after all. He took to the game like a politician to corruption. He soon discovered that one watched the players more than the cards. The slight frown that flitted on the face of the next player when a favourable card was discarded ahead of his turn told him about the possible cards that he was holding and what he was waiting for. Sometimes it became important not to discard the card that the next one wanted. He became an expert in looking out for sweating palms, palpitating hearts and an emerging smirk. None present there had ever heard about poker and the face that one needed to keep. Initially it was rummy, more like the five-day Test Match in cricket and soon it became 'three cards', the one-day version of the same. The stakes were erratic. The win or loss could sometime be more than Anand's monthly earning. He had the beginner's luck and an inherent talent for the game. He discovered his amazing ability to spend the whole day at the pump and most of the whole night playing cards with hardly any sleep at all.

This pattern continued in his later life also. He already started priding his stamina that allowed him to survive on so little sleep. All these abuses to his body surfaced in the form of various ailments in his later years. But he was then young and had already made the bribe amount that the broker wanted in a matter of ten months. So addicted had he become to playing cards that he started to get restless by seven in the evening. The last hour proved impossible to pass. The customer who drove in at closing hours was at the receiving end of so poor quality of service that it had become public and the owner would have terminated his employment. The pleasure he derived when the cards were in his hand was almost orgasmic. He would not have said so as he had not yet tasted the sexual pleasures, and the smell of money was intoxicating. The bribe worked like magic and Anand was now officially an employee of the state government. He had about a month left to join the services. He left the petrol pump job and travelled victoriously to Mullaikudi to tell the Lady the unbelievable news.

10

Relocation and Return

The first thing the Lady noticed was that the lips were black. The priest was not in the habit of smoking, for that matter no one in the village did, and the Lady could not come to the obvious conclusion. She attributed it to the sun and the work. This was, and would continue to be, a shortcoming in the Lady. She was generous to a fault. In her near and dear ones she was myopic and could not imagine the possibility of any wrongdoings. She started discussions about life from now on. Anand was not ready for any serious discussions. He came with the idea of enjoying his holidays and returning to Salem. Discussion on family and addressing responsibilities were not in his scheme of things. But no one said 'no' to the Lady. When she talked, the others listened. She wanted to know about Salem, whether it was a good place to settle down; would the children be comfortable there; would it be possible to find a dwelling that was big enough to accommodate all at the same time, and still small enough to warrant an affordable rent; what would his office hours be now that he was a 'government employee' and on and on. Anand was flabbergasted. He never thought even once, even remotely, about the whole herd following him.

It dawned on him that the Lady was thrusting the mantle of the head of the family on his unwilling and incapable shoulders. He should have said 'no'. That was the wisest thing to do. The nature of Anand must have become by now evident to all. Saying 'no' was not something that he had ever learnt, nor would he later on in his life. All that he needed at that moment was the comfort that only a smoke could deliver and he excused himself by going out on a fictitious errand. The discussions continued later as the Lady was perseverant, if she was not anything else. Finally it was decided that Anand would go first, join his duty and locate a place befitting the needs of the family.

The very word 'family' was a scary one. Anand somehow foolishly thought that expectations of him would remain at an annual get-together and the constant financial support, but the proximity of all of them was something he had not expected. He was counting them off on his fingers. He, his mother, the seven kids, some of them no longer kids and the hapless sister – a perfect ten. He somehow thought he would run out of fingers and was surprised at the figure he finally arrived.

He had a spare finger next day as his sister, the hapless one staying with them after losing her husband and father-in-law in a freak flash flood, died. It was actually that simple. She just did not wake up. It was the fifth death that the Lady was experiencing in her immediate family. Her husband, one daughter, the husband who ran to the Himalayas (the Lady had already pronounced him dead), one son-in-law washed away and now another daughter. Eight; she corrected herself after remembering the loss of three of her children. Was the loss only just two decades ago? It looked ancient.

Anand was not really close to any of his sisters and so did not really grieve much. He was even momentarily ashamed when he thought he had to now take care of only eight additional souls and not nine, when the family made its inevitable trip to Salem. How could one blame him? Which adult male would like to have his home shared with seven dependents, all children even before any serious thought about his marriage had been attempted? His perceived vacation turned into a complete disaster, first with the news of the family following him, and second with another death in the family. He had only a hazy recollection of passing off the remaining days and almost happily he returned to Salem.

The friends of his petrol-pump days had slowly faded into the background. Sometimes it was surprising that life could move on in the absence of friends who once appeared to be the very reason for living. There was no acrimony or fight. It was just that he was in a new environment and the social spheres of the two did not overlap. New friends happened – those who were as bad, if not worse. His courtship with the two vices continued – playing cards and making money were as necessary as the job because he had a huge family to support. At least this was his conviction. In gambling, the end is always negative. He was nowhere near the end. It was the initial phase and he thought he was always winning as the game provided him money at the worst of his crises with an uncanny regularity. The losses he made in good times were not recalled and he started living under the mirage that this was actually making him richer.

His association with schools resurfaced as his department needed to audit schools. Thus it was many of his friends, from then on, were from the cadre of school teachers. These teachers were the best of hypocrites. After imparting morals and commitments whole day at school, most of them assembled later in the evening to play cards and drink. It was on one audit trip to a school that Anand befriended Bhaskar. Bhaskar was different from the other friends of Anand. He was really educated, did not have many vices, surely not cards and booze, did not befriend Anand for money, did not mind telling him when he was wrong and became a constant presence in Anand's life from then on. He would later become the favourite of the Lady and help her settle down her business of papad and pickle in the new town. His genuine affection and the subsequent proximity to the Lady made him inseparable from Anand, though Anand was tempted to close off the relationship on many occasions when Bhaskar was becoming holier than thou in his sermonising ways. Bhaskar had become a rudder in the turbulent waters of Anand's life.

The Lady wound up her business and reached Salem with seven children in tow. Anand had found a house. Initially Anand found it difficult to sleep in a hall with eight other individuals. This gave him another excuse to spend more time at the club, playing cards and returning home almost at daybreak. His sleeping hours occurred between early in the morning till in the morning. The Lady began to curse the government for taking such a heavy toll on the life of her son. For her, the whole time spent *out of the house* was in the service of the government. This arrangement continued for a while and soon the Lady realised that running the household only on the fluctuating income brought home by her son was fraught with risks. She understood the need for additional money. She knew only one way of making it. Enter Bhaskar.

The loveable chap had a lengthy discussion with the Lady and assured her that the market for home-made delicacies in that area was a potential untapped, and she should go ahead. To initiate her into the circle, he promised to have his fellow teachers as her first customers. The factory came to life again. The initial sets of customers were a very satisfied lot and Papadam Mami became a brand with word-of-mouth advertising of satisfied and loyal customers. The children found it easy as the bulk of the customers was in the school itself. The additional trips to non-school customers were made after school hours and the kids took turn. Thus the Lady again found herself doing the same things in a different town.

The house was empty except at night when all, well almost all, returned to roost. The routine was pathetic and would have driven any other person insane. The Lady preferred a maddening routine to sure starvation. Life, as she saw it, was good. They had just about enough to survive. The son was employed. No one ever went to sleep with their stomach full but no one starved either. There was Bhaskar, the only friend who visited their home regularly, who was guilty of only holding back the true Anand from the Lady.

If everything was this close to normalcy, then it was time for the Gods to turn pranksters. This is what they exactly did when one morning, the Lady found Gopal standing on her doorway.

11

False Hopes and a Wedding

Anand was not used to Bhaskar calling him at his office. The official relation made it mandatory for Anand to visit the school and not the other way around. His first reaction was that someone, one of the children, had met with an accident. Anand stopped feeling shameful about such musings. It is alright to speak about compassion and emotions but the bottom line was money, actually the lack of it. The Lady had so far never found it necessary to contact Anand at his office and the only thought that occurred to her was to pass the information to Bhaskar, through one of the kids. The kids had a flexible time and none of the teachers minded it. Most of them were loyal customers by then. It was only after Anand left his office that Bhaskar broke the news to him.

Anand would have never been able to explain the surge and mixture of emotions that passed through him at that instant. Was it relief at someone sharing his burden? Was it exhilaration at the prospect of seeing his larger-than-life brother again? Was it anguish at his selfish act? Was it . . . what? He had no idea. All he knew was that he wanted to be home and Bhaskar, ever the gentleman, slipped away silently. The Lady was not very sure. She spotted something close to aloofness in Gopal. He carried with him an air of a traveler, only resting on the way. He did not say much, which was a surprise. He listened to the travails and miseries that the family had encountered, and were still undergoing, without any outward manifestation of what his feelings were. The children he fondled affectionately and the Lady could see that the affection was genuine. That was not fake. He appeared alright – a typical middle-class soul. He could easily be lost in a crowd. That's how ordinary he looked. The Lady was trying to guess his age and could not recollect. The way a mother's heart functions cannot be comprehended. She had no complaints about her son. If he had decided to stay on in the house, even as an additional liability, she would not have minded. For how could Gopal ever be a liability?

The silver-tongued prodigy – he was not forthcoming and neither did she probe. She thought it better for the two brothers to sort out whatever needed sorting out. The first few moments of the reunion between brothers were embarrassing. Each did not know where to start and how to proceed. The mother was not a great help either. Anand concluded that no conversation would amount to anything inside the house and decided to go for a walk with his strange brother. Somehow the close bond of admiration and love had not felt kindled as he expected it to. Gopal had apparently succeeded in a part of his ambitions.

"I drive a car now," said Gopal.

This piece of information was inconclusive and Anand decided to wait for more clarity.

"Actually I first worked in a garage in Trichy for a few years," continued Gopal. The gist of what Gopal narrated for the next two hours was this:

After a few years in a garage in Trichy, the owner of the garage engaged him as his personal driver. Gopal ended up being his Man Friday. There was very little that the garage owner could do in the absence of Gopal. Gopal attended to all his needs, which were surprisingly few. He drove the car for him full time. He left his menial work in the garage. In addition to driving the car, he handled the activities in all the four garages, maintained the accounts and even convinced his owner to launch a rental service where he saw the potential for earning good money. He was actually going to Bangalore with his boss for exploring the possibility of purchasing land when he spotted the Lady buying her ration of ingredients for the papad factory.

He took leave for three days on his return to Trichy and reached Salem the previous night. Anand found it impossible to believe that his brother had actually gone on driving to his destination despite spotting their mother. Gopal's strength was that he was better in controlling his emotions. You could not have expected Gopal to stop the car and leaving his master stunned while running, shouting, "Amma", amidst a group of startled and amused spectators. He knew she would not go anywhere and so return after completing his assignments. Anand was not sure why he came back. Even Gopal was not sure. It was very clear that Gopal was not going to stay. Anand would never be able to ask for help. The two brothers returned home for dinner and the Lady, when not told any thing explicitly, did not ask anything either.

Later that night with Gopal fast asleep, his mother asked Anand, "What does he say? Is he alright? Will he stay with us now?"

Three very simple questions. Anand wished he knew the answers although he was certain that Gopal would not stay with them. Anand did not feel very close to Gopal at this juncture and hence he did not confide in him about his smoking habit. Gopal would have been surprised for he had continued so far without any addictions whatsoever.

After Anand had gone to his office the next day, Gopal told his mother that he would have to return to Trichy and continue with his life. She was beyond shock. She did manage to ask him why he needed to go. After all these years, may be it would have been better if all stayed together. Gopal had ambitious plans. He could not be tied down by responsibility and a family. He promised his mother that he would return every year and she should not hesitate to write to him when there was a need. He was true to his words. He visited her every year. If the Lady had not asked him for help at any point of time, there was no point in blaming Gopal for neglecting his family. The episode of the return of Gopal did not have any long-lasting impact on the household or its functions. Both the Lady and Anand were too proud to seek help. Accepting help was vastly different from seeking help. Thus it was that Bhaskar became closer to this family than Gopal could ever be.

The time had come for Anand to marry. This was decided by the Lady. The reasons were not obviously the obvious ones – that Anand also needed a family, the one he could rightfully call his own, that here was a precedent being set, a younger one getting married ahead of his elder one, were all paling into the background. The Lady now had her priorities lined up square. She no longer was on the lookout for a help; she needed a bigger package. She now needed someone who would be wife, daughter-in-law, housemaid, chaperone to the children, procreator of the future seeds and most importantly, a breadwinner. This was unheard of – that a girl or a woman in an orthodox Brahmin family would actually be doing to a job; it was pure fantasy. Lady Bismarck did not get the sobriquet for nothing. She went about with a single-minded determination after the agenda that she conceived. She was ready to be patient. Anand by himself was not showing any desire to get married. He was taking each day of his life as a challenge and was not willing to spend his energy on contemplation, if it was avoidable. The Lady and Bhaskar set about executing the conspiracy. The specifications were laid out. The candidates meeting all of them or at least most of them were expected to be very few.

They were wrong. There was only one.

Jodhi was ideal. Whether she would agree to tie the knot was another question altogether. The Lady did not know the subtleties and did not waste time over them. She approached the prospective bride's father directly and laid out her plan. The father of the girl was an anachronistic of the times, when educating a girl-child was unthinkable, yet he was sending his daughter to work. Who did he think he was? He was almost ostracised by the ruthless community, the one which could never digest success in another, and was in fact wondering whether he had condemned his daughter to an eternal spinsterhood by his misplaced sense of liberation. He was desperate. Still he needed time to think over it as it would decide his darling daughter's destiny. The dowry demanded appeared reasonable. He had only one daughter and it was not a major concern for him. His gentle approach to anything in life was no match for the focused aggression of the Lady, the moment she set her mind to a task.

They agreed on a day for the bride and the groom to meet. This was a ritual that would look ridiculous now, but was a norm then. The Lady was considerate enough not to take the whole bunch of kids with her. The Lady, Bhaskar, the eldest of the boys and of course, Anand made the quartet. The reason for the Lady not taking all the kids was that she was certain that the knowledge of the kids and their physical presence were two different things altogether. The actual sight of all the kids could scare the girl even if it had no impact on world-weary elders. Anand had had a haircut and shaved for the occasion. The Lady and Bhaskar were singing his eulogy. He sat quietly with a stupid half grin pasted on his face throughout the proceedings. He managed to retain it even *while consuming* the refreshments. That was another part of the ritual. The bride's family served refreshments and the girl was expected to deliver the coup-de-teat by serving coffee at the end. Those few minutes were expected to be enough for the boy and the girl to size up each other and conclude. Those days the two involved had nothing to say. It was the parents who decided. Of course they knew what was good for the children. Here, on one hand, we had a father who was worried about his daughter remaining a spinster and on the other, the Lady, who had everything worked out. It was not expected to fail.

Anand really had no opinion. The whole idea of having a wife was yet to sink in completely. He also did not have much idea about what one was expected to do after the wedding. Sex was a taboo then. There was no one to discuss it with and very little by way of literature was available. The journalism available was yellow and the knowledge on the subject and one's willingness to discuss were inversely proportional. It was a miracle in fact that so many people married and produced children. As for Jodhi, well, no one cared. If one had ventured to ask her whether she liked the boy she would not have been very sure. She was not certain what to expect but this chap really looked funny with his pencil-line moustache and an impossibly lean frame.

The date was fixed and for once the Gods, whose main hobby was playing tricks with the Lady and her family, kept quiet. Gopal could not come to the wedding as it was not coinciding with his annual homecoming and the rest of the family was well represented. The last of the Lady's daughter came with her husband and four kids to grace the occasion. Every one in the family also got to meet the new member of the family – not Jodhi, but Bhaskar.

12

The First Few Years

The transition from the comforts of her home and her parents' affection to the harsh realities of life, and life with a group of people who never excelled in wearing their emotions on their sleeves, was something that Jodhi was mentally prepared for but even she could not accept it when it hit her full blast. The family did not know how to smile. No one smiled. Surprisingly not even the kids. They had nothing to smile about and hence it never looked out of place for them. She had the confidence that only youth could muster and went about trying to make things a little less gloomy for them. The family was certain of Armageddon with every dawn and it was not easy to dispel that. To be fair, it must be said that Anand was considerate. He pitied the girl, for who would willingly enter matrimony with seven children thrown in? The relation between the Lady and Jodhi was purely professional. The Lady made it a point to never let the girl come close to her emotions and always kept her on tenterhooks. The Lady was not the typical torturing, insulting mother-in-law but she decided not to be ostensibly kind either. She had expectations from the girl and was in no way prepared to jeopardise the outcome with silly sentiments, like affection and understanding. For the Lady it was meant to be and continued to be an employer-subordinate relationship. If Jodhi was naïve enough to expect frills and fancies, like affection and understanding, it was her problem. Thus she was pleasantly surprised once in a while when an act from the Lady that carried warmth, though her countenance remained impassive as always.

Anand did not know the correct decorum of behaviour. Anyway, the time he spent at home was so minimal that he did not have to grapple with the issue. His routine continued much the same way even after marriage. The only places that the couple went to were temples and to their individual offices. Jodhi was confused about the office hours that Anand maintained and the frequent camps and inspections that he needed to do at his office's behest. She was a working woman and could spot the difference of cigarette-smoking black lips from the lips that turn black due to constant exposure to the elements. Anand, the guy who was incapable of lying, at least to the near ones though he had been hoodwinking the Lady for years now, spilled all his beans to Jodhi and elicited a promise that the Lady would not get to know about the same. It was futile as even if he had not extracted the connivance, Jodhi would not have had the temerity to approach or confront the Lady with her new-found knowledge.

Two nails were driven in the opposite walls at the far corner of the single hall that was the house and a sari was draped over the twine that ran from wall to wall. This was the privacy that the newly-married couple had. On the other side were the Lady and the kids. At least those who decided to sleep inside. Often in the middle of the night, Jodhi would spot a hand or leg of one of the kids on their side of the diaphanous wall. The house was really that small. The intimacy or the consummation of their wedding in such surroundings itself was a miracle. There was obviously not enough space or time, the former due to the dwelling and the latter to the nature of Anand, to discuss anything at all. The marriage was actually a coming together of two individual, unrelated souls working towards a common enterprise. That was the whole idea anyway, right from the start.

Jodhi slowly came into all the plots and the sub-plots of the family. The good–for-nothing priest, the first son who was settled, in the real sense, in Madras, the dead sisters, their wards now in her custody, the sisters who were still around, so far at least not adding to the Lady's misery, the wanderlust of Gopal, yet surprisingly not married and the ever-reliable omnipresent Bhaskar.

She was amazed at the will power of the Lady and was full of admiration for her. She longed for her approval and did everything she thought was needed, but the Lady was not easily pleased. The Lady was justice personified. Though her motives in getting a working woman was for the extra money, but she never made Jodhi suffer the ordeals of the factory. Jodhi took over the kitchen, but not the backbreaking labour of making papads and pickles. She knew the task in front of Jodhi was colossal and as a woman who had more than her share of suffering, she decided to spare Jodhi a few travails that she could. It was a mutual admiration company and if only one had been more forthcoming in her expression of gratitude, the relationship would have been full and satisfying. Because of her determination to withhold overt affection, the Lady remained an enigma to Jodhi till her death.

The kids took to Jodhi instantly. Here was finally one with whom they could relate. She taught them, played with them, improved their appearances, taught them manners and was instrumental in most of them becoming something worthwhile in their later life. They were all singularly grateful to her and as if to emphasise that goodness was not dead, they remained loyal and truthful to her all their life. The life of each of them was a source of great satisfaction for Jodhi in her later years. She was initially scared at the presence of the kids. It was only later did she realise that she would have gone completely mad had the kids not been there in those initial years.

Life for Jodhi was to become such a dreary routine that she never could differentiate a Sunday from any of the weekdays. The mornings were a blur. She woke up at five, just an hour after Anand had gone to sleep most of the days, gave the Lady a steaming cup of coffee – the one luxury that the Lady retained till the end – cleaned, swept, took bath, cooked, fed the children, bathed a few of them, sent them to school, grabbed a meal on the run and just before leaving for work, woke up Anand at half past eight with another cup of coffee – her last task in the morning. Anand had the luxury of reporting at ten and was almost always lethargic in those hours between half past eight and ten. He normally missed his breakfast due to acidity that was a result of all night vigil and endless cups of tea and oily refreshments from the roadside stall that supplied the gamblers. He was a frugal eater. Though he would be later host to many ailments, obesity was never one of them.

The evenings were another blur for Jodhi. The first half hour after she returned from work was the best time in her day. The kids were normally out, dirtying themselves in the process of playing; the Lady would just be stretching her tortured limbs after another excruciating day of rolling papads and Anand would, of course, arrive only at close to seven for a period of anywhere between twenty minutes and two hours. The Lady would serve Jodhi her evening cup of coffee. This practice then was unheard of. A mother-in-law serving her daughter-in-law was one among the top deadly sins in any compilation. The Lady was known for being just and she practiced exactly that. She understood this was the least she could do. This singular act would keep Jodhi indebted to the Lady and the family for years amidst future turbulences.

Then began the usual chores, like cooking, feeding, teaching, cleaning and the last inhuman act – sleeping alone in a home that was still partly foreign to her. We should not misunderstand Jodhi. It was not the mere carnal pleasure of copulation that she was missing; she longed more for a shoulder to rest her head and an arm to comfort her. Seeking either from the Lady or the kids, even as an idea, was ludicrous. Thus continued this style of married life for Jodhi. The mere absence of happiness could not be called sad and hence she was not sad by that definition, but she was not fully happy either.

The first annual visit of Gopal after Jodhi's wedding made them see each other for the first time. Gopal was glad that his brother was settling down. His visits were always well anticipated as he brought lots of goodies for the kids. Giving and spending money was a trait of Gopal that the family could have learnt. The Lady was good only in earning and making money and any expenditure other than that went for food and offerings to the Gods, was considered an extravagance. Even clothes came under the banner of extravagance and all of them had only the barest minimum to keep themselves covered. Clothes were meant to cover, not to flaunt. Jodhi had a mental image of Gopal, with all the maternal and fraternal exaggerations that stemmed from blind devotion, and she was disappointed. Gopal was short and bulky. He also had no sense of dress. He defined sartorial disaster. He always wore a white dhoti and a white shirt – not an apparel that a young woman would be impressed with. Gopal had become subdued over the years and his much talked about gift of gab was not demonstrated. Gopal knew where to put them to use, and there he did, often with assured results. He, however, did not waste those talents on a household already sold. The topic of Gopal's marriage was raised and Gopal avoided it by saying that it was not time yet. Gopal managed to stay the whole period without committing himself to any long-term plans that the Lady could have been devising and left only to return the next year.

It was a week after Gopal's departure that Anand returned home one day at three in the afternoon with a sullen look. His face usually looked that way and the Lady did not see anything amiss except his time of arrival, which was most unusual. She had another hour of work and did not make any overt attempt of interrogation. It was only when Anand came and sat next to her, after an hour of dithering, did she realise that something was amiss and a closer scrutiny revealed his moist eyes on a sullen face. Her heart skipped a beat. She was used to the crying face of Anand as a child, but never since he had grown up.

"Amma, I have been suspended, pending inquiry in my office," blurted Anand.

Those were the first words that Jodhi heard when she stepped inside, back from her work. It was difficult to say who was the most shocked of the three.

Anand was really shocked as the suspension was on the basis of an alleged bribe. Anand was honest and he had never accepted bribe in his line of work. Many of his colleagues found the allegation strange as they knew his needs at home. Call it strange but Anand, who had embraced gambling wholeheartedly, shied away from corruption. Such double standards were very confusing for people who failed to understand him in his later years, including his very own son. He knew that truth would prevail, as that was what was written in the national emblem below the lionheads. The ignominy till the name cleared, rankled him, for he had no doubt that his name would be cleared at the end of the procedure. The red tape, and the enormously long periods that departmental enquiries took, unnerved him.

For the Lady it was a toss between whether to grieve for the loss of pride or the loss of income. She believed her son and was given to wondering whether all her efforts and beliefs had gone up in a whiff of smoke. She immediately cursed herself for even nursing such a thought. She knew it was attention and comfort her son needed and went about administering both in good measure, not realising that allowing Jodhi to do that would have raised her in her esteem even higher than the Himalayas.

Jodhi was thus left to grieve on her own. Even this moment of consoling her husband was not sanctioned to her. That was to be her fate. Her moments with her husband were always at a premium. There was always someone around. She hoped to elicit the charge and the truth from her husband later that night on the other side of the sari.

Anand decided to stay home that night as befitting the occasion. Jodhi would later tell her father and arrange for quicker turns of the wheels of government machinery that would exonerate Anand in a record three months' time. He would also receive his pay for the said period. Jodhi was in a way glad that her husband was home at decent hours, which did not last long, though the conditions culminating in that event could have been more to her liking.

It was on that night, against all possible odds, given the events of the day and the hopeless situation, that I was conceived.

13

The Hatchlings Learn to Fly

The next few months were quite traumatic for the family. Gopal had no clue about this period due to the fact that the whole event started and folded in between his annual visits. The kids had no clue either as, after a hiatus of three days, Anand started frequenting his club and his fellow gamblers. The duo of Jodhi and the Lady were too proud to seek help from him. Jodhi's father, with his influence, had set the wheels in motion and it appeared as if for the first time the mammoth lethargic government machinery would display some agility. The prayers to the Gods increased exponentially over the period of Anand's absence from the office. The Gods were used to such sudden spurts in fervent prayers, usually in direct proportion to the calamity encountered, and paid no attention. If they had acted on the size and frequency of the prayers, managing the world would have become impossible.

There were many days in those three months when many in the house would go to bed with almost empty stomachs. All of them were used to suffering pangs of hunger and it was just another nadir in their cycle of life. It was altogether a new experience for Jodhi. Though not from a rich family herself, she had never known hunger. Now she lived with it every day. It was during this period that she became pious. She was not expecting miracles from those above but she realised that the time spent in praying was peaceful and made her forget the dreary existence. There had been no record anywhere as to who invented closing of the eyes while praying. It was, however, a wonderful way to pray. The symbolic gesture reinforced the shutting off of the real world.

The factory was already at its capacity and even a superwoman like the Lady could not stretch it beyond. Techniques like creating a scarcity and increasing the price was not common then, even in established markets and such unethical thoughts could find no place in the household. Jodhi's willingness to enter the manufacturing sector to increase production was negated firmly. The Lady had very few beliefs but she was strong in what she believed. She knew what was not fair and she never practiced it.

It was during this period that the Lady became conscious of the smoking and gambling habits of Anand. If she had confronted him headon, may be his life would have turned out to be different. He might not have succumbed to further vices later on. For whatever might have been the strengths of Anand, standing up to the Lady was surely not one of them. He would have wilted and under the circumstances of his worthlessness, could have even given in. He might even have reformed, so to say. Here the Lady made the second of her uncharacteristic mistakes. The first was the one which ended up with one of her daughters landing in the well. She thought that indulgence must have been new and conceded that it could be diversion he needed, the solace he sought. She was probably grateful that her son was not drinking, which of course, Anand was not, not yet, and pushing him with the chips down might tilt the scale unfavourably. What if she pushed him over the brink? The definition of brink was then quite flexible, as it even today often is, and the Lady was fully justified in drawing the line where she wanted. She thought

Jodhi was not in the know and did not discuss it with her. The combined artillery of the emotional blackmail of the two would have been a perfect dose at that time to rein in Anand. Then, isn't life always written and viewed in chapters of missed opportunities?

Jodhi knew that the Lady knew, but the Lady did not know that Jodhi knew that she knew. In their game of misplaced domestic diplomacy, Anand escaped and sank deeper into the depths of his two addictions. When such an opportunity was overlooked, it would have been futile to later expect the already overworked Gods to show consideration again.

Anand for the first time in his adult life spent time at home when the sun shone and with the kids around. He was surprised that the eldest was no longer qualified to be called a kid and would be ready to enter some employment later that year. It was the second one who drew his appreciation for the first time. This guy, Ishwaran, was a misfit in the family. He topped in all his subjects. He had already come very close to the end of the school days, courtesy the two double promotions he had managed. There was nothing that he could do wrong; except for his health. He was most of the time unwell – not any descriptive ailment which could be attended and corrected. Just a general sense of being unwell and his colour was an anaemic offwhite most of the time. He was not good in any of the games, being equally incompetent in both indoor and outdoor games. He was smart to know what he was not good at and never wasted his time in pursuing them. He more than compensated the absence of athleticism with cerebral fitness. The fight in his class was always for the second spot. He had a gift for elocution. There was not one competition that he missed and he won every one of them, irrespective of what the topic was. Though he preferred the topic beforehand, for he believed in preparing his notes well, his excellence in extempore was equally high. He had his sights trained on higher education. The phrase was foreign in the household. School normally ended where it ended; at class eleven. It looked foolish and amounted to tampering with the nature of things. Higher studies were meant for those who had money and no job. That someone could willingly pursue for it was lunacy. Only Jodhi could commiserate with his ambitions. As she was the unofficial mother to all of them, the task of convincing the Lady fell on her. Anand was amazed at the boy's erudition. To be amazed alone did not warrant a face off with the Lady. It was not that the Lady was against any reasonable train of events. The problem could be equated with the mental make up of Adam as he gazed at Eve after taking a bite of the apple of the discord. It had no precedence and hence was difficult to comprehend and grapple with. The unknown was always labelled as perilous in the family.

Jodhi at first sought the assistance of Anand. Reason one being that it was his job as master of the family to ensure proper dispensation of justice to all; two being that she was scared. The reason was not that the relationship between her and the Lady would sour, but the failure would be unfair to the budding genius. Of course, Anand was of no help and she had to enter the battlefield on Ishwaran's behalf. Not all are gifted and to overlook one who possesses genius and not offer him the chance would be a sin unparalleled. The discussion was not going anywhere. Jodhi was explaining why Ishwaran should proceed and the Lady was not following. After nearly an hour of a long discussion, Jodhi hit upon the crux of the issue. In the Lady's mind the care that you took stopped when schooling got over. The subject then started being independent and did not need being taken care of. Simply put, you stopped spending on him after the allotted school-ending years.

The Lady heard Jodhi speaking of something called scholarship which would ensure that Ishwaran could continue without any assistance from the family. The Lady heard about such a scheme for the first time. No one else in the family subsequently would earn a scholarship either. The Lady considered it unfair that such schemes were meant only for aspiring students. The argument turned to why such a scheme was not meant for someone like herself when she was in abject penury, or for that matter for Anand, who now stayed without an income. The differences between a subsidy/charity and scholarship would mean another endless discussion fraught with moral obligations, so Jodhi wisely sidestepped, feigning innocence and ignorance in equal measure. Iswharan was elated at his prospects becoming a reality and that he could actually go on to become the first and the only double Masters graduate of the family.

While the issue of his continuing education was ensured, plans were afoot for getting the first one into some sort of employment. This task fell on Anand as he had two qualifications at that point in time. One of always being the head of the family and the second being the only adult at that time with complete time at his disposal. Anand went about knocking on the usual doors – a petrol pump, a cinema theatre, a shopkeeper and even a small pickle-making works. The imagination of the entire family was tied down to the limitations of their own experience. Ambition was conspicuously missing. You either needed adventure in your blood, a la Gopal, or inherent genius like Ishwaran to evade the usual choices. Thus it was that the first one joined a shopkeeper as a worker running the shop. Here his predicament was similar to that of Anand when he worked with the clientless lawyer. That he managed that job as well as his job of the papad salesman spoke volume about his perseverance.

Jodhi, who did not believe in limiting her vision like the rest of the family, was instrumental in preparing him for clearing one public service examination which made it possible for him to enter the state tax department two years later. That was a year after Ishwaran went to Madurai to pursue his higher education, and roughly a year after I was born.

It was to be an exceptional week for the Lady. As far as she could recall, she was never the recipient of two good news in one week. In that one rare exception of a calendar week, her first grandchild went to make an earning and her beloved Anand was reinstated. Anand got his name cleared and even had his pay delivered for the suspended months. The role played by Jodhi's father was not advertised as neither Jodhi nor her parents were the attention-seeking type. Only after the reinstating Anand in his job did Jodhi convey the news to her parents that she was pregnant. Things were finally looking up for the family. An additional earning member, one on the verge of leaving the town for higher studies, the remaining children promising no mischief, Anand back in his work, the seed for the next generation sown, the Lady was contemplating whether she could retire from her backbreaking labour, which was sapping her energy every day of the year. A quick mental calculation told her that she should continue this for a little more time. It was in the month of September that year I entered this world, born into a family that already had experienced enough in its lifetime, a lot bitter than better. Bhaskar was naturally my godfather. He became one without being labelled one as that concept was Christian and not common amongst Hindus. The Christian link to this family would come later when I grew up. It was with him that I would share a lot of my views while growing up and even as a grownup. This family then had no inclination at all about the pain that I would bring when it was my turn. Bhaskar, ever the astute one, was the first to spot this ugly side of me and would disown me. The only consolation was that the Lady was not around when I let loose my entire misguided wrath on those wonderful souls.

14

The Third and Fourth Vice

Jodhi and Anand decided that they would have only one child – a decision that they would live to rue one day. They had seen the plight of the children in their custody and how even a full meal at sometimes became a luxury. They decided that their son would have the best care they could provide and there would never be a compulsion to share what was available. The Lady, had she known of this conspiracy, would have scorned the very idea. One child was as unthinkable as a world without papads. This was just one of the changes in the society that the Lady would get to see in the new order of things. Things were finally looking up.

Gopal had come on his unfailing annual visits and this time the whole family, for the first time, had gone to their ancestral temple to thank the God for the arrival of the last child, myself, in the already quite overcrowded family tree. It was a religious necessity to undergo a tonsure for the newborn. The last sister also joined us with her family. The collective family could easily classify as a crowd. It was jokingly said then that the family could never go out together if there was a curfew.

There was a long debate about the naming process. By definition and precedence I should have inherited my grandfather's name or one of the Gods'. Anand was beginning to see himself as the new face of the new world and he wanted very little that reminded him of his humble dwelling and beginning. This did not mean that he had become wealthy, but a sense of stability was settling over the household and this could be intoxicating. I was named Amar. Why or what it meant, no one had any idea. It sounded different from all the names in the family and indicated a step forward into the new world. Or so Anand thought. It was easy on the tongue and was accepted. This was the first decision that was taken in the house without the involvement of the Lady.

The other children in the meantime were growing up and started the process of exodus to stand on their own. Each departure, though a relief on the household's straining economy, lanced Jodhi's heart with a hot spear. She loved them all unconditionally and had grown accustomed to their constant presence. The first one, the helper in the shop, was already under the tutelage of Jodhi in preparation for the public service exam that would put him in the state tax department. The Lady watched this with growing admiration. That such avenues existed was foreign to her. Her ignorance of the functioning of the outside world was as complete as her capacity to manage her home, amidst any difficulty. While the women toiled for the future of the family, Anand continued his carefree life. It was enough for him to pass on the salary at the end of the month. The losses and the gains from his other activities remained out of the Lady's radar.

The friends' circle of Anand was planning a weekend trip to Bangalore, the neighbouring capital. The reasons for the trip were: they had a surprise weekend with three consecutive holidays, there was no prohibition in Bangalore, Tamil Nadu was a dry state then, they had money to blow and there was a weekend high-stake horse-racing session. None of this made any sense to Anand. Wiser counsels prevailed and Anand declined the invitation.

The months went rolling by and soon it was time for Ishwaran to proceed to Madurai to pursue his studies for which he had received a state scholarship. The family sent him off with mixed feelings. Pride of the first scholarship was being consumed by the fear of the unknown. Jodhi was afraid of the streak of lunacy that touched all the intelligentsia. Her fears were prophetic, though no one had a clue then.

Soon after that, the elder one also cleared the exam and went into the state department of taxes. His success became a benchmark for the other children to follow and most of them would take the same route after schooling got over, and get themselves placed in some department of the state. Some would venture into private enterprise also. One would join Gopal as an apprentice in the garage. Of course all this applied to the lesser mortals and not to the apple of the eye of the family, Amar.

I was growing up almost to an equivalent of a rich spoilt brat; only we were not rich. I had not known hunger, hard work or any difficulties that the entire family had undergone incessantly. I was also a sick child, in the physical sense. The outbreak of flu or a cold in the town would start with me. For the first time, the family had found it necessary and located a family doctor. Anand never had the patience to spend time on such routine tasks and the waiting room of the doctor was always in the company of my mother, a constant, and either the Lady or Bhaskar. If one concluded that Anand had no affection, they would be wrong. The intervening hours for Anand, in the evening between his office and his nocturnal tryst with thirteen (or three) cards, were well spent on me. He would spend the entire time, we had seen earlier that this time was a variable, with me on his lap. Anand, who had not held any of the other children in his arms, would not let go of me. His was a love and affection that stuck to a time-table, in the allotted hours. I was also spoiled further by the household. After all, who did not love a small child and a handsome one as I was?

Life could have continued on this predictable course with each of the kids getting a job, leaving the house, the Lady getting comfortable enough to close her factory, Anand continuing in his own ways but not slipping any more, Jodhi with her sense of satisfaction at dispensed justice, if Anand had not accepted the invitation six months later to go to Bangalore. The moral standards of Anand were very flexible. He embarked on the trip with the same vigour with which he opposed it roughly a year ago. Bhaskar's advices fell on deaf ears. Bhaskar knew the group that visited Bangalore. All of them were rich. Making money on horse racing was not their purpose. It was the combined intoxication of liquor and the prospect of the stakes involved in racing that lured them time and again. The friends were rich and could afford losses that equalled roughly Anand's pay packet, stretched over two days of drinking and mindless gambling. Anand should have listened to Bhaskar and said 'no'. It was the wisest thing.

Anand went with them the subsequent week.

The first night that they arrived, Anand, who had his own strange moral standards, declined the offer of booze but took part only in the game of cards. Fate was playing its cruel hand and ensured that Anand won enough to fall into the bottomless pit of racing the next day. The horse is such a beautiful animal – flowing mane, rippling muscles, phenomenal stamina and a run that could look so majestic. Only man can devise a method of making the animal run for money and pride, both that it did not understand. He observed the rules and the money won. He bought just one ticket for the sense of participation and lost it. He saw people studying, *not reading*, reports about the horses. He understood that a lot of research went into understanding each horse, its pedigree, its equine family tree. He was introduced to terms like colt, mare, a leg, canter, the exotic names of each horse, the owners, jockeys, trainers, stud farms, standings, placing and most important of them all, the jackpot. This was the proverbial pot of gold at the end of the rainbow.

The third day saw Anand doing his homework and placing a careful bet on the five legs that comprised the jackpot. The four legs were over. Anand had come through. In the fifth and final leg Anand had *banked*. This meant that he placed his choice on one single horse. This was not the favourite. Anand would never know why he placed his money on a single horse and that too in the deciding leg of the jackpot. He never expected that he would be left standing with a stake in the final leg of his first racing episode. The board displayed that there were seven candidates left in the race for the jackpot, a sizeable amount. All his friends had lost much earlier, and had no interest in staying back. They wanted to get back to the hotel and start drowning their loss in whisky. But they stayed on, after seeing that Anand was close to winning his first jackpot. The last leg of the jackpot started. The race of about 1,200 metres by a good horse lasts normally less than three minutes. It looked like an eternity to Anand that day. His palms were sweating and his palpitations racing at an alarming rate. His vision blurred. Compared to this, the excitement, that one encountered when holding the winning suit in hand, paled into insignificance. It was heady, unbearable, tense, gruelling and fun.

It would have been absolutely fantastic if his horse had come first. It came seventh. Anand saw the jackpot amount going to three, who shared it and he never banked again a crucial leg later in his life. If he had won, there was a distinct possibility of his not returning. The sum that big would have raised questions at home and he would have been convinced not to pursue. The loss made him an addict. He went to horse racing as frequently as he could. He did later even when there was no need for quick money at home. It was never about money. It had always been about the burning that came from within, only to a gambler. Only Anand never understood it.

That night he added whisky to his list of compulsions. Whisky made him forget the loss. Actually he became unconscious. But that was his defence for continuing whisky later on.

He vowed that he would be better prepared for his next racing session and really put his heart into the preparation that saw him making enough money to sustain his infatuation with both the horse and the whisky. Here again, he remembered only the good times and the losses were covered up. That a gambler always ends up losing was never clear to him till his death. No gambler ever understands this; never.

15

Years of Stability

That period between my first year and my sixth year was when the family, sort of, stabilised. This was the period during which the remaining children finished their school, except the last one who still had another two years. He would be the second one in the house, after Anand, to fail to clear his school final. Officially the first one, as no one knew about the results of Anand. Not even Jodhi. This was one secret that Anand did not share with his wife. Call it male chauvinism, if you want. This last one would go and join Gopal in his garage, when I would be in my second year in school. Almost every one ended up with a proper employment to boast of. The Lady did not want any of their earnings. It was sufficient if they did not add to her expenses. This was also the period when the first one got married. Anand and Jodhi played the role of the groom's parents in the wedding ceremony. They would subsequently don the same role on five other occasions before they did that on mine.

An intelligent reader at this point would notice one marriage missing. Ishwaran did not marry and that story would unfold in due course of time at the appropriate juncture in the narration. It was during this period that Anand got his first promotion. The celebration was, naturally, in Bangalore. The family only had the opportunity to receive the good news. Celebrations were not the norm in the house. No one celebrated birthdays, anniversaries or promotions. My wife would introduce such a civil habit in the family and practice it almost singlehandedly. The Lady was by then (I mean when my wife introduced such civilities) dead and she was never a witness to one such family event. The additional income and the reducing burden of the dependents meant that the family had more money at its disposal and there entered for the umpteenth time in the Lady's mind that the family could stop 'the factory'. Jodhi insisted on that as she was a witness to the sufferings of the Lady from the beginning. It was getting evident that the Lady was getting old. It took her longer to get up at the end of the daily ordeal and the creaks and snaps were louder in her joints. Joints, that she did know she possessed, were aching. The family doctor, my favour to the family, observed that the abuse could not go on for long. He did not know the family background or anything about Bismarck. This comment alone convinced the Lady to carry on for seven months longer than what was necessary. Finally she threw in the towel. After informing all her customers and giving sufficient time for their palette to get accustomed to drab products that were available in the market in the name of her delicious papads and pickles, the factory was shut down around Diwali when I was four-years old. The sudden release from the daily backbreaking full time occupation left her suddenly with time in her hand. For the first time in her long life she had time and no job. The kids were all but gone. I was too young and, barring the continuing ailments that afflicted me with amazing regularity, did not need much attention. I had not a full-time job. If my parents had not made the foolish decision of stopping with one offspring, may be there would have been few more kids around and she would have had her hands full. She did not know what to do with her free time. Of course, she could have gone deep into religion; befriended the forty-two Gods. She could have channelled her energy and intentions into some social cause. She could have done many worthy things.

But she decided to become a mother-in-law.

There are things that one cannot explain in life. This is the reason we have invented Gods, fate, providence and other terms like these. How else could one explain Anand, the obedient son, loyal husband and the responsible uncle to all his nephews getting mired into all the addictions that destroyed him? How else could one explain the heartlessness of the parents-in-law who sent the Lady's second daughter home with four kids because their son ran away from responsibility? How else could one explain ....so many other things? Thus it was not possible to chronicle why the Lady became what she eventually became. But there were no grey areas there. She became the perfect mother-in-law, exaggerated in melodramas (of sliver screen; the TV soaps were still some years away) of that time, and made life miserable for Jodhi from then on till her last days. She would realise the injustice and even reconcile with Jodhi with only the little time left to live. That was a solace too late to have any meaning for Jodhi.

Suddenly everything that Jodhi did was wrong. The wayward ways of Anand was Jodhi's making. I was constantly unwell because of Jodhi. The sorry lives of her two daughters were due to Jodhi. Jodhi lived comfortably when the Lady was killing herself with the toil in the factory. Or so the Lady alleged. The early morning coffee was too hot; or too cold; too dark; or too light. The house was always dirty. The dresses always needed another wash. The food was bland. The list grew bigger and more ridiculous with each passing day. Jodhi was initially dumbstruck and did not know how to proceed. She thought that this would subside as she still greatly admired the Lady. It did not. Surprisingly or conveniently, Anand did not notice this. The Lady was dispensing venom in the absence of Anand to start with and with no sign of any challenges, grew bolder. It became her full-time occupation. She did not spare her even when someone was around. She made it a point to be at her sarcastic best when Jodhi's parents were around. They, like any stereotype of that time, first questioned Jodhi and even *advised her* against her non-existing lapses. When it became clear that this was purely one sided, and unable to spot or suggest a remedy, they stopped visiting their daughter altogether. This was considered as a victory by the Lady.

Jodhi approached Anand with this problem. She did not still take it to a level of complaint. Psychiatry could have been a solution. Their interaction with doctors stopped at physical ailments and they did not know anything about Dr Freud or his specialisation. Anand treated it like any other problem he had faced in life. He was a firm believer that if you looked at a problem long enough, it would go away. He listened to all the woes of Jodhi and told her that everything would be alright over a period of time. More like a sage delivering a discourse to his followers. It did not have any specific action plan or time frame. Anand became less patient with each subsequent outpouring of a tear-soaked Jodhi. She stopped telling him when it became evident that continued perseverance of this matter at this forum would alienate her husband *in addition* to her mother-in-law. This was the first time she thought about her as a mother-in-law in their years together. She started crying silently whenever she was alone, or in my presence. Thus even after growing up, my childhood recollection of those years of financial stability at my home had always been of a visiting father, a shouting grandmother and a weeping mother.

The atmosphere at home was becoming suffocating and troubling for Anand and he used every opportunity to stay away from home. It broke his heart to see the sorry plight of his wife. Her parents were too gentlemanly to ask him anything. He was still scared to confront his mother. Unable to hide his impotency to address the issue, he started advising his wife on correcting *her* behaviour. This sent her into a deeper shock and she withdrew more into her shell, where she had place only for me and her own pack of Gods. She stopped speaking except in the interrogative mode of asking what anyone wanted. Her answers became monosyllabic. She became jittery as anything she did, brought out a volley of insults from the Lady. At some point in time, she just gave up. She started existing, instead of living.

All the while I was growing up, with one new illness every month. My parents started travelling more due to me. The capabilities of the local doctor had been exhausted and I needed a new specialist for new ailments. I contracted all illnesses that were listed in the vaccination chart. I managed most of them just before the vaccination was due. Chicken pox, jaundice, measles, mumps, fits, laryngitis, tonsillitis and any other conceivable "itis". These journeys were a troubled mix for my mother. On the one hand she was happy to be away from her new tormentor and on the other, the state of my health was eating her alive. Most of my ailments lasted the stipulated time and went away, only to be replaced by the next one in wait. The doctors could do nothing to predict and prevent and managed to treat and contain only. The continued bad health was giving her other nightmares. What if I died? Suddenly their decision to have only one child appeared stupid. Anand was man enough to accompany her on these ordeals and did not leave the task to the Lady or Bhaskar.

Bhaskar had sensed and seen the transformation in the Lady and could do nothing as the matter was very delicate. He also stopped frequenting. The Lady felt her triumph completed with fewer people visiting the house. I, in the meantime, was almost on athe 'explore Tamil Nadu' trip with my medical tourism. I had visited most of the cities in Tamil Nadu by the time I was six and all I could recollect later most of the hotels, buses, trains and waiting rooms. Oral medication was as regular as the food I ate, and injections became the norm. When most of the children of my age would start hollering when the syringe was taken out of the boiling water, I could carry out a normal conversation with my mother when the doctor was *administering* the injection.

I was finally six. It was time for me to go to school. The expectations from me were greater. Ishwaran was the standard for me in education. Set by the family, of course. I had no such crazy ideas. The last boy, who would fail in his final exams, and I were the duo that went to school together. A far cry from the group of seven that was doing the job with a schoolbag on one shoulder and goods to be sold, on the other. If I had undergone a similar hard life, may be I would have turned out to be better.

In the meantime, there was good news from Madurai. Ishwaran had completed his first Master's degree in history and he was proceeding further. Why anyone would study so much, the family wondered! Jodhi by then had been so deflated that she failed to even appreciate the achievement of Ishwaran, given his beginning and surrounding. Ishwaran was grateful and wrote a letter to Jodhi, personally thanking her for what he had managed to achieve. He would continue his second postgraduation and at the same time, take classes for the undergraduates. He was already becoming popular by giving speeches on almost every topic under the sun. He also came into the sight of the district chief of a budding political party and was taken into its wings. They found their Hitler in him – small in stature, frail but with firebrand oration. There the similarities ended. For unknown to the family, Ishwaran had made inroads into experiments with marijuana. The suicidal streak of his mother, who jumped into a well, must have brushed on him. So far his indulgence in marijuana was at the nascent stage and had not become a life-destroying, image-shattering millstone that it eventually became to everyone. He was only seeking his journey into the realms of fantasies induced by the smoke at about two times a month. He had the tell-tale glassy look and trembling fingers that went with the habit. The family was foreign to such things and never noticed anything amiss when he came home on holidays. Also, was he not another child with a poor constitution? His erudition made him mumble words from the Beatles and Pink Floyd in his state of drugged ecstasy.

My school days were not exceptional and passed almost unnoticed. I did not excel nor did I fail. I was surely better than everyone else in the family except Ishwaran. To equal, or surpass, what he had achieved was impossible. None of my teachers ever failed to mention the excellence of him in prodding me to do further and I started hating him for destroying my sense of achievement at that age. My above-average performance was a soothing balm to my mother, who would hug me tight every night and murmur, "Please study well", amidst her silent crying. Neither the plea nor the crying would make any sense to me. I was too young to understand her reasons for crying. In fact who knew why she cried? For loss of innocence? Separation from her parents? The fluctuating health of her only son? For a spineless husband? For a ruthless woman she now hardly understood? If you had asked her even she would have been at a loss. It was heart-rending, however. No child should ever go to sleep listening to the silent weeping of its mother. Jodhi longed for the days of penury when she went to sleep with hunger every day but with a light heart. She cursed this financial stability which destroyed her life in other ways. Her husband was spending very little time at home. On the contrary, the Lady was spending every moment at home.

It was that time of the year when Gopal came home and Jodhi dreaded what would happen. She was scared to think of her reaction if the Lady continued in her merciless ways in front of Gopal. Gopal always remained an outsider for Jodhi and even after all these years, she could not develop any close bonds with him. She felt more comfortable in the presence of Bhaskar. Gopal came and this time he had news to tell.

He was planning to settle down in life. The man for whom he was driving the car had decided to become his father-in-law as well. He was so impressed with the business sense of Gopal that he decided to entrust his entire business to him. In order to ensure that the business continued to yield benefits to the family, he offered his daughter to Gopal. Gopal also agreed. He never felt it necessary to discuss this with his family. Why should he? None of his actions so far had been with any discussion or consent of the family. He was gracious enough to tell them before the wedding and it was planned the following year. That the girl was ten years younger than him did not matter. He had achieved his second ambition also. Now on, he would be driving his own car. Of course, this decision of Gopal to go ahead and decide his own life was also due to the influence of Jodhi as per the Lady.

Jodhi had already crossed a point where words hurt her no more.

16
Gopal Arrives

The marriage took place the following year. Gopal had not made any indications that he would get back to the original family, nor extended any invitation for anyone to stay with him. His association with the family had so far been an annual affair and that was how he wanted it to continue. His wife was a decent lady with none of the anticipated arrogance of a wealthy girl. She was down to earth and would anchor the life at various points later when the adventurism of Gopal was tossing the boat even in calm waters. The family returned after the wedding and Gopal started his new life. He would go on to produce five children, squander all the wealth he inherited and build it all over again.

There were no indications of any of these in the initial years. The ownership transferred smoothly and most of the workmen were already familiar with Gopal in a supervising capacity. The father-in-law retired early and devoted his life to visiting all the temples in India. He died within a year of the wedding and did not see his first grandchild. Gopal had a lust for land. He wanted to make a fortune in real estate. He would scout the satellite towns and locate promising patches of land. The paper work was unbelievable and frauds thrived in that field. Gopal sold all the assets except the main garage and the house, and converted all his assets into investments in land. Gopal was smart, but not smarter than the blood-sucking leeches in the real estate market. Duplicates were made on his original documents. The forged documents were made authentic with sufficient greasing of the corrupt officials and within a span of three years, Gopal reduced his inheritance to the single house in which he lived and added a child to his list of liabilities.

Life at my place, in the meantime, was inching along. I had been cementing my place in school. The last of the boys had already left after failing to clear his final exams and joined Gopal as an apprentice in his garage. He had no idea that the garage would be sold in quick time to cover the losses of Gopal, but fortunately for him, the subsequent owner did not believe in a complete overhaul which would have thrown him back at the doors of my home again. He continued even in the absence of Gopal.

The first one, who was already married, had started showing unmistakable signs of the family genes. He had already fathered a girl and the news leaked back that he was often seen in the vicinity of the unofficial places that sold liquor. His wife, who would often visit our home, had started complaining about his drinking habits. The Lady confronted him one day and poured out all her wrath on him for his irresponsible ways. She more than made up for her failure when the matter of Anand's drinking habits came to her knowledge. If the wife had expected any good results out of this, she did not know anything about those who drink. This spineless guy swore on all the Gods and even on his dead mother to plead innocence. It was easy to believe in something if the alternative was mired with only troubles and unpleasant consequences. The Lady took his word and started abusing his wife for tarnishing the image of her boy and the name of the family.

Jodhi smiled for the first time in years, looking at the irony of the phrase 'family name'. She consoled the girl and advised her not to open the topic again. When Jodhi questioned him, he could not lie to her and conceded to his addiction. Jodhi went into a long and patient monologue of all the tribulations that the family had gone through and beseeched his turning around into a better man. She added the poor plight of his wife and daughter for good measure. Here was a first daughter in the family after the previous generation that was full of sons and she counselled him to prevail over with better senses. He was tearful and was pathetic. He was disgusted with himself. He went home and apologised to his wife. He swore on his daughter that he would never touch alcohol as long as he lived. He begged for forgiveness. His wife was elated. She met Jodhi at her office and thanked her tearfully for saving her husband and her life.

Her husband came home that night stone drunk and became the first one (and the only one to the best of my knowledge) in the family history to earn the term 'wife beater'. He kicked the daylights out of the poor woman. She was lost. That such a change would take place in a matter of six hours was indigestible. The girl, a small child, watched with horror the flailing arms, thrashing legs and bruises all over the body of her mother. She was too young to understand what was happening, but was old enough to cry. This sound diverted the attention of the inebriated beast from the wife to the daughter and he started assaulting his daughter also. His wife, who hugged the child to protect her from the senseless husband, did not let her go, even after her husband had gone to sleep after such a tiring work. It was only when she was certain that the beast had fallen asleep did she attempt to get up and it was then that she realised she had a broken arm.

The doctor who treated the broken arm smiled sadly when the woman told him that she had fallen down in the bathroom. He wanted to point out that one did not get bruises all over the body, lacerations on the face and a black eye to boot falling down in a bathroom. He treated many women from the adjoining slums with tell-tale signs that revealed a drunkard for a husband. This was, however, the first time that he encountered the phenomenon from a proper locale. He knew Jodhi and the family well and later confided to her the news. Jodhi visited her home that evening and waited for the rascal to return. These guys have an antenna that is pretty strong and the chap avoided the house in Jodhi's presence. His wife finally told Jodhi to proceed as she had seen the worst the previous day and had come to accept life as a fatality that came very easily to women of my state. The why always eluded me but I had seen it repeated on countless occasions to be an authority on this topic.

This guy began to sink lower, if that was possible, and the poor wife finally told Jodhi not to bother about them any more. She, however, requested that the Lady need not be told about the same or the subsequent degeneration. Jodhi could not even bring herself to ask Anand to address the matter as how could she? That would qualify for the classic case of the pot calling the kettle black. Here she was wrong in her judgement. Anand never ignored his responsibilities and while he remained addicted to the habit, amongst others, his was not the sort to convert a private indulgence into a public spectacle. Anand addressing the matter would have had no difference but Jodhi was incorrect in her assumption of Anand as a wrong choice.

Liquor as an addiction could sound strange to many, who are in the habit of drinking as a cultivated refined habit. This sort could savour the finest single malt on every weekends and take anywhere between two to three hours to nourish about two drinks. Seeing was believing when it came to someone like the poor woman's husband's drinking. This cult had a very strange behaviour. Not for them the nuances and niceties. This group always bought the liquor in 'quarters', never a full bottle. This 'quarter' is roughly one-fourth a quart and a most common measure that is sold. The entire 'quarter' is emptied into a glass and after a good measure of soda splashed on the same, was drunk in a single gulp. No one wasted time in sniffing, swirling, taking a tentative sip, rolling it in the mouth or allowing the aroma to tantalise. The fiery stuff went straight down. While it started acting on one's system and numbing the senses, one would already be on his third or fourth drink of the evening. What exactly such a person enjoyed was always a mystery. With increasing addiction, one started going from a more expensive brand to a cheaper one and then to one that was still cheaper. At a point of no return, what mattered to him was the alcohol and nothing else. The few moments of sobriety were not enough to dwell on the collapsing household, or lives that he destroyed.

Jodhi felt a moral responsibility for the woman and her daughter and would insist on the daughter spending the time at her house often just to ensure a normal atmosphere for the child to grow up. The Lady was getting from bad to worse and even national and natural calamities were now attributed to the scheming of Jodhi. Then came the news that Gopal was coming down ahead of his annual trip and it spelt bad news to Jodhi. Gopal arrived with his wife and his first son. His wife was already pregnant with the second child. Gopal came with the news that his immediate return was not an option. He had sold the house to take care of the last of the debtors, and had arrived here to settle down and start anew. He had confidence in his capabilities and only wanted shelter for a month, at the most. The word 'no' was never heard in the household. If they had taken care of seven hungry kids when they had no money or clue where the next meal was coming from, what was the issue with three more in reasonably good times?

Anand as usual, had no opinion, Jodhi's would not matter and the Lady could not say 'no'. After all, was not Gopal her favourite from a very young age?

Gopal stayed for five months and of course, no one took 'one month' on the face value. But true to his words, he settled down quickly and with thousands of apologies and thanks in equal measures, left for his own life in another part of the town. The Lady declined an offer to join them in their new house and preferred to stay with my family. This made Jodhi happy, inexplicably. The five months that the family stayed together formed a strong bond between Gopal's wife and Jodhi and it stayed that way later. Both were grateful to each other. For Gopal's wife, it was the unconditional acceptance and the absence of embarrassing questions. The family never questioned their fall from wealth, nor enquired about future plans. It never made them feel as intruders. It was a show of matured acceptance of hardships of life as normal. For Jodhi, it was a brief period of peace. For reasons unknown, the Lady kept a low profile during the five months that Gopal stayed with them and spared Jodhi from her acid tongue.

It was about a month after Gopal left us to settle down that we moved into our new home. Not our own; Anand would never own a property to his name, but a very decent rented one, which had its bathroom (I mean a proper bathroom, not just a portion symbolically cordoned off as one) and a toilet *inside* the house.

17
Oral Exam

Cirrhosis was the first word I remember hearing after entering the new home. I did not know the meaning of the word; only the grave concern with which it was uttered. My mother pleaded with my father to have some control over his drinking, "Look at the state of ….." she trailed off on spotting me in the vicinity. I was intelligent enough to conclude that someone known to us was in possession of this cirrhosis, whatever that might be, and my father would get the same if he did not control his drinking, whatever that he was drinking. The next day before sipping my milk, I asked, "Mother, will I get cirrhosis if I drink this?"

She tousled my hair and asked me not to speak words the meaning of which I did not understand. Later in my life, I would not heed this advice and go on to write a word, the meaning of which I did not know, at least not in the entire context and would get thrashed to inches of my life. So I asked her the meaning of the word and she said I was too young to discuss such matters. This looked like an endless loop to me. All I knew was I would not get anywhere with my mother and I approached my father with the same question. You could have knocked him down with my little finger. He turned a deep red, not impossible, given his fair complexion and brushed me aside, vaguely mumbling. This was his answer to most of my queries anyway. The only thing new this time was his physical discomfort. His physical affection seemed to decrease with my increasing age. He, who would not let me go from his lap when I was a child, now hardly had any physical contact with me. I somehow always needed physical confirmation of affection and its absence led me to believe the absence of affection also. This was the first of my misunderstandings with my father. I never voiced them and so he never clarified them. I had drawn my own conclusions and he paid a price later.

The next word I remember was marijuana. Ishwaran confided in me when he was home for his holidays. I do not know if ramblings of a hallucinated mind can be considered as confiding. He pronounced it with a 'y' sound and for most of my life, I always misspelled the word. Not that any one noticed it, as I never had to use the word in its written form at any places where it mattered. I was also gently reminded by Ishwaran not to discuss this topic with anyone. Ishwaran's understanding of the word 'gentle' was strange and I never uttered a word about it. It was easy to link lunacy with the higher level of intelligence and I was scared stiff. I was closeted with Ishwaran as he was my role model. If I had achieved what he had managed in academics, my job would have been over. So I stayed with him when he was home on holidays, as if intelligence was transferred by induction.

Ishwaran was a delight for it was easy to be stunned by his brilliance. There was not one topic that was strange for him to discuss. He could talk on any topic for any period of time. Jodhi looked on him in silent admiration and longed for the same greatness in her son. Ishwaran by then was smoking grass quite regularly. While the family was immune to the signs of his new indulgence, I always enjoyed the pungent acrid smell of the weed on him.

These two words I remember distinctly because they sounded the death knell of the first two children that my mother moulded into with affection and love. The weekends were fun because both my mother and I would escape to Gopal's house, sometime with my grandmother, and at other times on our own. Anand's weekends were precious. They were spent either in the company of cards, or as was lately becoming regular, at Bangalore. The sense of fatalism that I discussed earlier was common to all women and my mother was no exception. She was feeling a little relieved as my tryst with the ailments seemed to be over. I was not strong and healthy in any conventional sense, but I was not ill and that was more than sufficient. Gopal's son and I bonded well and the second was a daughter. Anything that young was beautiful and we would spend the whole day playing outdoors with our sister. Both the mothers managed to perfect the knack of keeping their conversation and household chores going while keeping the corner of their eye trained on us. Invitation to spend the night in their home was turned down regularly as I needed to cuddle with my mother for my sleep. As I said earlier, affection to me meant physical and my mother had no problems in discharging that.

The new home was surely an improvement over our previous shack and here we had a room in addition to a hall. The room was meant for the three of us and the hall for the Lady and anyone who came visiting. The backside of this arrangement had a kitchen, a bathroom and the novelty of a toilet. The others and I in the house were spared the ignominy of leaving the house to go to the toilet. The long walk through your neighbourhood, with an advertising bucket of water that splashed water on your legs all through the walk, could be quite humiliating. Though we had a room to our self, I never recall spending a night in that room with my father. His timing was strange and unpredictable. Most of my childhood memories of the morning hours were with my mother in the kitchen, my grandmother in the hall cursing my mother, my father in our room fast asleep (at eight in the morning!) and myself getting ready for the school. Two things never failed to surprise me – my grandmother's perseverance and my mother's patience. I sometimes used to speak in a low voice just to check whether my mother was deaf, as how else could one explain this silent suffering.

This grandmother, who was devil incarnate for my mother, was an angel to me. She pampered me. This was the first time in her life that she had a child in her house with time and money to spare. When it became evident that I would be a lone child, an act for which also my mother received her vitriolic comments, her affection towards me grew. The other grandchildren she nurtured were only a responsibility and here for the first time she had a child to love. This Dr Jekyll and Mr Hyde persona of her left me confused. Every child likes to be pampered and I was no exception. Her pampering made me forgive her cruel treatment to my mother and I grew accustomed to the daily happenings. After all, if my mother did not mind it, why should I? Her pampering varied from goodies to eat, to money to spend, toys to be bought, protection on occasions when my misdeeds deserved a proper hiding. I was spoilt by her. And I enjoyed it. My mother would be left helpless on many occasions, unable to correct me, while I shamelessly schemed and sought my grandmother's cover. I was already becoming good at manipulating people to my end result. On each such occasion, my mother would unfailingly tell me where I went wrong in the hours before we slept. But who cared? I listened to all with a smug confidence that I would be able to repeat what I did, with the antidote clear in my mind. My mother was glad that at least I was not at the receiving end of the Lady.

The daughter of the drunkard, that was how I always recalled her though I might not have fully understood what it meant, Priya spent most of her days at our home. Her mother was happy at this arrangement. Many an evening I remember her coming to collect her daughter. It was pathetic to look at her. She was impossibly emaciated. Her husband had stopped worrying about them any more. Why they lived together was not clear to me. She started doing lot of odds-and-ends jobs to sustain. Not even a tenth of her husband's salary reached home. With no clear reprimand from anyone in the family, he grew braver. He began reporting to his office, partly drunk. There were whispers of departmental enquiry into his conduct. The speed with which anything moved in government offices was a boon to him. Priya would unknowingly relive her father's young days by living in our house. My mother's heart went out to her and she cared all she could. The Lady never had anything against children and Priya never felt unwelcome in my home. My mother asked for Priya living with us permanently as that made sense, but something fundamentally stupid did not allow her mother to allow that to happen. Except for the nights that Priya spent terrified at her home, she spent most of her days with us in our home.

There was now a sustained belligerence from the Lady towards my mother which was different from the open war when her transformation began. This allowed Bhaskar back into our home. He would teach me the difficult subjects. He would listen to all my exploits, carefully filtering out my exaggeration. Whenever I stepped into territories that were definitely adult, he would gently draw me away. He was willing to listen to anything I wanted to talk about. He taught me to play chess. He initiated my habit into reading. He made me remove the image of Ishwaran as my idol. He showed me there existed a world beyond academic brilliance. He might have been a reason why I never pursued marks and percentages, when that was the only goal of many of my contemporaries. I played chess with him regularly and, he sportingly allowed me to beat him at correct intervals, designed to keep me interested and at the same time not allowing me to become overconfident. We started buying newspaper in the home – the first clear sign that we could afford finer things in life, after my reading habit became steady, thanks to his persistence. Even later in my life, much after he disowned me, I could never fail to think of the smiling Bhaskar when I opened the newspaper in the mornings.

I was enjoying my life with none of the difficulties that the rest of the family had experienced. It was the time for my year-end examinations. I had already appeared for four exams. I had only one left to go. A weekend came in between and I went to Gopal's house as usual. We were playing in the ground adjacent to the house. Though I had one more exam left, my preparations were complete and I had no care in the world. One more exam and the holiday started. My mother was against going to Gopal's house that weekend as exams were at hand. I could be adamant if I wanted. I also had an ally in my mothers' nemesis. As I had pointed out earlier. I was already shameless in manipulating people to my needs, and she had no choice. We went and another usual Sunday followed at Gopal's residence. We were about to leave. My mother called me from the house and I turned midway during a climb to the top of the tree and fell. The pain was excruciating as if someone poked a red hot iron rod into my arm and the last thing I heard, before passing out, was the clear and unmistakable snap of a bone in my arm. My right arm, the writing hand.

The doctor was categorical that I needed rest and the snap I heard turned out to be three snaps together and they were from my fingers. The plaster would stay on for six weeks, roughly the period of my holidays and I would be ready to go to school when the schools reopened, the doctor assured. To the *same class*, I thought with horror! Those were not the days of child psychology – rods were not spared, and students, who did not meet the bare minimum, were failed. Children then had no inbuilt protection till class eight. I started crying. This gave my grandmother a new topic to harass my mother. She had managed on limited ammunition for a surprisingly long time. Here I gave her the equivalent of a submachine gun on a platter. My mother tried to speak sense into me. I would not listen. Latching on the doorway shown by the illogical Lady, I actually started blaming my mother for what happened. "If you had not called me, I would not have fallen," I said.

She was dumbstruck. "You would not have fallen if you had listened to me and stayed home," she retorted with a flash of anger that was new in her. This was because she was used to unfair allegations from her mother-in-law, but was horrified to see her son taking the same road.

It was Bhaskar who came to the rescue.

"We have the whole holiday to decide who is responsible for the fracture. We now need to address the issue of ensuring that Amar goes to his next class and does not return to his old class."

"How is that possible now? He did not listen to me," Jodhi wailed, unwilling to give up so easily. "He has missed one of his exams. There is surely no way that can be overlooked."

"I am not saying that it can be overlooked. May be, we can try to make some amends. I know his classteacher and Amar's performance so far has been good. We can do something."

It was decided that Bhaskar would approach the headteacher of the school and arrange for an oral exam for me, with a new set of questions. As the exam had ended, repeating the same question paper would have looked improper. You needed someone like Bhaskar to even attempt such out-of-the-box thinking. No one in my family would have thought of such a compromise and surely not my father, I thought unfairly. This habit of mine to blame someone for mistakes of mine would continue to grow with me. This allowed me to dump my responsibility on someone else and shamelessly walk away, even with the head held high. Bhaskar brought me to reality reminding that the idea was still only that and the headteacher might not approve of the same. It was alright with me. Even if the school had not accepted the proposal and detained me in the same class, it would not have mattered, as in my mind Bhaskar was already a hero, and my father a mere lump of flesh.

The headteacher must have got down from the right side of his bed, or his usually grumpy wife must have been nice to him over the breakfast of crisp dosas. He agreed to the proposal and he agreed to a re-test. Thus it was a week into my holidays I gave my oral exam on my last subject in front of a panel of five of my schoolteachers. Such an incident had not happened in the history of the school before and would never happen again.

The lesson that my mother wanted me to learn, to exercise restraint, went flying with the kites that Gopal's son and I flew that summer. My father reprimanded me for my carelessness with exams around. "What would have happened if we did not have some one like Bhaskar to help us?" he asked me.

I had no answer for this. I hated him for being so unkind. Here, for the first time, Anand was talking sense and his son could not understand what all the fuss was about. With my parents criticising what I did, any other parent would have probably skinned me alive; I sought solace in the comfort of my grandmother. For my grandmother, the opposite of anything that my mother did was correct.

18

My Early Years

I was a quiet child. But I had broken the accepted behavioural norms on many occasions, sometimes knowingly, and at other times, in innocence. My grandmother was a generous lady, where my mother was not considered and she always felt pity on the homeless and the beggars. In those days, the beggars used to come on a regular basis on a house-to-house basis. They were regulars. The same number of beggars came every day, at the appointed time, from about eleven in the morning to nine in the night. It was as if they were office-goers. They were so punctual that you could set your watch by them. It was unbelievable. Even today when I tell my daughter, she refuses to believe this. The Lady had a box full of small denomination that have ceased to exist today, and was in the habit of giving alms to every one of the beggars who came, every day – a strange custom but one which she practiced nevertheless. May be it was her idea of patronising a society. Miserly to the core, due to the times she had seen, she kept alms and temples as areas out of the orbit. There she held back nothing.

My school was so near to my home that I could actually come home *during* the recess. There was no need, but I did on the pretext of drinking water. In that duration, I would steal some coins from the box and rush back to school. The change was used in buying the most unhygienic edibles that money could buy, near my school. The stuff was tasteless, and the cleanliness of either the ware or the seller and his shop, was deplorable. It continues to be a mystery that I contracted no illness in consuming them. I never needed that stuff. It was, as I said, tasteless and I did not grow up with the difficulties the rest of the family had undergone. I was always well fed. I never knew or experienced hunger pangs. The thrill was in stealing the money right under the nose of everyone in the house, and not getting caught. I also became popular amongst my friends as someone who could treat them to that shit. This went on for a considerable period. The box was filled in the beginning of every month with a very fair approximation of number of beggars multiplied by the number of days. This I did not know. The beggars lost their earnings towards the end of every month.

The first time the Lady attributed it to a miscalculation and did not lose any sleep over that. The period that the beggars went without their earnings, it was so regular they would not have been mistaken if they had called it wages, grew slowly as I grew more audacious and greedy. The Lady was not stupid to make the same miscalculation every month and she realised that the money was being stolen. The first suspect in these matters is generally the hapless maidservant. The Lady was always known for being fair. She would never question the servant without concrete evidence. The safety around the box was increased and the servant was being watched with a Hawk Eye without making it too conspicuous. My success rate was falling down and I realised that luck had held out for long and called it quits. I would surely have been caught if I had continued. The end of the episode left the beggars happy, as they had their steady income all through the month, again. I never confessed to this even after years. This was another trait of mine. I never confessed, never accepted a fault when it was pointed out, and never discussed to sort out a controversy.

This was just one incident of a kaleidoscope that made up my early years. I was not built for sports and I abhorred outdoor games. I used my reading habit as an excuse for not playing any sports and most of the evenings I spent reading or playing chess with Bhaskar. Looking at my interest in reading, my father used to bring books from his office library. I was expected to maintain the books in a pristine condition and return them in the condition they were brought. I was not to fold the corners, keep the spine up or damage them in any way. All these were instructions from my father. As if he ever read anything, I used to smirk. For reasons not very clear, I was already inventing reasons to dislike my father. He used to bring books regularly. He would ask me my likes, and at other times, he used his own judgement. Whatever he brought on his own were bad for me. I was very scared of him as he could turn violent if instructions were ignored. I maintained the books in excellent condition, a habit that would stay with me forever. My books always remained fresh and I regularly used bookmarks later in my life, and was apoplectic if someone mishandled a book, leave alone my book. This perfect track record was spoiled with a set of three books that my father brought once. They were books by Gandhi. The choice was my father's. He expected them to be a proper influence on a growing boy. Though I was sceptical as usual, I was soon engrossed. Mr Gandhi was a powerful writer and he made many complex things look simple. His language was easy and his clarity of thoughts was equalled by the lucidity of language. What happened to those books was another interesting story.

Viji was a strange name for a boy. He was my neighbour. He was not exactly a boy and he was not a man either. His age was difficult to judge. He was not a normal boy, and his parents preferred him at home to avoid embarrassment. He was clumsy and a fool. He was also a pervert. This I did not know in those years. We used to often sit in the evening and chat as both were not in the grounds playing with others – I due to my dislike of sports, and he, for reasons I was yet to learn.

He took out a paper and drew a shape that looked like a heart, like the heart on a playing card, with the central dip not stopping at the top but running right through, sort of bisecting it. He offered it to me for inspection.

I thought he was on the way to becoming an artist, and was going to discourage him, looking at the clumsy sketch.

"What do you think it is?" he questioned me.

What would I think, I had no idea and I told him the only thing that occurred to me, when I looked at it for the first time.

He smiled at the same time, shaking his head in a 'no' on the horizontal axis and said, "Through this a girl pisses." He said this in a hushed voice and with furtive glances.

I also lowered my voice. This practice is called echolalia. You unconsciously imitate the one in front of you.

"So this is the penis of a girl?" I wanted full clarification. Wisdom does not pass you by every day and it is your duty to grab it.

This time he laughed. "Moron! Girls do not have penises; they have vaginas."

It is difficult to understand people like Viji. Why would they go around talking subjects to children who are not fully prepared? Why will they convert an organ of the body into an obscene art? Why will they convert a healthy sex education into puerile journalism? Why will they poison an impressionable mind with incomplete, but tantalising information? It is difficult to answer these questions. But there are enough perverts even today, may be more, who pose a threat to the civilised society. In a country where discussion on sex is taboo, such perverts have a clear field and innocent children fall prey to them. I was lucky to have undergone an experience that stopped at mere discussion.

Three years later this same Viji would molest a younger child, a younger *male* child, and would go to juvenile detention centre. I was spared of such permanent scars. The reader may be wondering where this is leading to. The episode with Viji ended there. Rather, it should have ended here. If I had not gone ahead and completed my next stupid act, a lot of unpleasantness would have been spared.

I was also a big show off. I needed to exhibit my knowledge and my skills. What I craved for was adulation. The showing off stopped the moment my erudition or skill was appreciated. If I learnt a new word, I would go on using it in all my conversations, even incorrectly, till someone asked me what it meant and allowed me to educate them. Ishwaran was not around to spot my incorrect use on the occasions that I did and the rest were not up to that. If my drawing master taught me a new trick of composing a face using five numerals, I would go on drawing that on my notebook, slate and even on newspapers. Someone had to spot and say "Wow" for that to stop. That night I practiced the clumsy shape that Viji showed me on the cover pages of all the books by Mr Gandhi. Why I chose a pen instead of a pencil is not clear to me even today. To make the illustration self-sufficient, I inscribed the words 'girl' and 'vagina' on the two halves. It looked natural and complete. Two halves and two words were meant for each other. After a thorough job that filled the cover pages of all the three books, I went to sleep peacefully.

The explosion that happened next day was a new experience for me; in fact for everyone at home. Anand went insane. He was incoherent. He could not believe what his eyes were seeing. My handwriting was unmistakable. I did not know I was doing something wrong and did not attempt to camouflage my writing. The sacrilege in front of him, and the fact that he had to *replace* those books, for they could not now be returned to the library, combined together and unleashed a fury, not seen before and not after either. The three books came and hit me first like a hurricane. He hit me that day with every conceivable and mobile object in the house – Foot scale, cane, broom, belt and bare hands. He would have gone on and killed me also if it was not for the Lady protecting me. My mother was too ashamed, at what I had done, to come to my rescue. The Lady kept me shielded after the initial damage, itself very considerable, and kept demanding Anand the reason for the thrashing. This was quite a situation. How could Anand tell his mother the reason? He paused for a while and the Lady misunderstood this as a halt in the hostilities and exposed me. The sight of me rekindled the rage and Anand started thrashing me again. The Lady took the role of United Nations again and demanded an explanation. In reply Anand thrust the books with my wonderful drawings in her face. This was comical, as the Lady could not read.

I received the next instalment of the assault as the Lady fumbled with the books in her hand in a way only those who cannot read are capable of. She threw the books away in disgust as it did not tell her anything and one of the books hit me on the back. The scene was almost comical. She went back to her role of my guardian angel. She knew that something was wrong, but was not sure what it was. There were only three people in the house who could tell her on what was on the cover pages of the book. Two were too embarrassed to tell her, and the third was on the verge of losing his life. Anand now wanted to know where I had learnt all this crap. I was not certain whether the answer would cease the barrage or renew them with my partner in crime, whatever the crime was, for I still was not sure what was wrong. As I was not certain of the outcome of the confession, I kept quiet. My intention was not to protect Viji; I decided that my association with him was over. No friendship was worth the treatment I was receiving. My quietness was mistaken for stubbornness and I could not remember when Anand stopped hitting me. He left the house in disgust. He drowned his shame in his usual manner. My mother was for the first time ashamed of me and did not speak to me properly for a week. If any of them had opened a discussion with me when things were normal, I would have told them the truth.

Parents assume and believe the worst in their children. Children think that parents are tactless and unreasonable. Most of the tragedies of life stem from this misunderstanding.

I did not understand the reason for the treatment I received as no one was willing to discuss it with me then. It became evident to me later, but the scars of an impressionable mind (and part of the body) are not easily erased.

I told the Lady what I had written on the cover pages when she was inspecting my bruises and she fainted, the only time I remember that happening. If my parents could forget it quickly, it was not because of their magnanimity but because what followed was even more catastrophic. There was a telegram the next day from the college in Madurai that Ishwaran had been expelled and was on his way home.

19

The Lunatic

It was the first of the college. Expelling students was quite within the acceptable. But expelling a faculty? Ishwaran had completed his second masters and was already a regular faculty. His time was more flexible than that of many others, mainly due to the political clout he wielded. It was this political connection that delayed the inevitable. He had gone deeper and complete in his surrender to the wonder weed. He looked disoriented most of the times. But his intelligence was as sharp as ever, when he was sober, and this more than compensated his other lapses. His dress sense had gone astray. He started smoking marijuana in the staff room. A member of the faculty smoking in the staff room was not a big deal, but dope? A section which was envious of his meteoric rise had been waiting for just such an opportunity. The principal of the college was finding it difficult to hold them back any longer. He was also afraid to tackle Ishwaran directly. What if he had become rude? The insolent ways and the devil-may-care attitude of Ishwaran was already part of the folklore. Finally, Ishwaran made it easy for all of them. With his last lapse of reason, even the political clout could not save him.

There was a girl doing B. A. in psychology at the university. She was a girl of an impressionable age. She was completely in awe of Ishwaran's genius. Topics which made no sense to her, when she tried to understand, or when others tried to explain, became clear as crystal after his explanations. There was nothing that he could not explain. She was also a very confused girl. She mixed infatuation with admiration. It is a common malady of most of the students. The world is full of students who would always remember either the mathematics sir or the English madam with amorous shades. Most students, at some point in their life, start falling in love with their tutors. Most of them remain sane and can fondly call back those silly memories because they had passed that stage of infatuation, like most, without any screw up, *literally and figuratively*. She was not one such girl. She was convinced her offering to this great intellectual should be nothing less than her own complete self.

One evening, after college hours, this desire became easier as Ishwaran was completely stoned when she approached him with another one of her endless doubts. The moral defence of Ishwaran was not in functioning mode and the girl was feeling very adventurous. It was a Molotov cocktail. Lust had no role on that evening's proceedings. It was an obsessed student's abject submission and the basic subconscious instincts of a semiconscious Ishwaran taking the lead. The journal remained unexplored, the questions on theology remained unanswered, but a practical on exploration of human anatomy was well under way. Passion is blind and first-timers are known to throw caution to the winds. These two did not choose their setting properly, as it was conceived in the heat of the moment and not premeditated. Thus they did not abide by some of the basic precautions that scheming adults would have undertaken. The open door, clumsy movements, grunts of passion, and stupidity only newcomers were capable of, all culminated in them being found much before what they, or at least the girl, set out to achieve. The shit hit the fan. The girl found it easy to turn into a wronged woman, than be a labelled one with loose morals, and Ishwaran was in no condition to defend or explain. As they say, it was an open-and-shut case. The girl gathered her dishevelled clothes, and Ishwaran, his belongings.

The presence of Ishwaran had never made the family this uncomfortable before. He was always the most liked and admired. If there was one person who was relieved, it was his elder brother, who, for once, was happy that the concern and focus was now redirected. Priya was thrilled as she was having a wonderful time listening to stories and anecdotes from Ishwaran. He had this wonderful gift of talking to a small child comfortably. He was not in the habit of making silly noises and a falsetto tone that many adults mistook as the standard for interaction with a kid. They may be surprised to find that children hate this. Here was a person finally who could talk to the girl normally. It was difficult to believe all that you heard about him. He looked very sane. But for some physical cravings that manifested at appointed hours, like Pavlov's dog, nothing looked abnormal about him.

My showing off had to be curtailed. I was, as it is, lying low after the last adventure that saw me looking into the jaws of death, and this guy's arrival quashed the remaining choices. With the King around, how could the lesser mortals strut? His brilliance remained undiminished. The numbing smoke of marijuana had not reached or maimed his cerebral faculty. Yet.

He seemed at peace with the world. It did not occur to him that he needed to get back to standing on his own. He was used to being a member of this family, and circumstances had forced him to return. It was as simple as that. From where he managed the money for the drug remained unsolved till the end. We were certain that he had stolen money from our home on a few occasions and decided not to pursue it but made his access to money an impossibility. This did not deter him. He managed. Surprisingly he did not have any other indulgence. He did not smoke, I mean cigarettes, or drink.

For the first time Anand took the matter headon and reasoned with Ishwaran. Anand spoke to him, explained the chances that were still possible given his credentials; it was easy to cover up the girl-at-Madurai issue, threatened him, tried to scare him and finally gave up. Ishwaran would listen to the entire conversation, if you can call a completely one-sided monologue that, and get up and leave, leaving

Anand feeling as if the opponent in a boxing match had just left halfway through a promising fight. Anand would continue to sit and stare at the place Ishwaran vacated, unable to understand how to move ahead. He would then give an accusing look at his wife as if it was her fault and leave. He changed the approach, merely juggling the order of reasoning and threat, toyed with alternatives, and even tried early mornings, or when Ishwaran looked cheerful. The result was the same. Sometimes Ishwaran would just go to another corner of the hall and sometime leave the house. I had never seen my father engaged in an activity in the house so earnestly. Anand's patience was very short lived and he gave up eventually. He was resigned to taking him to the ashram once again. He moved the item to one of financial inconvenience and stopped to acknowledge his presence.

Jodhi and the Lady joined forces after a very long time. The acrimony did not recede. It was only pushed to the backburner in the face of a graver crisis. He was subjected to a never-ending assault of emotions, sacrifices made, the poor start, the progress made, and now finally this sorry spectacle, all hammered round the clock. He had almost become a saint by then. In one crazy moment, the Lady even threatened to commit suicide and Ishwaran just lifted one eyebrow by an eighth of an inch in reaction. When such ultimatums are used so early, and fail, further progress is doomed. That was what happened in this case also. In the battle of attrition, everyone had to give up.

Such continued silence grew to an alarming level and suddenly turned into meaningless garrulity. It was then that the family first had an inclination of the extent of damage to Ishwaran's brain in the face of such non-stop abuse of a numbing addiction. Continued marijuana, and his current state of non-activity, combined with an incisive mind had all made him finally insane.

It was initially difficult to accept that he had become mad. The first few instances were nervously laughed away as pranks, though Ishwaran was never known to play pranks even as a kid, leave alone then, when he was such an accomplished grown up. He would wait for my mother to return from work and give her an elaborate military-like salute, and demand coffee with an impish grin. This grin was the reason initially that made us believe that he was joking. When the grin became a sheepish smile, which remained on him for longer and longer duration, till it became permanent, we were certain that we had a problem at hand. He would twist Priya's hand behind her back, and would not stop even when her tense laugh became hysterical with real pain. The Lady or my mother had to intervene. Such and other acts made Priya stop coming to our home. The predictable beast in the night at her home was preferable to this unpredictable fool. My school books and notebooks were vanishing, to surface later in most unexpected corners of the house. One day, he followed my mother all the way to her office and unknown to her, waited outside till the evening. He did not offer her any answer and returned with her like a dog, following her. The Lady was on the verge of going to Bhaskar's house, to go to a police station, to lodge a complaint, as Ishwaran was missing throughout the day. Bhaskar, on whom many unpleasant tasks of my family fell, approached the problem in full earnest.

Ishwaran was actually teasing him when he was normal, and started becoming violent when he became certifiably mad. On one occasion, he calmly went to the kitchen at the end of another attempt by Bhaskar, and returned with a jug full of water. This, he carefully dumped on Bhaskar's head, with all the precision and focus of a priest anointing a deity. Bhaskar liked the family, and did not stop his attempts immediately but even his interest started waning. The other members of the small colony, where we were staying, turned their whispers into open discussions, given my family's gentle behaviour. Many would come and offer solutions, as if everyone had a mad one in their family and had them treated successfully. I did not know there were temples, as centres of cure, especially for the lunatics. I would later go to some of these temples and was relieved that we did not heed the advice and sent Ishwaran to any of these places. These temples were like old age homes where you got rid of your parents. I do not think any lunatic ever got cured at any of these places, but the family was surely spared the trouble. Here you could enlist one and wait for the news that your boy/girl had died. The conditions were inhuman. The other children in the vicinity who were once, in the recent past, encouraged to go and sit with Ishwaran, to increase their brain power, were now barred.

I was also cautioned by the family to keep my interaction to the barest minimum. I was against it. My impression was that a person like Ishwaran needed company and constant engagement, to have any chance of a recovery. To leave a talented, but now disturbed, person like Ishwaran in solitude was a recipe for disaster. I was not old enough to phrase my thoughts well and even if I had, no one would have listened to me. As it is, I was just getting out of my 'persona non grata' status, post my tryst with female genitals in graphical forms. I did not want to endanger my status with any philanthropic attitude towards him. In my mind, he was already a goner. One of my friends told me, "This is what will happen if you study too much." I do not know why, but I believed this statement for a long time.

The Lady was complaining to her Gods for the first time – may be it was voiced loud for the first time, or may be I heard it for the first time. She lamented and wanted to know why she was being subjected to all this torture. She would rather die, she moaned.

"I have seen enough and suffered enough. I cannot withstand such pains any more. Please take me to your abode." With all her years of praying, she was almost on a first name basis with most of her Gods. Such dialogues with Gods were nothing new. But such unadulterated agony was new. She had never cried out to her set of Gods so openly even when the priest died, when her daughters returned, when her daughters died, when Gopal ran away, when Anand was suspended, when Ishwaran's elder brother became a drunk, when Gopal decided his own marriage, or even when I told her what I wrote on the cover pages of the books written by Mr Gandhi. Ishwaran was special. Here was God's gift in human form and she was lucky to be the chosen one. She silently celebrated all his academic achievements and now this unspeakable agony.

"Take my life but spare this genius. He has a lot to achieve," was she cry that night ? I smiled, because I had, by a sheer coincidence, read in my history book that day about King Babur praying similarly, willing to trade his life for that of his son Humayun. As if Gods listen to all this, I thought cynically.

Of course they were listening. It had been a long time since they toyed around with her. They decided to take a life, but not the one that was offered. That night, the well read and intelligent Ishwaran, who knew that slitting one's wrist was a sure way to die, went ahead and slit both his wrists. The blood-soaked bedsheet was the first thing that my mother saw, when she got up to open the door for my father, who, as usual, was returning at about five in the morning. Her screams woke up everyone in the house, except Ishwaran, and few of our neighbours too. Anand, for a moment, was embarrassed standing outside the door at that hour, when the other doors in the colony opened. He was more desperate to get *inside* the house than trying to find out what the screaming was about. The Lady, used to a life full of surprising tragedies, started to wail in a nanosecond. My view was blocked by my grandmother and I could only see blood-soaked hands of my mother behind her. For a moment I thought my grandmother had inflicted an injury on my mother, and was shocked that she would stoop so low. It appeared natural that I also should cry and I cried, though at that point I was crying *for my mother*, thinking she was the one who was hurt. Anand, who was *still* outside, was losing his patience and started banging on the door. The neighbours, most of them not fully awake yet, sensed good drama and joined my father and started banging the door. Only Ishwaran stayed calm, as he was already dead, amidst all this bedlam and with the departure of the Lady towards the door to answer the summons. I noticed that it was Ishwaran's blood on my mother and saw that sheepish grin on his face. It was impossible to look at that face and believe that he was dead.

With one job accomplished, the Gods turned their attention to the last daughter of the Lady.

20

The Final Shock of the First Generation

This family had a period of some uneventful years, thought the Gods, and proceeded to make up for lost time. The tragedy of Ishwaran was soon to be followed by another one, though the family had no idea about this. We were all in complete shock and disbelief over what had transpired. He had been moody alright and was surely mad in the recent past, but was it to the extent of taking his life? Seemed as if he had inherited at least one gene from his mother – the one who had jumped into the well. His elder brother was so far gone in his alcoholism that he went through the funeral rites with absolutely no sense or show of emotions. He wanted to be free by the evening for his sustaining quota of liquor. Ishwaran's was the first death in my family that did not go through the complete thirteen-day cycle, mainly due to his brother, who decided that the arrack shop was better suited to drown the memory. The Lady was in her first period of genuine grief. She had not felt so bad on any of the previous occasions. She considered this passing of life as completely cruel and senseless. If only Ishwaran had pulled on for some more time! Of course, nothing would have happened, as we did not have any specific remedy to his problem. I do not think any of us even understood what his problem was. Jodhi was shattered. Anand had grown to accept all that life could throw at him. He had other worries too. Of late he had been feeling a continuous discomfort on the right side of his stomach, but kept on ignoring it. Every time the pain became severe, he would assign another innocuous overlook, and resort to Digene. He avoided doctors till the time it was possible. He had already had his share of waiting rooms and the suffocating smell of disinfectant, courtesy me.

Bhaskar was as usual a relief. He was worried over a reticent Lady and this, for those who knew her, was a perfect paradox and started diverting her with minor matters, and tried to involve her in some religious events, in and around the locality. This eased up the Lady as expected and she was seen getting back to her former self, which was bad news for my mother. I did not know what was the correct official mourning period and tried to engage Bhaskar in a game of chess when he came home, a day after the cremation. This brought out angry protests from everyone and they all seemed partly relieved to have been offered an outlet for expressing their grief. My supply of books from the library dried up for obvious reasons. It was really very pathetic to be a child, or a young boy, in a place immediately after a death. The capacity for a young one to grieve is limited and the elders in the family pay no attention to this. They grieve longer. The grief is normally directly proportional to one's affection and the association. So it is that the elders are still grieving when a young one becomes normal after the initial shock. This overlapping period is hell. You are shushed and hushed as often as you open your mouth, and laughing, which comes naturally to a child, is suddenly taboo.

Ratna played an important role in the next tragedy of the family. The strangest thing was that we had nothing to do with this woman of questionable mental stability. The only time we came to know about her was when fate tragically interwove her into our life. This woman was one of those, who had not seen a happy day in their adult life. Her story might even make our history (the Lady and her miseries, I mean) appear a bed of roses. Without going into her past, in which we have no interest, and no knowledge, let us straight reach the point in her life which is of importance to us. She decided to end her life. We are not bothered why; only her choice. She decided to go to the District Collector's building in Trichy, as this was a fairly tall building then, with an easy access to boot. Her idea was to reach the terrace and jump; from there. That same day, the husband of the Lady's last daughter, had to go to the Collector's office to collect a document. He was about six feet away from the door when he suddenly felt a relief from the scorching sun. A shade enveloped him. Instinct made him look upward to ascertain the source of the shade. Before his head completed its upward sweep, Ratna, all 200 pounds of her, fell right on top of him, with a speed very close to a scooter in its third gear. As the cliché goes, the poor guy did not know what hit him. His neck broke before he hit the ground. Ratna was unconscious and broke quite a few bones and her ribs. Miraculously, she survived. An ambulance was called and it was after quite some time before the crowd spotted *another* body below the woman. The two bodies were taken to the general hospital and the police recorded a case of a couple jumping together in an attempt to suicide. The passersby dissolved the moment the police came and there were no immediate witnesses to the event. Efforts were on to trace the family and relatives, if any, of the *couple*.

My aunt, in the meantime, was getting nervous when her husband had not returned. Those were not the days of instant communication. When the evening had turned into night, she grew more worried and sent her sons out to find out. This was futile, as they were not old enough to make proper guesses of the places that their father would frequent, nor was my aunt capable of telling them specific locations. As a result, the boys went to the end of the street and stayed there for what appeared a decent time, before returning home. It was one of the longest nights for my aunt. The children were not old enough to lose sleep over imagined worries and went to sleep.

The police in the meantime located the office details of the man and went to the office next morning at ten, nearly twenty hours after the incident. The colleagues in the office were surprised to hear the suicide attempt of the couple as nothing in his conduct in the office ever gave them any reason to suspect such an act. Ratna gained her consciousness and revealed to the interrogator that she jumped *alone* and wanted to know why they had put cushions near the steps of the Collector's office. People jumping down from the terraces of buildings are not expected to keep their eyes open to spot the reason which arrests their fall. The peon in the office was given the unpleasant task of informing the news to the family of my aunt. And he was *surprised* to find my aunt at home; as he had been told a couple had jumped to their suicide. So after twenty-four hours, my aunt came to know about the freak death of her husband. She was not in the mould of her mother and became an atheist in that very instant. She neither prayed nor visited a temple for the rest of her life.

Anand did not know what to do. Fortunately the house that my aunt stayed in belonged to them and one of the children was eligible for a job in the department which was offered to the next of kin, after the basic qualification. My aunt, in the tradition of the first generation, was an illiterate and offering a job to her was out of question. She would not have taken one either, had it been offered. For the Lady, life was on a complete play-back mode. All her past life appeared to be happening all over again. The family, all the elders, cried together and wondered why all these were happening to them, but could not find.

My aunt and her family needed care and shelter. Taking them into the fold once again was not considered practical due to the presence of the house which belonged to them, and here at least one expense was taken care of. Gopal took part in addressing one of the family's troubles for the first time, due to his feeling of indebtedness towards the role played by Anand in his time of crisis. There were discussions, possibilities and more discussions but no solutions. The Lady could only think of her daughter setting up a factory in her house to churn out papads and pickles. Her expertise was limited and she could not think beyond that. It was Jodhi and Gopal's wife together who came up with a solution. It was decided, actually recommended, that starting the next academic year, due in another three months, the two children of Gopal and I would come and stay with my aunt and do our schooling from her place. In principle, my aunt would be the caretaker of seven kids, a near perfect action replay of a role played by her mother. Anand and Gopal were to support this enterprise. The third and the fourth kids of Gopal were too small and did not qualify. The fifth was not yet born. It suited everyone and the occasion.

Only no one found it necessary to ask how I felt. I still needed the warmth of my mother when I slept at night. The morning coffee of my grandmother's was as much mine as it was hers. Going to my aunt's place for a vacation was okay, but to stay there full time? When would I meet my parents? Twice a year? When we returned home, I complained to my mother and expressed my inability to accept this proposal. My mother explained to me the necessity, the sacrifices that we needed to make so that someone got a new lease of life, how it would not really matter much, how the family would use all the excuses for a get-together and more of how..., how...and still more how. It might have made some sense if I had listened, but I saw her expression and knew she would anyway convince me and did not listen to a single word.

It looked totally unfair. I had to leave my home so that someone would say later that my parents were good people. Bullshit! The decision was collective and was accepted by the elders and to be fair, the parting had to be as painful to them as it was for their kids. In fact, the seven children would form a good comradeship and soon were actually enjoying the stay together, I included. But at that point, I as usual placed the blame on my father and found one more reason to dislike him. I told Bhaskar that I was being sent to my aunt's place because my father did not like me. Bhaskar was shocked at the seriousness with which I spat out the accusation and tried to warn my father about a drift that was taking shape between father and son. Anand was basically a simple soul and rubbished my worries as anxiety, and Bhaskar's concern as exaggeration.

When everything was packed and the day arrived for leaving home, for what appeared to be easily a few years, no one noticed that I had smuggled a sari of my mother in my bag. The next few years I planned to sleep with the garment next to me. The rustle and softness of the sari would make me forget the actual physical separation.

21

My Life away from Home

The beginning of the following academic year saw a motley group of children assembling under one roof. The four children of my aunt were decidedly the quietest. They had just lost their father; only someone who undergoes such an experience while still young can ever understand the feeling of helplessness. Those of us who normally grow to a fairly mature age, physically if not mentally, never realise the precious gift of always having our parents at their disposal – so much of what they do is considered as what is expected of them; we fail to appreciate what they are doing and never express our gratitude. When we come to realise it , it is normally late. Two of Gopal's children and I joined this hapless four. With one daughter from Gopal and two from my aunt, the ratio of the boys to girls was four to three. My family had been known to be boy-oriented and this ratio fell into the pattern. I settled down easily with the new group and the surroundings within the first six months. I could have done the same thing from day one except for my self-conceived deliverance of injustice. Why had I to come here when my parents were both still alive? My father and my uncle had done their honourable duty in the eyes of the society and in the process, sacrificed our childhood and happiness. These were only my thoughts for I do not recall the children of Gopal ever expressing such sentiments. I am made to suffer so that this family of my aunt can survive. I thought unfairly.

I could have made the whole stay pleasant and meaningful right from day one but you could count on me to complicate a simple arrangement. I was rude, disrespectful and inconsiderate in the initial period – all without any reason or provocation. The other children, four of them elder to me, could not have been more accommodative and they started ignoring me when I remained adamant. This cut off woke me up and I became one with them, passing the entire tumultuous period with clear understanding and good camaraderie that would remain within us in later years. It was this period that could have taught me the value of putting the family before self. This period was also very formative as it imbibed in me an independence I would never have gained had I been under the shelter of my parents and a dominant grandmother. In this period I would learn the meaning of give and take, competitiveness and pure, unadulterated and selfless affection. Most of these virtues evaporated fairly quickly when I became an adult. But that is another story. Though it was my father who was responsible for this valuable lesson, I would credit myself with the lessons learnt. I never missed an opportunity in my life later to remind everyone that I lost my childhood due to my father. During the actual period he did not know my feelings. When I started voicing them, a lot of water had flown under the bridge to pay any attention.

No one was more impartial in my entire lifetime experience than my aunt under whom I was fortunate to live those precious years. How could one lady treat her children and children of her brothers same? She did not go overboard and smother the three of us with extra affection and allowed her children to be robbed of that rightful liberty. Fortunately she was not overwhelmed by her sudden widowhood nor was she embarrassed at living under the help and guidance of her brothers; at least financially. She had accepted what life had thrown at her and taken it headon. Here she had inherited the iron will of her mother. She also was more comfortable with the arrangement due to the close-knit large family with each supporting the others as during her childhood. She knew that demonstrating gratitude and dispensing the job assigned would be enough and there was no need to become servile, nor was that demanded. The love and affection that flowed so naturally amongst that generation would forever remain a mystery to me.

I was always calculative. Life's give and take was maintained in a mental account book with me and I had to always equal the score. I never wanted to remain in debt and I made it a point to collect all that was my due. My aunt would instil discipline and a sense of time in all of us. Here, for the first time, we learnt to live by a time-table. There was a time for everything – from getting up to getting ready, to going to school, to playing, to studying, to retiring for the night; there was a clearly marked time-zone. The meals were also served on the allotted time every single day. We remained active, played well, and studied harder as each had to prove better than the other, ate on time and had proper sleep. Though suffocating in the beginning as it looked too regimental, the routine grew on us. We all learnt to like the predictable clockwork precision of this life and started being dependent on that. There was a different time-table on non-school days. My aunt knew how to keep the children occupied. She encouraged us to borrow books from the library, egged us to start playing various games and insisted on our participation in every function or competition that the school organised. This magnificent seven would lap up most of the trophies and shields in all the school engagements. For the first time in our family, after of course the unbeatable record set in academics by Ishwaran, one corner of the house was cluttered with our rich haul.

Trichy, even today, is remembered for its imposing hilltop temple of Ganesha. That is the image that comes to one's mind, to one that knows the place. I do not recall many Sundays that we did not go there. With her self-imposed atheism and joints that cried for relief, after toiling endlessly throughout the day, she never accompanied us.

After our morning meal on Sundays, we would all march out unfailingly towards this hill. The climb was arduous but not to the sprightly young ones and we would often race up the hill on its perilous steps. In our mad zigzag rush to be the first, we were responsible for many normal devotees losing their balance and dropping their offerings in their frantic grabbing for a proper grip. Their curses would never reach our ears as we were fast and careless in equal measures, which are possible only for children. The winner was never the same one as the stamina and techniques made a huge impact on the outcome but I was consistent. I never won. Not even once. The joy and the healthy competitiveness was so complete that one never felt bitter. Reaching the top was a goal by itself and the ranking mattered less. We must have been a strange group because in all those years of climbing the hill, almost every Sunday, we never went inside the temple. Our goal was to reach the top. We needed a hill and it was by sheer chance that this hill housed a temple atop it. It did not bother us nor did it interest us. Most of my generation would grow up indifferent towards Gods and temples. With an earlier generation completely sold out to Him, this was surprising. We would rest there catching our breath and come down even faster. Not one trip was complete without someone scraping a knee, bruising an arm or at least falling down and dirtying one's dresses.

The lunch on Sunday was always sweet after such an eventful morning. We hated rains as only the rain could find us home on Sunday mornings. Life with others of our age in a new place could be intoxicating and the first vacation spotted me counting the days to return to Trichy. Bhaskar was happy with this change in me and encouraged me to develop a hobby in addition to whatever I was doing. This was too general an advice and I did not heed it further. Individual hobbies in collective living were not possible. My mother was impressed with my grooming and it was she who cried when I went back after my first vacation.

Another experience we shared would remain with us forever. There is no English equivalent word, or phrase, to convey what could be so easily be said in my native language in two simple words. All of us would go to the open terrace on a full moon day. My aunt would bring the dinner to the terrace and we would all sit in a circle and have our dinner under the blindingly bright moonlight. There were no rules and we could talk as much as we wanted during dinner and with our mouths full. This monthly dinner had no specific end time and we continued till we were sleepy. None of us ever cared to help our aunt in cleaning up the place or getting the stuff back to the kitchen. We took too many things for granted. On the face of it, this looked like an open-air dinner. But the experience stayed with us for a long time. Later, when I grew up and settled in a busy city, with a busier lifestyle, and a terrace that was the property of one hundred and five apartment-owners, this concept was unthinkable. This was something my child was going to miss. The hilltop Ganesha, who was never visited, and the moonlight dinners were the fondest memories that I carried from my years in Trichy.

The new school was also an eye-opening experience. You were no longer known by your family and did not have the presence and support of Bhaskar all the time. Here I learnt to really stand on my own merit. Never a topper, but I still managed a performance that was more than acceptable. In fact all the children would do well under the stewardship of my aunt, who herself was illiterate, and this was her great pride. The only time I ever saw her angry was if any of us did not do well in our studies. The exams were regular and by a sadistic design, were arranged in such a way that you either got your results before a festival holiday or you had to study during the festival holiday. In the former occurrence, you just would not be able to enjoy your festival if your marks were poor as nothing displeased my aunt more than a poor academic performance. Promises would not satisfy her and you were condemned to spend that period in penance. To rub it in, she would be so sweet with others who managed well that this became a great motivating factor for all of us to do well. In the case of the second possibility, the iron regimen would be enforced and there was no way we could think of any festivities with exams round the corner.

Without sermonising and intimidating, she had nurtured us all to take our schooling seriously. Due to the routine that we stuck to, and may be because we ate well and spent more calories than we consumed, we remained healthy and I do not recall any of us ever falling sick in the entire period we stayed there.

Soon the first son of my aunt finished his school and landed a job in the state treasury department and my father heaved a sigh of relief. Though he and Gopal continued to support the enterprise till the completion of school of all the three of us, it was a clear signal that another family would now be on its own in a matter of time.

The remaining three children of Gopal never had an opportunity to go through what we went through and thus the intimacy that existed between the three of us was never extended to, or shared by, the other three. Three years had passed since my first uncertain move to Trichy and I was already worried about getting out of my aunt's place in another two years. The relationship we had with her was one which we would never have had with our parents, with the unwritten code of conduct that existed. My parents were also busy making a living and running a family. While we were all having the time of our life, something wonderful started happening back at my home also.

My grandmother who became a perfect copybook mother-in-law without any provocation, decided to become human again. She must have become tired of a non-reacting daughter in law as it was equal to punching a sandbag. My second vacation was a sweet surprise because for the first time I felt something strange in my house. For two days I could not locate it. Years later, when I went to Europe for the first time, I would have a similar unfamiliar feeling while travelling. After a full week in Europe, I realised that I was missing the sound of a car horn on the roads. That strange feeling I felt but could not place immediately at my home was the absence of my grandmother's cursing and shouting. She had become normal. Either she ran out of steam, which I doubt, given her capability, or she finally felt the unfairness of the treatment she was meting out. My mother finally felt vindicated and her faith in the Almighty went up by ten times. I do not know whether I became indifferent in religion due to the overdose of Gods at my home or the stoic atheism of my aunt. I was only glad to see my mother smiling again and it was long due.

Anand had a busy life and he distributed his life amongst all his activities but the family took the smallest part that was on the offer. I even challenged Bhaskar on my second vacation that my father did not even know which standard I was studying in. The truth in the challenge and my growing indifference towards my father combined to put a heavy responsibility on Bhaskar. He approached my father again after I left and was brushed aside with the same casualness that he exhibited the first time. Anand was an optimist and incapable of harbouring ill feelings. He mistakenly assumed the same characteristic in all. Here his judgement failed – on his son, that is.

22

The Lady Departs

Anand finally hit a jackpot; his first ever jackpot. All his years of perseverance had paid off. He felt like a student who had scored the top rank in his class; though as a student he never scored anything worth talking about. He would never win one again. But this tantalising win after years of association was enough to keep him hooked on for the remaining period. The sum won was substantial. The occasion called for a celebration. For this group, celebration only meant booze and more booze. This group surprisingly had high morals when it came to promiscuity. Either it was the typical south Indian morality, or the lack of interest. The group retired that evening and Anand threw the biggest party of his life. The bill ran into roughly the amount that was sufficient to take care of his household for three months. But that day, money was the least of his concerns. In fact after that party, and the loss the next day, he would get to see only half of what he had originally won.

Anand never showed the accounts and the family was not in the habit of accounting for money. For all her other qualifications, Jodhi was poor in finance. Her interaction with finance had only two facets – the first was to hand over her salary to Anand, and forget about the same. She had a box in her cupboard, bearing the portrait of Goddess Lakshmi, the goddess of wealth, with the hope that the symbolic gesture would result in actual appreciation of wealth. This box was meant to store cash at home. Her second interaction with finance was that she needed to locate money whenever she opened the box. She was not extravagant. In fact, no one in the family was, except Anand. Her periodic association with the cash box was always in genuine need. Here Anand succeeded and even exceeded her expectations. He would ensure enough money in the box, by hook or by crook, and Jodhi never had a reason to question him. She was a simple lady. Her needs were meagre and she knew that sustained questioning on Anand's means would only end up in a fiasco. So she studiously avoided it.

The party was in a high-profile hotel called 'Blue Fox', which the group had never dared to enter before. The first time Anand looked at the prices against the items mentioned in the menu, he was sure that something was wrong. No amount of quantity and/or quality could justify the prices mentioned. By nature a frugal eater, that day he almost was on a fast. His sense of outrage was limited to solid offerings only, and on the liquor front he splurged. It was an insult on some of the finest single malts that day. He and his acquaintances raped single malt. They first added ice cubes, and as if that injury was not sufficient, they added the insult of splashing club soda. Single malt with ice and soda! The spirit of Scotland could have survived these two anomalies but gulping them down with a war cry of "Bottoms Up!" was the final nail. The skeletal remains of many of the founders of some of the finest distilleries in a Scotland cemetery were actually on a rock 'n roll that night. The restaurant manager, with a trained hawk eye to locate naïve idiots and relieve them of their money, approached Anand with a cigar menu. Anand had no idea what the list was about. He thought he was being offered more choice in whisky and politely refused. The hawk eye persisted and started blabbering about Havana and aroma. It made no sense to Anand. He had to order something, if only to get rid of this hawk. He went through the menu with great difficulty. The print in front of him was moving on its own will, and his effort to rein it in were proving futile. On a normal day Anand would always order the cheapest item on the menu. Today was celebration day! So he reversed his intuition and ordered the most expensive one on the menu, still not knowing what he was ordering.

Anand, who was expecting some aromatic native dish of Cuba, was hence surprised when he saw a cheroot on a platter. His numbed senses conveyed the word cigar properly this time to his brain. The damage was done. Someone instructed him, he could never recall who it was, to bite off the tip and demonstrated the right technique of lighting a cigar. The instructions were not complete, either lost in the state of intoxication or due to plain ignorance. Anand ended up chewing and swallowing the bit that he bit off, and lighted the cigar. It was horrible. If Anand had started his smoking habits with the cigar, he might not have continued. The barrel of the cigar was too big and he could not support it in his mouth without an additional prop, and he needed his hand continuously *even when the cigar was in his mouth*. He felt like a homosexual giving a blow job to his partner with that huge smelly thing in his mouth. His feelings were not appropriate and would not have been accepted by cigar aficionados. If the pride of Scotland was buried that night, how could Cuba escape?

The actual payment of the bill, the physical separation of money, sobered him a little. The loss on the race course the next day sobered him up a little more. But it was the unconscious Lady who brought him completely to ground Earth when he returned home after a weekend of unbridled fun and adventure.

In sheer contrast, the day, after the great party night of Anand, was pure terror for Jodhi. He was home, that being a weekend. Preparations were on for my homecoming that week after the mid-term exams. The festival of lights, Diwali, was also round the corner. Diwali is exported as the festival of lights to the Western world. Those who hail from the Indian subcontinent will vouch for this as festival of sound, as the deafening noise of bursting crackers adds actually decibels, not illumination. It was just after Jodhi finished her endless, indescribable activities that always took most of her morning hours. The meal was over. The radio was belting out some mellifluous instrumental strains. Jodhi approached the Lady to ask whether she would be interested to go to Gopal's house as they had nothing significant to do for the rest of the day. The Lady nodded her head in the negative, saying she was not feeling comfortable, stood up and fainted. This was the second time that the Lady had fainted in her life. The readers might recall the first time; when she was told what was written on the cover pages of Mr Gandhi's autobiography by me.

There was a noticeable difference between the two. While the first one was in a pure cinematic fashion, on hearing the least expected; the second was pure dynamite. She fell like a tree uprooted. She was not thin and years of hard work had ensured that there was not an ounce of fat in her eighty-five kg weight. The absence of fat proved bad, as it could have cushioned her fall. Jodhi was too stunned to react and arrest her fall. It was good because Jodhi might have suffered her own injuries in such a foolish attempt. The Lady broke her hand and suffered a deep gash on her forehead. The fall followed by the flow of blood, drove my mother into a frenzy, and she screamed. The screams brought in the neighbours. She was good at screaming. The last time she screamed was when Ishwaran had slit his hands and the neighbours could not get in. One called the doctor while the other one ran to inform Gopal. Bhaskar arrived in less than thirty minutes. No one was sure who informed him.

The presence of Bhaskar in times of crises was so natural that it did not look out of place. The brothers had one thing in common. They were never home when you wanted them. Gopal was out on one of his endless tours. The two daughters-in-law never stopped crying that Sunday and the doctor did not know whether to attend to the Lady or control the weeping women. In a very poor attempt at humour he remarked, "Why are you crying? She is not dead yet."

When he received incredulous looks, coupled with horror, he realised his faux pas and did not utter another word to the women. He told Bhaskar that there was nothing to worry about. He concluded that the Lady was fasting quite too often. Lack of sufficient intake, coupled with an unusual October sun, combined to cause the drowsiness and the fracture was an unfortunate occurrence. He added that the Lady would be up and about in a week's time. The broken hand was plastered and there was no sign of the Lady regaining consciousness. She remained that way on Monday when Anand and Gopal returned. It was full three days before she came back to her senses. This was a misnomer. She came back to her senses in the medical sense of the phrase. The fire of life that was burning in her eyes was gone. She had a vacant look. She recognised people but lost her voice. Either that or she decided not to speak. My mother was certain that she had lost her voice because she was a witness to the Lady's attempts to say something. The Lady remained in her bed for the longest duration of her life in that period.

I had come home and was shocked to see the Lady so helpless. We had never seen her lying down, even in sleep, as she went to sleep much after any of us children did, and was already awake before we woke up. Children could be callous. One like me, who was also a scheming kind, could be downright nauseating too. My first worries were that if the Lady died before Diwali, then I would not be able to celebrate the high point of my vacation. In my later life, I loathed myself for harbouring such thoughts, though briefly. Nevertheless, those were my thoughts then. I also learnt about the hapless situation of the two women, who were left to handle the situation. This gave me immense pleasure in practicing my mentally-aimed blows on my favourite punching bag, Anand. I blamed him for the predicament. This would not have happened if he had stayed at home. How? I had no idea. But I was certain. It never occurred to me to blame Gopal. It was all Anand's fault.

A week had passed since the Lady's fall and she still had not spoken a word. Her hand was mending well as per the doctor. I never understood how he managed the diagnosis with the hand still encased in the plaster. She was showing definite signs of improvement, as per him, and I started having doubts about his ability for the first time. In the three days that I had seen my grandmother, she remained the same and what I saw on day one, was bad. I started believing in the word premonition when my relatives started arriving slowly as if some emotional current conveyed to them the state of my grandmother. For the first time since the early days of forced togetherness, the family had assembled again; everyone, except Priya's father, who was too far gone by then. His presence would have been an embarrassment for the Lady as he was one sore apple in her breed. That is, among the living, as Ishwaran was no longer counted. It was the first time I saw my father at home for such duration. His crying was legendary and he gave a free demonstration to those who came in late. My aunt was crestfallen. All the Gods, present in the house, regally hung on the walls as well as in the general vicinity, were invoked. Bribes were offered. My aunt steadfastly remained an atheist and kept a one-sided conversation going with my grandmother. Ten days after the fall, the situation was becoming a little complicated. If she died, people could cry their anguish out and go ahead with their life. If she had shown definite signs of a revival, then everyone could proceed to their respective vocation in life. Things were becoming a little more complex with Diwali just two days away.

That evening her face glowed like never before. She looked like her former redoubtable self. She even smiled, exposing all her healthy teeth. She was an example that our doctor would refer to some of his patients in their thirties, with cavities. He did not know that my grandmother never used a brush or paste in her life. She called me and held on to me with a grip that was surprisingly strong. I winced at her grip and she relaxed a little. I was relieved. My grandmother was safe. Diwali could go on. I was even then often ashamed at my selfishness, but never found a way to overcome that.

The next two hours witnessed a visible relief amongst all my family members. A few rushed to the nearest temples to confirm timely payment of bribes promised. My father stopped crying and Gopal and his family began to get ready to go back to their unattended house to prepare for the function.

My grandmother called out "Jodhi" very clearly which was heard by everyone in the house as it was uttered in a small period of quietness. This was the first word spoken by her in the last ten days. The smiling faces were now beaming. My mother actually blushed on being conferred the honour. Her joy must have been very close to how she must have felt, when years before I must have uttered my first word. Her smile and blush turned into horror when my grandmother did not respond to her queries after approaching her. I was the first one who realised that my mother's name was the last word my grandmother uttered. It took most of them a longer time to realise that she was dead.

A few things irritated me at that moment. I knew the worth of the last spoken word. I knew that the word would be discussed often in future in connection with my grandmother's death. I wished she had called out *my name* instead of my mother's. I knew the ill treatment that my mother suffered at the hands of the Lady. Then why was she crying so much? So what if the old woman had mellowed down a little of late? Should not my mother's feeling be one of good riddance? And could not she have pulled on for three more days and died after Diwali? I had not only to forego the Diwali celebrations but the vacation also. All these thoughts ran in my mind.

I had conveniently forgotten the early morning coffee, the times that she saved me from the fury of my father, the innumerable fasts and offerings that she made for my health, and the countless times I shamelessly manipulated her to my advantage. Tears did not come to me and I made no attempt to put on a show. This drew unexpected attention.

"Look at that boy! What control on his emotions at this age! No wonder he is as shattered as the rest of the family, but is able to carry himself so well. May God bless him."

So I carried on in the same vein, enjoying my spot in the limelight throughout the period of official grief. Bhaskar, who could read me like a book, saw through my charade and was repulsed at what he saw. He was the first person to spot the ugly side of me so early in my life. He would of course, try his best to guide me but give up later.

My grandmother's was the only body I had ever seen on a funeral pyre with one hand cast in plaster.

23
Additional Liabilities

I was back with my aunt for the second half of my penultimate year in school. The home looked absolutely strange when we left after the holidays. For the first time in their married life, my parents were alone in that house. The lifestyle of my father ensured that *my mother* would be alone for most of this period. She, in fact, wanted me back but this was ruled out as my aunt and her family were still not self-sufficient. Anand expected to extend the support for two more years, which meant I could return for my pre-university course, to my home. I also was not very much in favour of going back as the bond was getting stronger with all of us at my aunt's place. Home would only mean me and my mother and I was not comfortable with the idea of having to spend time in the presence of my father. With the Lady gone, it was next to impossible to expect my father to return to normalcy. I also knew that closeted together with my mother would mean her lamentations. I had always been specific about getting only the creamier side of life. The affection and attention were alright, but to listen to grievances and meaningless old sacrifices was not exactly my cup of tea. I could have understood the need of my mother to talk to someone as she had no one to talk to. Then I could have done many things which I did not.

Youth is a wonderful thing. Nothing lasts in its mind forever. Ecstasy and agony spent equal time on the mind and very little at that. The death of my grandmother also did not dwell for long and we were soon back to our carefree life. We were mature enough to put on a solemn face in the presence of the elders as decorum demanded. Everyone in the family learns to tide over the tragedy of the dead. The young get over it quickly and the elders never understand this. Because of this gap in the course of recovery, the elders in the family inadvertently teach the children to cheat by showing false bereavement. Children are fast learners, if not anything else, and change their masks with dexterity. If my mother had not gone insane in those eighteen months, it was because of the sorority that she developed with Gopal's wife, complete surrender to the Gods and the presence of Priya. She became the daughter my mother never had and she was compensating on behalf of the family.

Priya's father followed the footsteps of my father in getting suspended from his job. While it was a false allegation against my father who was finally vindicated, the ground on which he, Priya's father was suspended, was more concrete. Dereliction of duty and misconduct were the charges levelled and no one could contest them. He did not know how to go about initiating remedial measures to get him reinstated and sank deeper into alcohol. He pawned all that could be pawned in the house and his wife decided to leave Priya at my home for longer durations due to the presence of her husband at home. She was too scared to leave that poor child in his presence and asked my mother to take care of Priya for a few more weeks.

It was a sorry situation for a girl to grow up. To have parents and still be forced to live with someone else is a tragedy only such a child can grasp. She had now grown big enough to understand the realities of her family. A mother on the verge of death due to physical exhaustion and unbearable shame and a father, who would happily sell his own daughter for a bottle of liquor was a combination that permanently scarred her young mind. She had been growing up to be an exceptionally quiet child. I had never seen a child who never laughed, except for Priya. Sadness and melancholy were her constant companions. After a period of ten days, her mother was too embarrassed and decided to take Priya home, if you could still call the shack by that name, for a few days. My mother reasoned against it and she did not want to humiliate her further by stating the obvious and heartlessly relented.

It was a mistake.

That night Priya witnessed what no other child should ever be exposed to. Her father came home completely drunk. He had been summoned by his senior officer and been summarily told that his suspension had been confirmed as termination, after the findings of the committee. It was news he was expecting but the actual realisation still hurt. He knew only one way of drowning his pain. There was something ominous about him the moment he entered their house that night. His wife could not exactly put her finger and carried out the normal routine every housewife has been trained to do. One had to always respect her husband. Proverbs equated one's husband to the Lord Himself, and even if he happened to be the lowest form on earth, he still had to be respected. Balderdash! Scum like him got away because of servile wives like his. As she prepared to serve him the dinner, the inebriated beast pulled her down and indicated his desire to have sex with her, there, in front of his petrified daughter. Horror, revulsion, helplessness, disgust, shame and an intense fury swept through her. Physically she was no match for him and her futile efforts were becoming feebler by the moment. She kept shouting, asking her daughter to leave the house immediately. Priya was seeing all her worst nightmares coming true in front of her own eyes. Terror does different things to different people. Mostly it paralyses. Priya was numb with shock and was incapable of moving. Her mother was losing her battle and the shame was engulfing her. It ended as abruptly as it began – with the thrust of the kitchen knife right through his heart. There was no time to weigh the alternatives. She knew that the longer she delayed, the more difficult it would be to end her life, adding to the ignominy of a trial and the publicity. She felt absolutely no pain when the same knife cut through her breast and stopped her heart from pumping blood. A waste of an additional life, as cirrhosis in him was so advanced that he would have died if he had lived another two days. But isn't it this that gets labelled as fate all the time? Priya did not utter a cry or even a word. She sat like a stone next to her mother's body, refusing to even look at her father's corpse.

She would tell my mother years later the horrific events of that night. As the child was incapable of saying anything, the event was closed as suicide of a couple in the face of poverty. Many could easily guess what had transpired, but were held back from assuming such a worst possibility; and in the absence of any confirmation from the only witness possible, the case was closed thus. The bodies were confined to the flames and Priya moved to my home as a permanent resident. Fortunately for my parents, none of the other children that they had brought up had degenerated to such depths. Still the passing away of the first two of their flock was a severe blow to their morale.

Priya offered my mother the appropriate diversion she needed. She found a new mission in her life. Priya would grow up in my home, finish her college and settle down with a steady and handsome job in a bank. She would never marry. The efforts of my parents and even from the rest of the family, including myself, were of no use. Her wounds were deep and expecting the eternal healer – time to take care of those wounds was a misplaced notion. It was tragic, as she was a very sensible and quite girl. My mother was her idol and benchmark, and she would have become an excellent mother herself. In fact the children of the next generation which included mine would find her a great companion and sought her advice when we parents were too delicate on certain matters.

The presence of Priya made it easy for my father. He stayed *out of the house* for the same number of hours and was frequenting the house only in odd hours. A lodge or a hotel would have served his needs without much difference. Now he was doing it with a clear conscience as he knew his wife was not alone at home. It never occurred to him that it was during this period that my mother needed him most in the house. His life was a simple routine – office, club, friends, racing and booze. But even I, his strongest critic, would admit he never let the family down. Though my mother was glad that she had Priya at home, the circumstances could definitely have been better. She has had enough. She started praying earnestly for a stop in this continued assault of surprises. She was tired of bearing the burden of the family by now. She was also getting older and the moral support of the Lady was missing. She needed a normal life with no shocks at every turn. She longed for the simplicity of her small family – husband, wife, Priya and I. She could take only this much and not any more. She knew it was a matter of another two years for my aunt to be on her own and she wanted to devote her time in taking care of her son. She did not want to fail in her son. The calamities that befell her first two wards had unnerved her.

That was the last time she prayed for anything with a selfish self-centred request. There was no connection whatsoever with her prayers and what happened to her parents, but human mind can be quite unpredictable and is capable of linking two completely unrelated events with a strongest correlation. She blamed herself unnecessarily and endlessly. She was convinced that her parents died in a bus accident because she prayed for a small family. It was God's way of offering what she wanted, with a macabre twist. One had to know what to ask for. Fortunately my maternal grandparents were not known for their power of procreation and we had no liabilities from my mother's side.

It was an eventful year. We were never allowed to grieve one death for a decent duration. Death was a constant visitor in my family that year. I had seen more dead bodies in that year alone and it was sickening. I would not see another death in my family for a very long time, but the next death taught me many things that I never understood in my life. And as it usually happened, the realisation came a little late.

24
Growing Up

It was my last year in school; I was already worried about spending the next year at my home. The separation which had been so painful when it was initiated, was now playing in the reverse. I did not want to leave my aunt. The sari of my mother, that I had brought, was confined to some corner in the house and vanished over a period of time. I took comfort from it for about six months and then it looked silly. I had grown to be independent. While the company of my cousins would keep me happy, their absence did not affect me. I learned to enjoy solitude. I was becoming capable of looking after my needs without assistance. All this would have remained a pipe dream if I had been under the shelter of my parents. I would have continued to be the timid, shy and nervous kid that I was then. This transformation would not have been possible were it not for my father taking that brave stand of sending his only son away. I owed it to him. But at that point I did not have the opportunity of retrospection, or introspection, to appreciate what he had made possible. He was my punching bag for everything that went wrong. Only I was fully responsible for all the positive aspects. I was certain that any other child in my place would have failed miserably. I could be, and at sometimes still am, capable of being incredibly naïve and stupid.

We walked to the school every day. Any other mode of transportation was not heard of. There was also another school in the vicinity, exclusively for girls. I spotted this girl in one group, one day, for she had an uncanny resemblance to a popular actress of that time. The fantasies of most of the boys and men were woven around the public figures – an actress, an athlete, a tennis star or the latest winner in the beauty pageant. After some days, I started noticing her seriously. Every day I would wait for this group to pass and locate her with racing palpitations and sweating palms. I started finding excuses to leave my house alone and not with the regular group, but also managed the time in such a way that we passed each other. My mornings became meaningful only for this activity. The day she did not turn up would be unspeakable hell for me. I would be short-tempered the whole day at school and remain sullen at home. What if she did not turn up tomorrow? Only this thought would occupy my mind the whole night. The relief of seeing her the next day was almost physical. I would search for her amongst the regular temple-goers on Sundays on the hilltop temple of Ganesha, but she never appeared, not even once. May be she was also an atheist, I used to think. It would be good to have both husband and wife with same principles, I thought. Yes, I was already nursing intentions of telling her of my pure love and to ask for her hand in wedding. It would be a perfect match, I convinced myself. I did not even know her name.

This group of girls was surprisingly quiet. The inevitable giggle was always there, but nothing else. It was quite natural for a group of five girls who walked every day not to address each other by names. It looked unfair to me. My dreaming was handicapped as I had to address her only by endearments and not by a specific name. It was easy for Shakespeare to rubbish the importance of a name and write nonsense like rose smelling as sweet and all that, but I was certain that he never had to follow a girl for close to ten months and not know her name. That was correct. It was not that I did know her name; I did not know anything about her except that she went to such and such school. I was not even certain whether she was my junior or senior. What if she was elder to me? This was another paralysing thought. I told myself that it would not matter, and if necessary, I would stand up to anyone. All this bravery was only in my mind. I did not even have the courage to approach her or ask her to be friends. What did I know about her? Only that she resembled an actress. This was all the qualification I needed to visualise someone as my future life partner.

I was ignorant about sex, like all boys of my age at that time. I knew that a man and a woman married and produced children. The exact process of procreation was a mystery to me and the movies of that era remained quite subtle. The camera would zoom in on birds pecking each other; two flowers bouncing against each other in a gentle breeze or a painting of a couple in embrace in varying stages of disrobe whenever the hero and heroine started getting amorous. If the movies were hopeless in educating, correct literature was not available. Of course, a few of the authors like Wallace and Robbins could have helped me. I had just started reading English novels and as was the tradition, I started with James Hadley Chase. Mr Chase was as bad as the movies when it came to describing carnal pleasures.

This pointless exercise of looking at this love of my life every day continued throughout the final year of my school. I imagined that the feeling must have been mutual. A few glances of hers in my direction had been conveniently misinterpreted by me as passion burning on the other side too. That was a strange situation. I did not know her name, nor her age, nor where she lived and worst of all, did not even know for sure whether she harboured similar thoughts. Her face would never leave my mind. I had vowed that one day I would marry her. If that was not possible, I would remain a bachelor forever.

It is so easy to make all sorts of stupid resolutions when you are young. As it had to happen, the last day of the school was on me, a little too quickly in my opinion. That day I followed the reason for my living to her home. What I wanted to know was not clear. I just wanted to add a little more information to my dossier. One by one, all her friends left the group and soon only she was left walking, so sensuously, towards her home. Here was my chance to approach her and make the introduction and do all the spadework for our future life together. I was terrified. A lot many 'what ifs' crossed my mind. I could not imagine a negative answer to even one of them. So I just followed her as if that in itself was the mission. She crossed a railway track and took a narrow winding road towards a cluster of houses that was very ordinary looking. There was danger here. Walking on a road populated with about hundred people was alright, but if she decided to turn around and question my reason for following her on that narrow path, I would have had no option other than to blurt out the truth. I was half expecting that to happen, as I was capable of doing things only when left with no alternatives. At the same time I was not comfortable with the task and was fully prepared to turn about and walk the other way at the slightest inclination of her turning around.

She reached her home and went inside after washing her legs outside from a garden tap. An orthodox family, I deduced. I stood there like a moron, watching children play marbles on the dusty street. The children were aware of my presence and turned to look at me with uncertainty. After a scrutiny of few minutes, they decided that I was harmless and had no intention of separating them from their marbles. They went on with their game. I tried to locate if there was a future brother-in-law of mine in that band of urchins. I had no specific plans on what I would do if I had spotted one.

The most unexpected thing followed next. The darling of my dreams came out of her house, and hollered "Baaaalllllooooooooo……." That must have been my brother-in-law, whom I failed to spot. All students must have undergone the experience of having goosebumps on the back of their neck when the chalk makes a screech on the blackboard when the master underlines a point. That noise was nothing in front of her voice. I stood there, unwilling to believe that the sound came from the slender throat of my beloved, my future better half. She repeated her clarion call. I was across the railway track and back on my way home, before she finished her second call. Was that possible? Was that really her voice? Could one live with such a voice every day for the rest of one's life? Suddenly my resolutions needed a relook. I decided at that moment that looks of an actress would not be the only criterion in my future endeavours.

I reached home almost an hour later than my regular arrival time. My aunt was worried. An earlier occasion, when her husband did not return on such an evening, ended tragically had made her worried. Her relief was palpable at my return. I mumbled something indecipherable on her query. It was much later, when I was playing the whole efforts of the last year in my mind and its cacophonous culmination that evening, that I started to laugh. It was no longer about my well-guarded future and so I shared it with my cousins. My aunt was wondering what we were laughing about that night in her house. I left for my home the next day, along with the two children of Gopal. I would not return as per the arrangements already decided and the other two would spend a few more years with my aunt. I did return whenever I could as some of my best years were spent in my aunt's place. The secret of the screeching siren was a joke that all of us would share and the one I would tell my wife when I was married.

Home was not the same any more. Whatever might have been her drawbacks, the Lady had an aura and a presence. That was missing. My mother, who was not used to such freedom, became difficult to manage. Suddenly she wanted to be a part of everything. She wanted to know whether I would become an engineer or a doctor. A boy from a Tamil Brahmin family had only these two alternatives. He was branded a failure if he was anything else. I had to do mathematics and science and get into an engineering college or a medical college. That was decided. My opinion did not matter. It was another matter that I had no opinion of my own. Here was another classic case of Amarism. I would not decide, and whatever anyone decided for me was wrong. It was impossible to tolerate me and I sometimes wondered why my parents ever put up with all my unprovoked sullenness.

Priya was a relief. She was already a schoolgoing girl and I could show off all my intelligence on this innocent girl. Due to my performance in my last year in school, it was easy for me to get into pre-university. I was warned straight away that the next step, that of an admission to enter the portals of a reputed engineering college, would not be an easy one. My mother, who had this irritating habit of repeating the same set of instructions, never failed to remind me of the onerous task ahead, nine times a week. She was not a nagging wife. She never had an opportunity. She made up for that by becoming a nagging mother. I perfected the technique of turning myself mentally off and used to watch only her lips moving.

That was also the year our house became the first one in the colony to buy a television set. We only had one national channel then. If my memory serves me correct, the programmes were only for about nine hours a day. There was a huge argument between my father and my mother, one of the few I could remember, about the necessity of the TV in the house. The bone of contention was that the TV would be a cause of distraction for me from my goal. It was ridiculous. I was never addicted to television, not then and not even today, and would happily spend my time reading books. Reading was not a habit in my house and my mother was happy so long as I was reading an English book. A novel in English was considered to be an equivalent of my studies, for reasons unknown. It suited me. I had just discovered Harold Robbins and had already come to the conclusion that he was the best author who ever walked this earth. It was sheer sleaze. It appealed to a young and perverted mind. If Priya had been a little older, I would have even seduced her, using a few scenes from the novels. I had no scruples and anything that made me happy was alright. Bhaskar would spot 'the Betsy' one day and express his surprise about my choice of books.

"Why do you not read someone like Somerset Maugham?" he asked.

I had never heard that name before and developed an immediate dislike to him without ever reading even a single book of his. I saw my mother looking through the pages of the book soon after that episode. It could have been a natural act. My mind immediately conjured an image of Bhaskar pouring out the lurid details of the book to my mother, with shock written all over her face. I had not forgotten my earlier episode of the anatomy of a girl's private parts on the cover pages of my father's book. The mark left by the buckle of the belt was still there on my right shoulder. My mother could jump to her conclusions.

My dislike spread to Bhaskar also. I started being curt with him. I answered him mechanically and sometimes pretended as if I did not hear him. My mother would feel embarrassed at every such occasion and would step in and say something to make Bhaskar feel comfortable. This made it all the more difficult for Bhaskar. He was willing to play chess with me "just like old times". I had lost my interest. However, I would play for hours with Priya and teach her all the tricks which Bhaskar had once taught me. These things did not go unnoticed by Bhaskar. His attachment to the family and my parents was so deep that minor insults like these bounced off him. He would continue to patronise me and guide me on the reference books I needed for the exams, guides that would prepare me for the interview for admission into a good engineering college, and various courses that were available in engineering and which college would be most ideal.

For a boy who was in his pre-university, I was especially dumb. I had thought engineering only meant civil engineering where you ended up building bridges and buildings. At that time, most of the engineering colleges offered at least six disciplines. This was a new headache to me. I had to choose again. Why could not life be simple? In my characteristic way, this confusion was attributed to Bhaskar, who brought up the whole topic. I had decided on one thing – the college will be far from my home. I felt imprisoned at home. Hostel looked the best option where I could be on my own. (And catch up on all the remaining Harold Robbins.)

"Why do you think of a hostel? There are better colleges nearby," said Bhaskar.

"I do not want to become another frog in the well" I replied with an unnecessary but well-intended stress on the word "another". I had already indicated that I could be nasty when I wanted to be. My mother was scarlet with shame. She did not believe what she had heard and did not know what to do. She tried the universal advice of the need to be polite with one's elders and well-wishers. I was thinking of another barb when Bhaskar said that it did not matter and I was big enough to decide what was good. He said it with his usual smile. My mother was relieved. I was observant enough to note the tinge of sorrow encase that smile and I felt victorious. I had scored my first point in insulting an older person, with no provocation or reason and walk away scot free.

My mother later asked me whether I was serious about the hostel. She had missed me for a long time. The earlier years were drowned in responsibilities and my poor health. When I was normal, and the house bereft of all dependents, I was packed off in an act of philanthropy. She wanted to be with her son. Her son wanted freedom. He was not clear from what or for doing what.

Anand was told that weekend that I was becoming a bit of a loner and a little strange to understand. She was worried about my short temper, acid tongue and swinging moods. Anand was never good in addressing complex issues. The man of the house should ensure money for the household and the rest would take its own course. He was also a simple man. He convinced Jodhi that she was worrying without any reason. The deaths of Ishwaran and his brother were not her making. They were not because of her; they were in spite of her. He convinced my mother that I was a boy with good education and good background and nothing amiss could happen. He believed in Providence. He was steadfast in his faith that good things happened to good people.

"Aren't we good? Did we not take care of all those children when they were orphaned? Did we not as recently as a few years back even support my widowed sister, and sacrificed our closeness to our only son? There is a God above. Do not worry. All will turn out well. We will reap tfhe benefits and enjoy our years together when our son grows up. We will have no responsibilities other than playing with our grandchildren."

He blabbered like this for about half an hour. It actually sounded good. Even he started believing that all this would happen. That was what would be fair. Because she did not have any better arguments, she gave up and prepared for a few more years of solitude. Of course, she would have Priya – the one steadfast loyal child from this family.

Anand was satisfied. When the problem was first thrown at him, he was equally confused. Like a conjurer performing tricks, he kept elaborating his fantasy of a perfect world, where he himself was finally more convinced than Jodhi.

They had no idea that I would grow up with my own perception of what was fair, and what was not. Bhaskar was my first victim. My list would grow and engulf many more in my family.

25

The First Sign

The routine of this new life at home was murderous. After the designated hours spent with my college studies and the preparation for the engineering college interview, there was a big void. If Priya had been elder by another four years, things could have been different. I soon lost my interest in her. There was very little I knew about chess which I transferred to her and I soon discovered that she had a natural ability to play chess, while I withdrew before the infamy of a defeat, which started looking imminent. This was another trick of mine. I withdrew from any competition where I did not have a fair chance. It never occurred to me that such contests would sharpen me more. I needed to be the winner; if not always, at least most of the times. A young and intelligent opponent did not fit into it. This frustrated her initially. I would demand and get most of my jobs done through her before consenting to a game. The poor girl gave in to every demand of mine just for a game of chess. Of late, my mother started harassing me if I spent too long with a novel in my hand.

"These novels will not feed you in future. Only good education will take you far. If you concentrate on your studies now and become an engineer and land a good job, then you can read all the novels you want. No one will tell you anything then."

"So you want me to read this novel after five or six years? I might as well not read it," I would dump the book and walk away.

This would work like magic. The next sequence was always the same. She would come to me with the book, clarifying what she meant.

"Am I asking you not to read this? I am only telling you to finish studying before you devote your time to this novel. I am asking you to distribute your time judiciously. That's all."

Then came the final plunge.

"After all it is your life. I do not want the society to blame us for being uncaring parents."

This parrying would go on. I would continue to stay from the novel and wear the sullen look. I could have patented it. I would stretch it to a breaking point and, I knew when to stop, then I would gracefully accept the novel as if I was doing her a favour. Despite the blatant emotional blackmail I was resorting to, the episodes repeated with surprising regularity.

The absence of my cousins was a huge drawback as I had no one to discuss anything with. I did not make friends easily. Given my nature it was not surprising. A new student is always destined to be a loner and one with my idiosyncrasies was certain to be one. I kept most of the fellow students at a mere acquaintance level and never allowed any of them to become too close to me. I was going to be there only for a year and I wanted no serious commitments. That was my version. The truth could well have been that none of them wanted me as their friend. I was eagerly looking forward to my vacation. I was planning to go to my aunt's place and wanted to have another good laugh on my aborted first love. I was also interested to find out if the others had something going.

You could count on my father to screw up the whole thing – the infrequent jab of pain that he was experiencing on his right side, just in the region of his stomach, had started becoming frequent and then constant. I had started noticing the constant massaging action of his in the few hours he spent in the house. My mother, who was panic stricken in normal times, went into an overdrive. Anand had to cancel his precious trip to Bangalore for an appointment with a doctor. This first investigatory appointment gave birth to further and more specialised appointments and the doctors were not able to conclude anything. He was given a lot of symptomatic medicines. Those doctors, who knew my parents well, equated his lifestyle with this predicament and advised a slow down on his abuse of his body.

There was no medical proof at that time to convert this advice into an order. Most of the medications was painkillers and gave temporary relief which lulled Anand into delaying a thorough investigation. If he had done one on time, I could have gone on my vacation as planned. He delayed to the extent possible and when the pain became unbearable, even to a normally stoic Anand, emergency measures were needed. The teacher appears when the student is ready. Similarly the correct doctor appeared when the patient was ready. Biology had never been my favourite subject. So when the doctor mentioned something very grave about a gall bladder, and was talking about a potential surgery, it made no sense to me. Where in the hell is a gall bladder located? The doctor was a curious one. He spoke with his eyes half closed, as if in a dream, and years of cutting up people and correcting what was wrong inside gave his voice almost a professorial tenor. He must have spoken about this on hundreds of earlier occasions. I was an opportunist. I had to show off my knowledge and display an eagerness to learn new things, even if my father was gravely ill.

I learnt that the bile created by liver is not very concentrated. This is sent to an intermediate storage pouch. This pouch is the gall bladder in question. Here the concentration of the bile increases. The gall bladder, if it were functioning as it should, releases the bile in to the digestive tract whenever food is sensed. The job of this bile is to emulsify the fat and neutralise the acids in the undigested food. I would write it down and memorise it. I would educate everyone who later visited my father. I was not able to explain to someone what 'emulsify' meant.

In my father's case his constant abuse of his body coupled with either lack of food or untimely food collaborated to convert his delicate gall bladder into a mass of useless mush. It atrophied and withered inside. The doctor decided to operate upon him immediately as the presence of the non-functioning organ was a bigger nuisance. The Hobson's choice, my father had to live without the gall bladder, but that also promised relief from the pain; what about the function of the gall bladder?.

"That is all right. The organ is superfluous and a man can live without a gall bladder. He just needs to control his diet," the doctor asserted.

My father and control his diet? I smirked knowing it was easier to ask Hitler to love Jews. I kept this scepticism to myself.

Bhaskar was livid when he heard the doctor say that a part of the human body was actually superfluous. "God is not a fool. Human body is one of the finest examples of his creative ability. There is not one cell which is superfluous in the body, leave alone an organ." He could not bring himself to accept the necessity which arose because of my father's philandering way of life. I still respected him for his depth in almost all subjects, and was aghast that I could not think of such an outburst first. There was only one way to get into the limelight. Counter attack!

"I am sure the doctor is capable to decide on his field of specialty," I mumbled, but loud enough for my mother and Bhaskar to hear. It was an open challenge. My mother was too worried about the surgery to pay attention to this emerging skirmish. Bhaskar was nonplussed and decided to ignore me, and for the first time left a conversation without a proper ending. He would complete his withdrawal over a period of few years, but the separation had its beginning here.

There were no alternatives given. The surgery was a must and the sooner we did it the better. It was decided, by my parents, of course, to plan the operation during the vacation time so that it did not clash with my college. All my enthusiasm in learning about the functioning of a gall bladder vanished as I saw my vacation plan disintegrating. Even I was smart enough to realise an expression of desire to proceed to my aunt's place while my father underwent a surgery would not go down well with my mother.

So I stayed. Laparoscopy was not known then and the doctor slit my father across his midriff and removed the unwanted, non-functioning organ. The recovery, which would take three days at the most today, stretched to three weeks, the entire duration of my vacation. I spent the whole duration shuttling between my home and the hospital. This was the longest I stayed with my father. He was in great pain and could not carry out a normal conversation. My warped mind mistook it for lack of affection and I was curt in attending to him. I would read my novels, study my books and pretend not to hear his calls for a sip of water, readjustment of his pillow, or my help for a trip to the bathroom. I would wait for his call to become a supplication before attending to him. My poker face would not reveal the sadist within and my father was too simple a man to even start to guess the monster that was shaping up.

To the visitors I would explain the diagnosis, the functioning of the gall bladder, life after surgery without it and attend to my father before the request left his mouth. I had planned all this well. In future, if my father and I ever crossed swords, I wanted the sympathy of the outside world with me. I should be painted as the wronged son and not the other way about. Priya was the only one who noticed this disparate behaviour of mine and was initially confused. She was a smart girl in the making and in the later years only she would stand besides my parents and tell me on my face for what I was. The vacation in fact had turned out to be more entertaining than I first feared.

My mother was busy with her prayers for a speedy recovery, and stopped nagging me. I could sleep during the night in the hospital and sleep during the day at home on the pretext of having spent the night by my father's bed. The capacity of the youth to sleep is unbelievable. I did have my distraction that I wanted. Out of sibling affection, and a gratitude that was overwhelming, my aunt came over to visit her ailing brother along with one of her sons, who was roughly my age. While my mother and my aunt took over the hospital vigilance, my cousin and I had a blast. Bhaskar was aghast at this, as it did not look apt, what with my father still not declared out of the critical zone. He asked me to behave in a subdued way as that looked proper.

"I do not think I have to wear my emotions on my sleeve," was my reply. It was a straight rip off from one of the novels I had recently read.

He nodded his head sadly sideways, and as I was preparing for my next repartee, left me and slouched away. When my cousin told me that there was no need for me to be so rude, I told him I knew better.

Did I?

The vacation was coming to an end and my father returned home after his discharge. It was strange to see him at home. If there was ever a chance for the father and son to get to understand each other better, this was it. I decided to take part in a local chess tournament to avoid staying at home, and spent most of my time in preparation, and in the actual competition. To my surprise I reached the third round, and looking at the draw made me go weak in my knees and my mouth water, at the same time. If I cleared my next round, I would run into Bhaskar. I decided to give all I had and ensure that I would eliminate Bhaskar. I studied all his previous games; went through all the strategies we discussed. I was a monomaniac. I had only one purpose. I prepared my best defence and even started playing with Priya again, just to hone my skills. My father, who was watching me play chess for the first time, was impressed. He did not follow the game but was smart enough to follow the general scheme. He knew Priya was good as the communication between the two was excellent. Priya's affection was unconditional. I was preparing myself in anticipation of the disgrace that I planned for Bhaskar. I even had my curt one liner ready for the post match handshake.

I ran in to a new player I have not played before, and lost comprehensively in twenty-seven moves. I was so focused on my tryst with Bhaskar that I made the cardinal error of not sizing up my next opponent. This was one lesson I learnt from that tournament. This helped me to be systematic in my professional life and brought me success.

I also stopped playing chess from that day.

I was surprised to see the changes in my father after the operation. He came home from his office and *stayed* home.

Hitler was beginning to love the Jews.

Weekends were at home. He even started showing interest in my college work and in my preparation for the interview. My house started resembling a home for the first time in years. Even a diehard cynic like me would have softened if this arrangement had continued. My mother prematurely thanked all her Gods and my grandmother's Gods. I was spotting a constant smile on her face, like the one a groom wears on his marriage reception. She became bolder with the presence of my father and started ordering me, whereas in the past, she would have requested or said. I had to hold back my natural instinct for I was still shit scared of my father. It was alright to discreetly dislike him, but to show disrespect on his face was unthinkable. Harmony reigned.

It was too good to be true. It was only a matter of time, I knew. Only my mother could be foolish enough to believe this to become *and stay* permanent. A wounded lion stays with its pride, licking its wounds, gathering strength. When it becomes agile and able, it goes hunting again. So did Anand. His convalescence lasted exactly two months. His regression was slow, but steady. He started his nocturnal tryst with his cronies gradually and soon reached his peak performance. My mother spinelessly glided into her routine of getting up at five in the morning, *to let him in*. He was a non-resident on the weekends as usual. He had, however, showed some restraint in smoking, and his food habits were far better than what they used to be. Considering what it was, anything would have been an improvement. Our household slipped back to its routine of an absent father, forlorn mother, hapless Priya and the incorrigible yours truly.

Further ailments would befall my father befitting someone who ignored the first warning bell so callously. Only someone like he could and he did.

26

My College Days

It was a dream location. The college I managed to get into was a picture-postcard location. A national highway ran through the campus. On the one side were clusters of indescribable trees and palms, followed by a virgin beach. The seashore was not commercialised like the Marina in Madras and the stretch of this unpolluted sand belonged only to the students. And to some love birds, I later discovered. On the other side, the four hostels, one for each year, formed a crescent. The beauty of this had to be viewed in three dimensions as the crescent climbed, as it curved. Beyond the crescent, were the football ground and an open air theatre. The main building stood at the centre, majestic in its width, albeit with the most rudimentary architectural design. The design was more functional, than ornamental. It was a college; not some auditorium for performing arts. On the far side of the main building, away from the hostels, were the staff quarters and the forbidden land – the ladies hostel. It was, as the cliché goes, love at first sight. In the void formed by the crescent was another ground, which was an all-purpose one. We would play cricket, jog, run around clad only in our jocks in the middle of the night as freshers, make our juniors repeat the same, when we were seniors a year later, lie down and star-gaze, or simply sit and talk most of the nights in that ground. All that later; my first day to the college to finish the formalities of joining, read payments, went smoothly.

We ran into some seniors near the administrative block. My father had accompanied me, which was a surprise. This was the first parental duty he had dispensed towards my academia. May be he felt he needed to make up at some time and found this to be one. The journey was thankfully short. We left around ten in the night and reached the college at nine in the morning. We returned the same evening and I was saved any awkward moments, which would have arisen if we had stayed there overnight. My father, the concerned one that he was, enquired with these seniors about the quality of education at the college. As if someone studying there would say anything improper about the college, I thought to myself. I had to find something wrong with every act of my Dad. After assurances on that front, he, almost apologetically, asked them if there was any severe ragging in the hostels. I chipped in here. My urge to display my knowledge at every chance did not let this moment go.

"The government has passed an ordinance branding ragging as illegal. Ragging, now, is a punishable crime. Did not you read it in the papers? In fact there is a notice to that effect near the entrance of the main building," I conveyed with a complete authority on the topic.

I was not certain whether my father was more relieved, or the senior students more surprised! One of them, Sujay, told my father with a comforting pat on my shoulders, that I was right, and he had no need to worry. I beamed and my chest swelled to the point of exploding. The formalities were over and we returned the same evening. I was to return about a month later for my first semester. The intervening period flitted by with shopping, packing, purchasing new clothes (no more uniforms!), my first pair of shoes and endless advice from my mother on what I could do and what I should not. Priya in a rare gesture of emotion gave me a steel bracelet. Not a very subtle gift but my first gift. I was also touched by the show of affection. I would wear it for the rest of my life, even when we stopped talking to each other cordially.

My parents accompanied me and we stayed in a hotel, as we reached a couple of days earlier. On the first day, we went and moved my belongings to my hostel room. A bank account was opened in my name. We returned to the city and stayed another night in the hotel. The next morning, my parents left for home and I was scared, as suddenly the gravity of the situation dawned on me. *I would be on my own.* There was a difference between staying with your aunt and staying in a hostel on your own. I returned to my hostel room. In the first year, three students shared one room. The room had three cots, no mattresses, separated by three desks and chairs. On each desk there was a table-lamp, with no bulbs; we had to buy one and fit. There was also a common lamp that threw a sick, dull, yellow light in the room. This left the corners dark and even the table-lamps, when lit, could not completely brighten the room. On the far wall, away from the cots, was a three-door wardrobe – one door for each student. Our dresses into the wardrobe, and our books and notebooks on the table, was the understanding.

Three terrified, out of the city, students immediately became friends. Pattabi and Mukund were the other two. Pattabi was from Madras and Mukund from Trichy. The three of us became friends easily and with Mukund, I could share a lot of my best moments from Trichy. Pattabi was a quiet one and would remain that way over the next four years. We spent the day, and part of the evening, in setting up our goods around the room. Each of us was too polite with each other and offered the other the privilege of choosing his cot. This went on with no solution in sight and we drew lots at the end to decide who would sleep in which cot. We did not know then that none of us would sleep that night in our room. We explored a little and found that we had one sanitary block per wing. That meant four washbasins, three bathrooms and three toilets for thirty students! We wrinkled our noses in plain disgust and came back to our room. The frayed edges of the picture postcard were already in plain view.

The word 'mess' was the most appropriate one for our canteen. The place had the unmistakable smell of stored vegetables and overcooked spices. The rice was of the quality that a beggar in my hometown would not have accepted, and the preparation of all items was uniformly bland. It was impossible to believe that food so tasteless could be *prepared.* It had to be an accident, we consoled ourselves. The food would continue to be the same for ever. We had a choice of opting for messes in the other hostel blocks, but it was mandatory for the first-year students to spend the first month in their hostel mess. We changed the mess from the second month itself and enjoyed reasonably better food for the rest of our four years. But that first month we had no choice and so we suffered.

We were back in our room after this unbelievable dinner and spent the next thirty minutes exaggerating the poor quality of the food that was supplied, laughed politely at everything someone said even if it was not really funny as we wanted to be nice to each other, heaped accolades on the quality of our respective homefood, again an exaggeration and after getting sick of being too proper for an artificially long stretch of time, decided to sleep as the classes began next day. The college started at eight in the morning. This came as a shock to all of us. We were used to ten in the morning to four in the afternoon with a recess of one hour for lunch in our schools. Eight to twelve; one to four-thirty, six days a week! Very unfair! Each of us said this to each other and tried to get some sleep when there was a loud knock on our door.

"Open up! You motherfuckers!" called out a voice, which was definitely drunk.

We looked at each other, surely a mistake, or a case of mistaken identity, and did not move.

The banging was repeated and we became "sister fuckers", in the next terms of endearment. We became "bastards" by the time we opened the doors, with a false bravado and a sense of indignation at being called such names.

The scene outside the door was terrifying. There stood a group of about seven students, surely our seniors, almost all of them with a cigarette in their hand and three of them surely very drunk.

"Come to the ground within five minutes. If you want to, you can pray before coming" said their spokesperson, spitting bits of tobacco and spittle as he barked his orders. The whole group laughed hysterically and went marching towards the ground in front of our hostels, where we spotted already some activity – too vague from this far to discern.

I do not recall whether any of us questioned as to whether we had a choice. All those ordinances of government and notices on the boards vanished. None of them stayed back to see whether we complied, as it was pretty obvious that they were used to obedience. That night was quite a night. The interaction with seniors under the name of ragging was formless. It did not follow any pattern. The ones who were in their second year were, usually, the most active and sometimes, violent. It was a first time for them and they took the plunge. The final-year students were clearly disinterested and showed up only for some free entertainment.

"Strip!" barked a visibly excited second-year goon. We thought we did not hear properly. I did not know about Pattabi and Mukund, but I took my bath with my bathroom door closed. The last one to have had a clean look of me, unclad, must have been our family doctor, and that too several years before. The order was repeated, this time accompanied by a resounding slap. Pattabi was standing first in the line and his eyes watered immediately on receiving the slap. He would tell me later that even his father had never slapped him. I was envious. I wished I had his father. Then Pattabi did not draw female genitals on the cover page of a book. I was careful not to tell the whole story. No one ever knew me fully as I was always careful, and a ruthless editor to boot. I ensured that people heard about me, just what I wanted them to hear. The slap clarified matters hours of lecturing would not have. We stopped at our briefs dreading that we would be forced to divest that also. You always feel defenceless when you are naked.

"Five rounds, on the double!" My days at NCC came to my mind. This was simple, though a little humiliating. We expected to return to our room after the rounds. That was how naïve we were, that first day. The run was designed to drain us of any resistance and the process of degradation continued. Pattabi had to smoke a cigarette. I had to romance Mukund, enacting a scene from a movie that someone recalled. We were made to dance. It was all very childish. Each gave an order that came to his mind. There were clashes amongst them about what needed to be executed first and an unsaid competitive spirit was evident as to who could be more innovative. They became tired sooner than we expected, and we were dismissed. We picked up our clothes and started dressing up before returning. If we had returned with the dresses bundled up in our hands and marched straight back, after all we did run around the ground that way only hours before didn't we, I would have escaped. We were brought up in that fashion. Before you went anywhere, you dressed properly. It was while I was buttoning my shirt, Sujay spotted me "My! My! Who do we have here? Hello friends, this is the incredible guy I was telling you about all these days. The guy who wrote government ordinance banning ragging in our country! Okay, all you guys can go back and Mr President here will stay back."

That moment I felt pure terror. Why could I not have kept my trap shut the other day? I was ready to cry as others made their way back to the hostel. The conclusion that I needed special treatment was unanimous. I was saved only because of lack of imagination on their part. I was slapped, pushed, shoved, kicked and punched. To hit someone who can not react gets tiring after some time. I was made to do a lot of stupid things like walking like a chicken, strutting like a peacock, and sound like an elephant, sing a song and the tasks became more unimaginative with progress of time. I returned to my room at dawn. All the students of the first year were half asleep in the classes on day one. This continued for fifteen days. We had never lived on so little sleep in our whole life. The ignominy on certain nights was at its zenith, when a senior would bring his girlfriend to the carnival. The ordeals of the night made our dinner even more tasteless. We had no appetite. There was no one we hated more in those fifteen days than our seniors, who took this sadistic pleasure as their birthright. The three of us vowed on the seventh night that we would never indulge in such a barbaric act the following year. We would set an example for others to follow. We were very serious about our pledge.

After the first month the ragging stopped completely and suddenly. When we were children, we were often confused about the seasons for games. No one ever knew when the marbles went in and the tops came out, or when the tops went in and the kites came out. The ending of the ragging season was as sudden, not that we had anything to complain about it, when it ended. The seniors who humiliated and tortured us on all those nights became our friends and mentors. Most of us would benefit immensely from the interactions and they helped us unconditionally. It was amidst this bonhomie that the three of us buried our pledge of 'no ragging' and already started devising methods for the freshers next year. We found our seniors lacking in imagination and we would correct this anomaly.

Suddenly the first assessment was on us. The marks we scored here mattered in the semester and there was no way one could ignore this. The college had a system of bombarding you non-stop with assessments, practicals, and more assessments and before you realised the semester exams were around the corner. We would spend whole nights in empty classrooms and at the library (till 11 p.m). We had two shops, on the other side of the road, on the way to the beach. These were typical college-hostel shops that served tea, cigarettes, omelets and clandestine pouches of marijuana. We used to frequent these shops, more for a break from our books and figures, than for the comfort of tea. The shops were run by two of our canteen staff, Bhaskar and Shiva. I had always stayed with Shiva's shop for obvious reasons. If the other guy had a different name, I could have divided the business.

The first semester exams were over and we were on our first vacation. The first semester had been a mixed bag and our attachment had not become deep, or any of the friendships, strong. Both would take place in the following years and many of us would cry unashamedly when the time came to part. The celebration of the end of the first semester had only one location – the terrace teashop of our main building, aptly named '*Samudhra Darshan*'. This was another dream location. The terrace of the main building had this small teashop, where we could get only a cup of tea; nothing else was served here, and look at the panoramic view that spread in front of us – from the main building to the lawns to the winding road to the groves to a small strip of beach and the vast sea. It was breathtaking! We used to stand there for hours together with the tea turning cold in our hand. We had more adventures still in store; the beach, the open air theatre, the ladies hostel and our favourite movie hall, Natraj. But we never had enough time to taste any of these in our first semester.

There was a small temple, atop a huge rock, just as the beach began. It was a temple of Lord Shiva. The backside of the temple faced the sea and to sit there and look at the horizon was absolute bliss. The endless waves, crashing against few rocks strewn all along the seashore, would make philosophers out of some of the most intellectual students. The temple was busy during the exam times as even someone, as indifferent as I was, would be tempted to put in a supplication in the face of 'engineering drawing' and 'strength of materials'. These two subjects were specific nightmares for most of us average students. I had no inherent talent for drawings and 'strength of materials' would not have been that scary, if we had had an ordinary professor. We had a sadist. A. S. Subramaniam. His initials formed a convenient and an appropriate acronym. He would recite the poem of Hiawatha and expect as to calculate the velocity and trajectory of the arrows, which the brave warrior shot. I was particularly worried with my performance in both these papers in my first semester and that robbed me of a proper vacation as I was really worried about failing in a subject for the first time in my life. Another example of this guy's sadism was in the assessments.

"Divide the length of your question paper measured in millimetrers by your roll number and the nearest whole number is the question you have to attempt," was one such instruction. Most of us could not deduce the question that we needed to attempt for a considerable period of time.

Not that it mattered.

All his questions were unanswerable.

After the last exam got over, most of us were eager to return to our respective homes, if for nothing else, at least for some sumptuous food.

27

My Lovee

It was lust at first sight. The moment I saw her, I wanted to take her to bed. She was not beautiful in the classic sense. But boy! she was attractive. I had read Lady Chatterley's Lover during my first semester, thanks to Pattabi, who was the most well read amongst the three of us. He introduced me to many new authors, most of them controversial, or from the beat generation. There was a sense of rebellion, just reading those books. The real fact was I did not understand many allegories, and implied insinuations, but I was always good in covering my ignorance. A phrase "stirring in my loins" from D H Lawrence stayed with me from that book. I *felt* it when I saw this girl. She was staying in the vicinity and I happened to notice her when my mother sent me to the grocer on one of her endless errands. I was wondering as to who ran these errands for her, when I was in college. I went grudgingly but after seeing her, I became very obedient and would be *out of the house* even before my mother completed the list of what she wanted. She was not accustomed to such compliance but did not pry deep into the motivations. I recalled my stalking the 'screeching siren' days and was relieved when I *heard* her make an enquiry from the shopkeeper. The voice was not pure music but husky. I liked husky, slightly masculine, voices in girls.

I was not shaping up badly either for a boy of my age. Regular games, I started playing badminton, courtesy Mukund, and jogging on the beach that made me wiry and fairly muscular. My arms were no longer matchsticks, dangling awkwardly but were reasonably moulded. The shirt did not rip at the seams by my rippling biceps, but the muscles were noticed easily. I took up jogging twice a day with a fond of hope of running past her and impressing her, but it yielded no fruits. The only place I would run into her was at the grocer and for a freaky moment I thought that she was the *grocer's daughter.* Try as I might, I could not deduce much about her and I returned to my college at the end of the vacation, no wiser about her.

The return made me realise how much I missed my two friends and the tea at our hang out. We returned a day before the classes were to start, and were having a jolly good time recounting our vacation exploits. I was careful not to mention anything about the nubile nymphet; once bitten twice shy. We were planning an early dinner, followed by a night on the beach. One of the studious guys had come running, telling us that the results of the first semester were out and the list was on the notice-board in the main hall. There was a mad rush. I had my stomach in knots. There was an uneasy feeling which I managed to ignore in my unsuccessful pursuit during my vacation. The demons of 'engineering drawing' and 'Hiawatha' returned to take their position of tormentors. Thankfully, the crowd in front of the notice-board did not make it possible for me to go closer and Mukund, the real sportsman of our group, muscled his way in and came out with a wide grin pasted on his usually cheerful face. I was already composing a letter in my heart, explaining to my parents why I had failed in two subjects. I apportioned the blame on the food, ragging and tactless tutors. I was cursing myself for not having laid the base during the vacation. I could have hinted and prepared them a little better. The composing of the letter was dropped when Mukund told us that we had all passed. I could not believe it. I did not stay back to check the percentage. The relief was physical.

The plans for the night on the beach suddenly appeared more appropriate, befitting the occasion. We finished our dinner and went to the beach. It was unusual to spot Pattabi carrying a bag with him. We found three bottles of beer, when we reached the beach, inside that bag. Pattabi looked very casual, sipping the beer. Neither Mukund nor I drank. I would not go near anything that had alcohol and would stay that way. The tragedies in my family had ensured I developed an inherent aversion to tobacco and alcohol. I remained that way and never was tempted. Mukund was not that resolute, may be his family history was different, and he joined Pattabi when he finished the second bottle. I enjoyed that night as much as they did, without the help of alcohol.

I just managed to clear both the subjects, but some good performances in other subjects meant that I had a decent overall percentage to write home about. I was specific about the overall performance and carefully avoided the unpleasant, poor marks, without actually lying. This was not school where you needed your parent's signature on the progress card.

The college life went on, with nothing much worthwhile happening. The weekend nights (Saturdays), at the open air theatre, were becoming more enjoyable, with a student body being given the freedom to organise the movies. We would arrange for outrageous movies, designed to embarrass the families of the faculty and the girls from the hostel. Our criterion for selecting a movie was mainly focusing on the presence of at least one rape scene – the more graphic the better – one song with the heroine clad in white, drenched in rain or waterfall, and vulgar comedy. It might sound atrocious but it was easy to fill all the thirty-five weeks with movies that fit the bill. The open air theatre was built more like a Roman amphitheatre and we used to stretch ourselves in the open space between the arc of the steps and the concrete screen. When the movie moved to the second half, and towards the end, most of us would have fallen asleep. On many occasions, we would get up on Sunday mornings in our open air theatre, not having bothered to shift to the hostel after the movie ended. We were sure that the faculty and the girls enjoyed the movies, as much as we did, because they were as regular as we were in showing up. It was after one such movie night, the central theme of the movie being a younger boy seduced by a bored housewife (the director relied on being explicit instead of choosing to be subtle), consumed by the thoughts of my nameless lass around the grocer shop that I masturbated for the first time. Amateur books with lurid details and the sick theme of sex in abundance were easily available in any hostel, and ours was no exception. The experience was unbelievably exciting and a thousand suns exploded in my head when I ejaculated. I quietly left my room and rushed to the bathroom, thinking I had spilled blood. I inspected myself very closely and cleaned myself before returning. I repeated the act many times, but chose the toilet or the bathroom for the subsequent occasions.

We had settled into a predictable routine of our activities. We would end up on the beach on Sunday nights and used to return, using the longer route that allowed us to pass the ladies hostel and the college building. We hoped that one of the girls would be around outside their hostel, in the middle of the night, when we returned. Like most of our other fantasies, this was also formless, as we really had no idea on what we would do if one was ever present. The exciting thing about a fantasy is that it remains in the realms of our imagination. On some nights, without any planning, we would decide and go to Natraj to watch a movie. This movie hall was very close to our hostel and there used to be a regular overdose of poorly-made Malayalam movies. The Malayalam film industry was a mature film industry with some laudable movies in their repertoire, the college-going teens fraternised them for clumsy movies, which revolved around sex and seduction.

College life now had settled into a pattern and we managed to juggle our activities adroitly. Just before the second semester examinations, there was a sudden craze for sporting a shaven-head look, and the three of us had ourselves tonsured. I returned home for that vacation sporting a look of a concentration camp inmate. I did not have the courage to appear in front of my fantasy woman in that shape and the first thing I purchased after reaching home was a golf cap. I was restless and itching to go out to increase the probability of meeting her. Surprisingly my mother had no errands for me. Murphy's Law at work!

That vacation was going to be shorter as I had plans of going to Trichy, to catch up with my cousins and visit Mukund. Priya was in class seven, an age where I could not confide in her, and the day to leave for Trichy was coming closer. My heart was in my mouth when I saw my dream girl with Priya in the lane where we lived. I ran and stood like an idiot in front of them. Priya looked at me with 'what' written in her eyes and the angel looked at me in a neutral way. I mumbled something to Priya about finding her there and would she please come over to home quickly. In an act of bravery, even I did not know I was capable of, I turned to my angel and said, "Hi, I am Amar, Priya's cousin. I am home on my vacation. Can't say I have seen you before" – all in one breath. I almost extended my hand for a shake, but withheld the urge with Himalayan restraint. She was shocked, no doubt about that, but it must be said that she regained her composure pretty quickly.

"Hello! I am Maria. I have been here long. In fact I had seen you during your last trip home. I live nearby. Nice to meet you," she said, as if she was reciting from her notes. The revelation that she had seen me last time was satisfying and I was sad I could not be as forthright as she was. Of course, she could afford to. For her, I was just a cousin of someone she knew. The fire of passion was not obviously lit, yet.

I again mumbled something that sounded like "hemgrphfehf" and left. I was walking on clouds. I was whistling a song with hardly a care in the world. In my mind I had already cancelled the trip to Trichy. I would wait at all the possible places and increase our acquaintance to a level of friendship, and possibly light the fire in her before I went back to college for another semester. Suddenly Priya went right to the top of my favourite people list.

How was I to use her? My mind was already finding out ways. Then it struck me as unfair as she was hardly twelve-years old. I had some amount of decency left. My mind was planning a lot many things at the same time. I would have to write a letter to Trichy, informing Mukund that my father was not well. I could use my father for this purpose. The coming semester I would open up this matter with both my best friends. After all I needed some support in my pursuit. She did not have to remain nameless, now that I was in possession of her name.

I stopped dead in my track. The whistling stopped halfway through a note. My hand went to my forehead involuntarily, in the universal gesture of dismay. "Did she say Maria?" I scratched my head, trying to recollect. There was no need. How could I forget words from those lips? Maria, it definitely was. And even my limited intelligence could not fail to grasp the significance. Maria was definitely a Christian name. No two opinions about that. I was devastated. Why? I questioned myself the rest of the way home. It never occurred to me that there could be such a twist in the tale, right at the start. I was wondering whether to write that epistle to Mukund or proceed as per the original plan. No way could it work out. My parents would never agree to it. As usual, I was looking at a very distant future. I did not even know whether she was interested in me.

Something wild and original woke up inside me. Enough of being timid and getting used to be a loser. I decided this time I would make things happen. The very idea of resistance from my parents egged me on (all those novels of the beat generation, even with my limited grasp) and I decided to go all out in wooing Maria, and ensure that I married her, and no one else. That week I happened to see

'Sound of Music', and suddenly Maria was sounding all the more beautiful, and the movie remained my favourite forever. Years later, when I bought a DVD player, 'Sound of Music' was the first movie I bought, though by then Maria was legally my wife. At that juncture, however, my love looked unrequited.

As luck would have it, her father happened to be working in my father's office, and this gave me further hope. That holiday I planned out my conquest well. I frequented my father's office (it was quite common then for the children to visit their parents in their work-places, and in a governmental agency no one cared two hoots) for the rest of the vacation and befriended Antony, my future father-in-law and impressed him with my half-baked knowledge. My father was curious at first, and as usual nothing retained his interest for long, and he chose to ignore me. He was, however, proud when Antony complimented him on his fine boy. It was easy to be impressed by me. Longer association alone could reveal me to be a selfish, egotistic, incorrigible and adamant imbecile.

My plan was a well-thought out one. I needed all the support when I sprang my intention four years later. All the while I had no idea what Maria was thinking about. Did she care for me? Was she also smitten by the lovebug? I corrected myself. It was lust first, which blossomed into love. I was sure of winning her heart, all in good time. To be honest, if her name had not been Maria, the possibility of revolting against my parents would not have risen as a possibility and may be, I would have lost my interest in her after a few more vacations of pointless one-side love. The future looked challenging and thrilling. I would be the first one in my family to marry someone outside of the caste, and a Christian one at that. It would not just create waves in my family; it would be a full-fledged *tsunami*. The controversy and the rebel act intoxicated me. To add to all that, was the voluptuous Maria. If there was one thing I was certain, it was that she would be my wife.

That Sunday, my mother was surprised to see me going to the church for the first time. I never showed any interest in going to a temple with her and here I was on the way to a church. I told her I was just curious. Maria and her family did not visit that church, and it would have looked foolish to keep going to different churches every week to find out. Without another meeting with Maria, I left for my second year in college. We did not meet, but I looked at her enough number of times from various vantage points, as I had her routine by heart by the time my second vacation was over.

The entire journey to the hostel was spent in arranging and rearranging disclosure of the news to Pattabi and Mukund. I ran various combinations in my mind. I thought of various locations and how to build up the whole scene to the climax before reaching the name 'Maria'. I made my decision. It would be the first night, at the beach.

28

The Birth of Another Son

The year ahead promised to be interesting. Firstly, the demons of the uncertainties of the first semester were buried and we soon learnt to crack the examination system to ensure that we got away unscathed. Secondly, the prospect of ragging the freshers, as we were officially the seniors, was looking good. We had planned out a long list of new insults and ignominies on our fresh batch. But that first night, we were found at the beach after our dinner and a hot cup of tea. Pattabi had started smoking grass and the smell reminded me of Ishwaran, but I was sure that Pattabi's shoulders carried a firm head and he would never step over the precipice.

Our respective narrations began and Mukund cursed me for opting out of the holiday tryst. He was so much looking forward to that. This gave the perfect opening to launch into the adventures of mine. While narrating, I realised that I had spent more time *with Antony* and not my beloved. I exaggerated for better effects – in my narration, Maria and I had already held hands and promised undying love for each other. I kept avoiding the mention of her name as I wanted to build it to a point where I would be posed the question. I had practiced the delivery of the name on the journey the day before. I would keep a poker face and tell the name as if it did not mean new complications. Mukund fell into the trap and asked me her name. My moment in the limelight!

I delivered the information with a dead-pan face. It was an anti-climax. Neither of them dropped whatever they were holding, nor did they jump up as if a scorpion had stung their testicles. Pattabi finished the long draw on the pipe and said, "So we have a rebel here!" Mukund reacted slightly better, "Do you think this will work out?"

I suddenly had my doubts, "Come on guys, I was counting on your support and there is no way I am retracting. I am committed to this. She will be the only one I can ever marry. It's either she or I remain a bachelor," I announced. It sounded hollow even to me. Pattabi, the philosopher, said, "Look, infatuation at this age is common. We all know about our resolves. We promised that we would never rag our juniors and here we are already waiting for the herd to arrive like hungry wolves. Commitments and promises at this age are impulsive, not to be taken seriously."

Looking back, I knew it was that precise moment when I took the final decision. I would marry Maria, at least to prove Pattabi wrong. But we were friends, and they pledged unwavering support in my amorous adventure and we returned. We had work to do.

New room in a new hostel – we took one room again as the thought of sharing our room with another one was unthinkable. We had to make preparation for the freshers. In the third year, it was two students per room and we took different partners. It was unthinkable for two of us to stay together, without the third one. In the final year, we each had a room to ourselves and we were in room numbers forty-seven, eight and nine.

The ragging proved to be boring after the first few days. We concluded that the food in their mess for the first month was punishment enough. That someone patronised that mess after the customary first month continued to be a mystery. We soon lost interest in the freshers and got back to our own worlds. In my case, read 'our own worlds' as dreaming on the future with Maria. Shamelessly I fantasised Maria and I in various positions and locations on my increasing instances of masturbations. Somehow this fascination of mine with Maria never dwelt into any matters sublime and remained purely carnal. I was often worried whether this physical attraction would wane off and prove Pattabi's prophecies true. How much ever I tried to infuse a sense of pure unadulterated love in my imagination, the labours failed miserably.

The "stirring in the loins" remained constant and thinking of Maria without an act of copulation remained as elusive as ever. I gave up any attempts at some divine form of love, and considered a mere mortal, albeit carnal, version would do. Advice from my two trusted musketeers, though genuine in intention, continued to be useless. Their own lack of personal experience and amateurism was evident in their attempts. For once I was not blunt and started sieving the advices carefully. I had my job cut out and the road was already strewn with enough landmines, without me screwing it up with another wrong move. Amidst all the eroticism, and over-the-head philosophy that comprised my reading habits, it was sheer providence that I managed to read The Love Story by Erich Segal. The book was surprisingly thin and the title led me to believe, coupled with its size, which I was about to read another book to act as a stimulus to my oversexed and perverted mind.

That book changed my life. I read it and was stunned by its simplicity. I must have read that book at least twenty times in that semester. It was an instant decision to gift that book to Maria, the next vacation. But how? In the town and locality where I lived, it was not common for a boy to gift a girl a novel, leave alone one with such a misleading title. The decision was made. She would read that book, which was certain. I just needed to work out the details. With the amount that my father sent me every month, I needed to sacrifice a few trips to a restaurant and two trips to Natraj to save enough money to buy a new copy of The Love Story. Of course what my father sent was enough for a decent living after the regular expenses, but you could not expect one's father to fund his son's amorous adventures too. I was, as usual, very self-centric and here I found another reason to find fault with my father. The third semester went by fast and I started to believe that time, or precisely how one perceived time, was relative.

The Gods, who were notorious for scheming nasty tricks on my family, for once conspired in my favour. Maria was in her pre-university year and the next year would see her entering college. Her father, for reasons known only to him, concluded that my English was good and Maria needed some coaching in spoken English and some help with Wren and Martin. He approached my father and wondered whether I could spare some time in the vacation with Maria, and my father, who agreed to almost *everything* so long as it did not clash with his routine, said 'yes'. I thanked the first son of my aunt who had taught us grammar during our stay in Trichy. It was a different thing that we cursed him every evening and often prayed for some permanent disability to inflict him.

She was very studious and it was evident that she had no feelings for me from her normal behaviour. I was worried about making mistakes due to the constant distraction of her presence. Correcting her spoken English was challenging, as removing sixteen years of the peculiarities of our region was not easy. She had all the faults that were unique to our state in spoken English. After 'G' it was 'hech' and it was never 'zed'; always 'ejed'. In the word 'independence' the stress was on the second syllable and not the first. She pronounced physics as if the alphabet 'h' did not exist. Pattabi was my tutor in correcting most of my flaws, and I shamelessly corrected her as if I grew up in the Buckingham Palace. She was a keen learner and a bright student. Sometimes she took umbrage over the air I was putting on, but was smart enough not to let it show. The simple act of handing over a novel was not executed till the end of the vacation. If I had not been guilty of vested interests, may be the act would have been easier. I was not, and the act was getting to be impossible as the days grew. I still was not sure whether I loved her. One look at her and the next moment I was rolling with her in the bed, the bathroom, the beach or a swimming pool (I did not know how to swim) in my fantasy. As she bent down to solve the exercises, I stole glances at her delicate nose, full rose lips, lustrous black hair, her bursting bosom and the silhouette of her shapely thighs. She was totally unconscious about her sex appeal and this made her more desirable.

With just two days left, I loaded her with grammar lessons to keep her busy till the next vacation and used the pretext of the 'power of simple writing' to give her the book. My hands were trembling and if she had as much as raised an eyebrow at the title, I would have plucked it back. She took one look at the book and asked me, "Will it be too difficult? I do not want to read a book and open the dictionary for every third word." I could never be this honest, not then and not ever. I rubbished her fears and told her that if she found that interesting, I would encourage her to other books. I stressed on the word "interesting" but she showed no emotion whatsoever. I walked back with her to her home and told Mr Antony that he could convey her progress and difficulties, if any, to me through my mother.

In my unpredictable college hostel life, letters from my mother were one thing that stood out. She wrote a letter every Sunday and posted it on a Monday. My friends would joke "Oh it's Thursday!", when my mother's epistles reached me. I never replied. I had been regular in not reciprocating affection from my parents.

The letter came on a Tuesday. It was raining that afternoon. In fact I remember every detail about that Tuesday afternoon. The dress I wore, the lunch menu, the practical that I missed in the afternoon, everything. The handwriting was vaguely familiar and there was no "from" address. My mother's letter would not come on a Tuesday. She was a stickler for routine and would never change. It was half way through my fourth semester. The letter was from Maria! Her father had been more liberal (or more stupid) than I thought. He asked his daughter to write a letter directly, hinting that it would improve her written English! The letter started without any endearments. Just

Mr Amar! She mentioned that she liked the story very much, thanks, and she cried at the end. Could I please suggest some more simple reading and a few questions that were because of Mr Wren or Mr Martin? Hardly a letter to send one into raptures of ecstasy. But I was smitten by the lust bug.

After lot of mental debate, I showed the letter to Pattabi and Mukund and drew the expected dose of laughter from them. Pattabi was more dismissive, "Amar you forget this girl. She is crazy! At this rate she will ask you to proofread her marriage invitation."

He was right. The letter had the air of a student to her teacher. But that was what it was. My mind, consumed by desire, would not see it that way. I took four days in writing my first letter (she had mentioned the address for communication inside the letter, her father's office address) and so carefully concealed my intentions in so much of double speak, lest her father read it and blow his top, that even I found it impossible to judge what I was trying to say when I read it carefully before posting it.

If Antony told my mother about my prompt reply? I posted a letter to my mother also, my first in nearly two years, rewarding her perseverance in order to camouflage my real intentions. Maria's reply came a full three weeks later. There were no differences in her letters. It was actually a course in written English for her, and my letters were increasingly becoming obtuse.

We were officially meeting each other during every vacation and she joined college when I was in my third year. The need for honing her skills in English was long forgotten and our letters became a little friendlier and less ridiculous in my third year. Pattabi once remarked, when we were in the sixth semester, that it looked a little hopeful now. Coming from him, this was a great stimulus. My father never found anything amiss in the two of us spending time during vacation, discussing novels most of the times. The antenna that women possess worked overtime and my mother started expressing her displeasure in the time I spent with Maria. She started very innocuously and built it to a regular sermon that the two of us spending such time together did not look appropriate. I wished that the doubts that were forming in my mother's mind would make its presence in Maria's mind. Either she was really innocent or she was the most consummate actress I had ever seen. I could not come home in my last year as we had our project, campus interviews and industrial visits. Maria was nowhere close to my mother in writing letters regularly, but I was prompt in replying, to Maria, of course. I had gotten through my campus interview and was assured of a job even before I started my eighth and final semester. This reduced the pressure on the final semester and I had more time to dream.

My parents were overjoyed and paid me a visit in the hostel and proceeded to a place of religious interest nearby. I gave the twenty-three letters of Maria to Mukund for temporary safekeeping, as the neat pile of those letters in my room would have surely looked out of place, when even the letter of the previous Thursday from my mother could not be located. I could trust my two friends with anything in my life. I told my parents that I would be spending very little time with them as I had to leave for my job. Pattabi and Mukund had both decided to pursue their higher education. Pattabi would go to Bangalore for his Masters and Mukund was accepted in a university in USA. I had my eye squarely on Maria and did not want to waste my time any more with education. My parents wanted me to know that it was all right with them, if I wanted to continue with my education and there was no tearing hurry for my earnings to support the family. Priya was in her final year in school and was already showing signs of a brilliant future. Her education would keep my parents occupied for at least five more years, and I used that as an excuse for my lack of interest in further studies. I was suddenly very considerate of my parents' hardships that I did not want to be a burden on them longer than what was necessary.

The parting was painful; more painful than we anticipated. Mukund would leave the country in two months' time. Pattabi would go to Bangalore after six weeks. I would have to go to Madras for my posting in three weeks' time. It was agreed that I would stay with

Pattabi and he would help me to settle down in Madras. We spent two days together after the exams, living it up. Those were the two days I did not think about Maria in the last three years. We felt no shame in crying and bade our hostel, and the college, goodbye. We promised we would return to the hostel every year. It was one of those promises you make when you are young. None of us would ever return to the college.

I reached home and the preparations were on for my imminent departure. My parents were disappointed that I preferred to go alone and stay with my friend. They wanted to accompany me and I was curt in saying 'no'. For the first time I saw an emotion close to being hurt on my father's face. The packing was a fiasco. I threw out everything that my mother packed as necessary and Priya was aghast. Parental concern or the approval of Priya was far from my mind. With less than a week left, I was rehearsing the most important moment in my life. I avoided meeting Maria in the last week and I met her on the day before my departure. She wished me good luck. With two years in college, and the casualness that can never be seen in a Tamil Brahmin girl, she offered her hand for a shake. I grasped it and asked her, "Will you be my Jenny?"

It did not register on her immediately. Her smile froze and her hand went limp in my grasp, when it registered. I let her hand go and it dropped lifelessly to her side. I prepared myself for this moment and did not waver in my determination. I held my gaze. Those were the few moments when I acted without hesitation and concrete determination. She could not look at me any longer. Her gaze fell down. Her glistening moist lips trembled. She was trying to form words but was failing. She finally found her balance and started to say something. With theatrical precision I held up my hand to silence her, "Maria! Do not think I have not thought about it. I have. In fact I have been thinking about only this moment over the last four years. I do not want an immediate answer. Take your time. I will be back in a month to get your answer. I am confident that we are meant for each other. Give it a good thought." And then I added, "God bless you." I did not know why I said that, except it sounded good and made the scene poignant.

I turned back and walked home. I had to go on a pretty long journey, both literally and figuratively, the next day. At the corner of the street I turned to look at her. She was standing exactly where I left her, in the same stance. The falling sun was behind her and I could not see the emotions on her face.

The next day I set out on my new life. I expected to meet Maria somewhere on the way to the railway station, but she did not appear. It was while I was on the train bound for Madras, after all the waving of the hands, after the same advice repeated for the seventeenth time, after everyone in my compartment slept, did the gravity of my act, the previous day, sank in. I had asked Maria to be my wife!

I still was not sure whether I loved her. Was it love that would stand the test of time or was it only a product of base desire and the intoxication of a rebellious act? Would she say 'yes'? What if she said 'no'? What did I have that was different to offer? Some half-baked command in English, a very shallow grasp of good literature and mediocre knowledge that any engineering graduate was capable of offering. Looked like I would have my one month to get my answer.

29

My Life

Madras was hot. Pattabi told me the usual joke that any newcomer to the city is cursed to hear. "We have only three seasons; hot, hotter and hottest". Irrespective of when you landed, the native always told you that this was just hot, and the worst would follow. The weather of Madras could start rasping your nerves from day one. The temperature remained constantly above thirty-six degree Celsius, and the energy-sapping humidity never fell below eighty-two. The crisp, ironed shirt that you donned in the morning was reduced to a damp, dripping rag in less than thirty minutes. Pattabi helped me to find a paying guest accommodation. I was given a room with an attached water closet-cum-bathroom and with it a long list of things that I was not expected to perform. The list banned smoking, drinking, bringing girls to my room, playing music loudly, reporting late in the night and consumption of non-vegetarian food in the premises. I had no problem with any of them except the music; so I included a pair of headphones in my initial list of purchase.

I saw a potential problem in my future life as I was scrutinising the list. I was a vegetarian and was never inclined to try meat even in my hostel. Maria being a Christian posed a new complication. Would it be fair to expect her to give up eating meat just because she married me? Life should be give and take. I decided to make my first compromise and with the help of Pattabi tasted chicken for the first time in my life. The Indian way of cooking rested on killing any original taste with abundant spices and the non-vegetarian menu normally took it to the limit. The chicken was rubbery and required a surprisingly long time of chewing before passing through the gullet. I never found the actual taste of chicken. It was spicy and made my eyes water. You could count on Pattabi to deflate any situation and he did by asking, with a straight face, "Will you continue with this fare even if the answer from Maria is a 'no'?"

I choked on the last piece. My look was sufficient to silence him and he decided not to press it further. There, I broke my first tie that tradition had imposed on me. I spent most of that first month with Pattabi and there was a surprise weekend when Mukund came to Madras in preparation for his journey to USA. There was a moment of envy when I looked at them. Did I let these opportunities go, the chance of higher studies, in pursuit of money and a good lay? This would become a habit with me. I would keep on questioning all my actions, in retrospect, and debate on all the 'ifs'. This would drive anyone, who cared to listen, insane.

The support of Mukund was what I needed to pull the legs of Pattabi, about the omnipresent stink of the city's seen-to-be-believed huge open drain. This went by the name 'coovam'. There was no corner of Madras that escaped this stink. This was an unbelievably huge sewage flow. At places it was wide enough to be labelled a river. Covering such a vast expanse with something similar to a roof was an impossibility and the citizens of the city had no respite from the assault of the stink, round the clock, seven days a week. Many in the city had learnt to live with that smell and I was not one of them. I knew for certain that Madras would not be a place for me to settle down and never made any concrete plans towards settling down. How could I subject my delicate Maria to such an ignominy?

This was the longest period I stayed with no letters from Maria. How could she? Not willing to accept 'no' for an answer over a piece of paper, I did not give her my address where I could be contacted. I was willing to wait for my journey home after the first month. With two days left before my travel, I received a letter with the unmistakable handwriting of Maria. I was nervous. It must have been Priya from whom she could have collected my address. The opening of my heart automatically removed her father as a possible source for obtaining my address. Young ones in love consider their parents as natural enemies. Here I was already considering the two of us in that situation; while the fact was I had no clue about what she thought. I kept looking at the letter and was scared to open it. Could not she have waited for two more days? I sensed something wrong. An answer in the affirmative would have been more appropriate in person and the choice of an impersonal piece of paper confirmed to me the presence of bad news within.

When the rest of the office broke up for lunch, I stayed back, mumbling something indiscernible and opened the letter. It had only three words. No salutations; no endearments; no signing off. It simply said, "I HATE YOU."

The capital case was hers and not me trying to emphasise. I was devastated. I read those three words over and over to understand whether it could mean something else. What could it possibly mean other than what it clearly conveyed? Did I move too fast? Should I have waited till the end of her graduation? Unanswerable questions were flooding my mind. The questions were immediately followed by a surge of pure panic. Had she spilled the beans to my parents or her parents? I was ready to confront my parents assuming she would say 'yes', and with her by my side, very much in a theatrical fashion. I always assumed she would keep the matter under wraps if her answer were to be a 'no'. This appeared cruel. She had an option to say 'yes' or 'no', no doubt, but could she not have been gentle and open and in person? I looked at that letter for the last time before putting it away; Pattabi would never see this letter I swore to myself. Something caught my eye. The upward curve of the last letter 'U' had a clear smudge, as if by a drop of water. Then it struck me. It was not a drop of water; it was a teardrop. She took nearly a month to write and she had cried while writing that letter. This meant she was still soft in her heart. My hopes were rekindled. I was now certain that she would melt like wax in my manipulative hands. With a renewed hope, I set off two days later for home and my future wife.

The train made it possible for me to reach only late in the evening. So any chance of getting the issue sorted out had to wait till the morning. I did not sleep well that night. My answers were in monosyllables to all the questions that my mother posed. My father was not home, which was normal. Priya was unusually quiet and was giving me loaded looks, which convinced me about Maria getting the address from her. There was still hope. She had not gone to her parents or mine. I was pleased with the way things had shaped up so far. I was sure of Priya's support when the moment came. None of these were good enough to give me a good night's sleep.

The next day, after my parents left for work and Priya to her school, I ventured out and placed myself in a spot, where I was certain to encounter Maria, and at the same time away from any prying eyes. Our locality was still small and gossip was in the blood of every inhabitant. I could see she was crying when I saw her. What did she tell at home or were her parents not bothered about the puffed eyes? She decided to pass by me and go on walking. For once, I was playing my cards right. I did not stop her, nor did I call out to her after she passed me. She slowed down, as I knew she would, and turned slightly and I was there, waiting. She exhaled sadly, approached me, and stood in front of me. "Why are you doing this to me? Is it some kind of perverted joke? Can't you see it's not possible?" she broke down and could not say anything more.

I must admit that her spoken English was becoming better.

A thousand seraphims were dancing in my mind. She did not say she did not like me; she was questioning the possibility, *rather the impossibility*, of the idea. Did it mean she was not averse to the proposal? I had to be careful. "If you are done with this silly crying, I have something to tell you," I said with no trace of excitement that was building up inside me.

She wiped her eyes and looked at me, with no resistance.

"I do not care about this society, or what my parents or your parents would say. I decided four years ago that you would be my wife. I still mean it. All that matters to me is what your opinion is?" I was carrying more conviction as I continued. I did not know that I could be this precise, "Say yes and I am willing to wait for your graduation to get over. We will break the news when the time is right." I was also improvising. I was slowly turning the first person singular into plural, drawing her into the vortex. As I was speaking, I was certain that it was just a question of time, and only the 'when' mattered. It was no longer going to be 'if'.

Then I sprang it on her when she was listening to my blah blah without any warning, "Do you like me or not? I repeat, will you be my Jenny?" It sounded ridiculous even to me.

It is difficult to judge the way a woman's heart functions. At this most stupid of all statements, she blushed and a smile crept in to her face. That was the happiest moment in my life. It meant she was willing. May be I should have got her confirmation before going to Madras. It was unfair on this poor girl to weigh all the combinations and oppositions, all alone. I told her to keep quiet about this episode and asked her to write to me regularly. It was agreed that it was possible that I could write to her at her college.

The next day Mr Antony came home and I was ready to flee. It was purely a casual call on my father, as he was passing by, and he also learnt that I had come. I breathed easy and even asked him about the well- being of his wife and Maria. "They are alright. Only Maria looks a little preoccupied; but she is not coming out. May be her exams."

You had to be a parent to be such a fool. I said yes, it was possible and I would have loved to meet them, but was in such a tearing hurry, and would he be kind enough to convey my regards? He and my father left soon after that. I was in the hall, reading the latest Ludlum. My mother had gone to the temple when Priya came to me and asked, "Has she said 'yes'?"

I jumped and immediately scanned the house to see if my mother was around. She told me that my mother was not in the house and repeated the question. I did not have time to ask her whether Maria confided in her, but I needed some support from within when the time came, and answered in the affirmative.

"I do not know whether it is correct or not. I do not even know whether our parents or her parents will give their consent. All I know is that Maria is a wonderful girl, so don't break her heart." Grave words and delivered with complete conviction and for the first time I noticed that Priya had more maturity than anyone of us did.

I returned to Madras after another tryst with Maria and could meet Pattabi only at the railway station as he was leaving for Bangalore. Getting him away from his parents was a huge task, but my beaming face must have hinted to him the victory even before I blurted out the truth, amidst the cacophony that is normal on a platform. He gave me his sphinx smile and wished me well. All of a sudden, I was feeling claustrophobic in Madras. My friend had left, and I did not like the city, and the unfinished business with Maria had been cemented, and what needed to be done was only the eventual showdown, with possibly the inevitable result. Maria became more regular than my mother in sending letters. Old habits die hard. Her letters still spoke about her academics, imminent exams, recent results and her future plan, again in academics, after her graduation next year.

I had to be very imaginative, or needed a magnifying glass, to spot any hints at the love that was blossoming. I, on the other hand, was becoming bolder with no one to censor my activities and poured out my love in all my letters. She had preserved all my letters and it was looking very silly when I read them once, after my marriage. Her letters slowly became to bore me and the continuity only helped me to rest in peace, knowing that the embers of love were still glowing bright in her also.

We decided that she would continue with her Masters also as I needed another two years to settle down. I had no idea what it meant. I needed time to confront my parents and in the most likely event of being thrown *out of the house*, wanted to be sure that I could live on my own with Maria. I had appeared for an interview and was selected for a job in Bombay in my second year at Madras. Maria had started her post graduation and hinted to me her worries, as her parents were on the look out for a suitable boy in their community. 'Idiots,' I said to myself. Were they blind? My parents, who began their career and were about to retire from the same place, were finding it difficult to understand this change of job culture. They were against it in principle. Loyalty mattered to them most and they were trying to convince me as to why I should continue where I started. They were also worried about Bombay. Bombay, for them, represented the nadir of human existence, where morals were loose and conduct unspeakable.

I had made up my mind. The money was better and secondly, I had vowed that I would never let Maria suffer Madras. The money part I could not explain to my mother because any amount more than the daily expenses made no sense to her, and the second part I could not tell her, not yet. There was a brief period between leaving the company in Madras and joining the new one in Bombay. I spent that time at home and convinced Maria to postpone any firm steps by her parents towards her matrimony, citing the postgraduation course. We had agreed that the coming year, when I return home on my annual trip, we would break the news to our respective families and seek their consent. Maria was particular that the wedding would be with the consent of the parents and we would not do anything foolish like protagonists in a movie. I teased her by asking what if their answer were to be a 'no', and she replied that would never happen. I wished I could have shared her confidence.

It was another year, at least, before I had to face the prospect and I was a grandmaster in procrastination. I did not want to spoil the one year with unnecessary complications. Our period of courtship was markedly absent in any physical contact. Maria was firm that we would not tarnish the dignity of pure love. 'Rubbish!' I thought, but did not voice it out. I, who normally found errors in everything that my parents said, was totally in agreement with all that she uttered. I was grateful to her for accepting me.

If Madras assaulted my senses with its weather and the stink, Bombay knocked me out with its indifference. No one paid you any attention and none volunteered any help. You were on your own. The money, which looked good, began to lose its sheen when I looked at the rents and day-to-day living expenses. I managed another paying-guest accommodation and after a few days of eating out, decided to start cooking at home.

You face a hurdle in every act. And for every hurdle, Bombay provided you with an easy solution, not always legal. Few years in Bombay taught anyone to ignore rules and regulations and become an expert in *getting a job done.* If you had money, and knew whom to approach, the job was done. I had discovered the many layers that Bombay offered. For every restaurant that charged preposterously, there were ten food joints where you could get a full tasty meal for a pittance. Shops near King Circle and Flora Fountain offered you books at throwaway prices. The topics ranged from Camus to Nancy Friday, Nietzsche to Anonymous. Most of my famed collection of books, and some very rare ones, were from these pavements of Bombay. The city did not allow you to rest. That was a luxury you could afford within the confines of your house, but outside you had to move, else you were jostled and pushed along or out of the way.

The experience of travelling in a local train in Bombay is indescribable. One has to experience it. The weather was as bad but the promenade of Marine Drive could lift the spirits of even the most pessimistic and a stroll along that curved footpath, finding precious old books at Flora Fountain, walking to Gateway of India and sitting in front of The Taj, with the book bought that evening open in your hand, for a quick assessment was a perfect way to unwind in an evening, before embarking on the nightmarish torture of the journey back in a local train. I was enjoying all that Bombay had to offer and identified locations to take Maria when she arrived as my wife to the great metropolis. I had never before fallen in love with a place like I did with Bombay. I simply loved Bombay.

Then came the rains! Rain for me till then was an annual event around Diwali time, lasting for about a week. We never even maintained a proper umbrella. If you waited a little, you could venture out in less than forty minutes (the longest known duration of a rain). Many a time the rains stopped in the time you took to locate an umbrella. In Bombay it poured. It rains non-stop from end of May to middle of October. Not mere drizzle, but torrential. The whole city became a common single sewer. Marine Drive became inaccessible for safety reasons. Barring a few, the other shops on the pavement vanished. It was impossible to commute. The trains ran, but never could maintain their famed schedule. There was one day when I was stranded with three hundred other passengers in a compartment, meant to carry one hundred and ten people, for fifty minutes between Dadar and Matunga station. For someone who had been living in Bombay, this was normal. Almost everyone had something to do, even while stranded. Housewives cleaned the vegetables they bought, groups of four played cards – a very complicated game that I never followed despite trying hard, another group started singing hymns with accompanying musical instruments, sick in mind youths peeped into the ladies compartment and many would read Times of India for the tenth time. It was an art to hold a proper size newspaper folded, in the small space that you occupied, and read. Humans are adaptive and I also got into the groove of the 'Bombay way of living' during the monsoon. What is more, only a city like Bombay is capable of the fervour it displays during the Ganesha festival, in the middle of the monsoon.

I was enjoying my new job. While no one helped, no one interfered either; and I had a free hand to do my job. I was methodical (the lesson I learnt from my last, last as in final, chess tournament) and was blessed with normal intelligence. I could not only manage well, but also make an impression. What I lacked in creativity, I compensated in diligence. Fortified by a favourable appraisal by my boss, I set off for home, afraid for the first time at the enormity of the task ahead. Maria was in her final year and she would not be able to put off moves by her parents any longer, and we had to go ahead and have the cat out of the bag. My mother was no less of a nuisance. She had been hinting at my 'settling down' in all her letters. She was never direct and I never bothered to answer her indirect volleys.

I told Maria that I would break the news at my home and try and approach her family through my parents. She, when asked, could just accept and there was no need to bring to the surface a combined conspiracy. It was difficult to get my mother alone at home as Priya's presence was as constant as my father's absence. With no option available, I arranged to have Priya visit her friend and prepared myself for the ordeal ahead. I was prepared for all the emotional blackmail and balderdash about society, norms and culture. I was prepared for a long-drawn battle. I knew I had to battle my mother for a few days before the matter ever reached my father. Then the second half of the battle would begin. If successful, the battle would shift grounds to Maria's residence.

Maria had no clear plan on the course of action in case of a refusal, and I did not want to burden myself with that thought. I would be careful, I told myself, to break the news gently to her, build a good base by a calculated preamble and indulge in worldly-wise talk about the changing times and iconoclasm. I did not know the Tamil equivalent of the word 'iconoclasm', and was not sure whether my mother would understand what the word meant if I said it in English. One thing I was certain: this could not be rushed. One had to handle this with velvet gloves.

"Mom, I would like to marry Maria," I said. "Antony's daughter." I added as if that was the required additional qualification.

Mothers live to dread this day all their life. Due to a combination of many factors, the mothers are always the recipient of such news in the house and they are expected to carry the whims of the children to their husband. It is not fair to them. The sons or daughters despise them if they do not convey it properly to the father, and the husbands blame them singularly for this debacle, as if suddenly all parental obligations and responsibilities are no longer a united effort. "I love" is a statement no mother wants to hear from her unmarried children. If it is used to appreciate a movie or a book, or to express affection to a dog or to appreciate food, it is alright. But as in loving someone, with an intention of marriage, the word is strictly forbidden. The double whammy for my mother, as expected, was romance with Maria.

It must be said that she carried herself with more restraint than I thought she would. She kept the book, she was reading, down. She looked up and I was startled to see her eyes glistening with imminent tears. I was never comfortable with tears. I was not prepared for it so early in the scenario either. The battle began. Each argument was met with an arrogant counter argument. There were hints from my side bordering on the extreme, should there be a negative answer. I left the extreme steps in the realm of the unspoken, as I was sure an implied threat worked better. I expected the battle to last long and my miscalculation was only in the apportioned slots. A nominal day or two with my mother, a long-drawn proxy war with my father and an equal period when the battleground was shifted, was how I had predicted its run. The duration of the battle was as I expected, but my mother took almost the entire period. She tried all her tactics – refusal to discuss, sentimental to the core, the family history, the social banishment that was certain to follow, and anything that occurred to her was put to use. She was actually hoping to avoid this matter going to my father, which I did not realise and started disliking my mother for being so adamant.

When it was clear to her that I would not budge, she told my father. She was scared of Anand's mood swings and asked me not to be present when she broke the news to him. Though shocked, my father did not object to the choice once my mother made it clear to him about my determination. He did not like it, of course. He also saw it would be better off if the marriage went on with their consent, instead of without the fact Mr Antony was his colleague could have helped a little. I would never know why my father agreed without the anticipated fiasco. I was thankful that I did not have to face him and explain.

The next day he asked me if I was serious, as he would need to talk to the girl's parents. I recalled that it was a first direct conversation between us in quite a long time. Our interactions normally remained very formal and personal conversations were not in recent memory. I still could not look him in his eyes when I spoke to him and said 'yes' looking at the bathroom door. With a sigh of resignation, he walked out. I could have spoken to him as a grownup son and tried to find out whether he really accepted my choice. If his answer had been a 'no', I could have explained to him. I could have told both my parents that while I realised the pain I was causing them, to marry someone other than Maria would have been more painful for me. Did not they also think and agree that Maria was a fine girl? Would not they also be interested to know that their son was granted his choice?

I did not.

It was enough for me to know that my mission was successful and I was now confident that the matter ended. No more twists and turns. Bhaskar came home that evening. I had not met Bhaskar after I went to Madras (after my confirmation from Maria that her heart also longed for me) and I was worried. Did my father give the job of discouraging me to his friend? I just courteously wished him and walked *out of the house* before he could start his assigned job. I was at the grounds, near the railway station, worried about this new turn of events. I could be indirectly rude to him but my parents would never tolerate outright antagonism, and if it came to the worst, I had to complete my interaction with him. Differences of opinion never gave the freedom of insolent behaviour in my household, though I was granted more liberties in this area.

I saw Maria running towards me and my heart skipped a beat. Surely Bhaskar had completed the damage at her place before he ventured into mine. How could my father stoop so low? I noticed the smile only when she was almost on me. She regained her balance and propped herself on the wall in front of me.

"What is so funny?" I snapped at her.

She was too happy to note my tone or the curtness. She narrated how Bhaskar had come home about an hour ago. The gnashing of my teeth could have been heard if she had been paying attention. Along with my father. It was Bhaskar who did all the talking, while my father only gave the support, by his presence. Not once did Bhaskar reveal that it was my wish to marry Maria. He presented it as the desire of my parents to ask for Maria as their daughter-in-law. The two families had known each other for a long time and they could not think of a finer girl than Maria, their religious beliefs notwithstanding. It carried more conviction. It was no longer a marriage being sought by the children; it was an act of parental desire. Bhaskar conveyed that Amar had accepted the proposal, and if they and Maria agreed, the families could proceed on further arrangements. My father could never have thought about it. It must have been Bhaskar's idea. Presented thus, the element of iconoclasm was blasted away and they shook hands surprisingly fast. Maria was asked, of course, and no prizes for guessing what her answer was.

I felt ashamed for walking out of my home when Bhaskar came in. May be he came in to tell about the confirmation. I did not care. At that moment, all I could see was Maria, still so voluptuous, still so attractive and to be all mine.

Soon.

30

Neelam

The 'soon' turned out to be another fourteen months. The date was decided in December the following year to allow her to complete her education and time for me to take root in Bombay, whatever that meant. Gopal's family was the first to be informed about the proposed match. The arrangement was explained to the whole family as an agreement conceived by my parents, and gracefully accepted by me. The love angle was removed and my parents were left to answer many questions, some unpleasant, at this strange matchmaking. I could have stepped in and bailed them out. I could have told all – that the choice was mine and my parents were generous enough to accept it. It could have saved them heartburns and restored my pride. I saw an easy way out by keeping quiet. My purpose was over and fourteen months on, though it could have been shorter, Maria would be Mrs Amar. So why bother about clarifications?

Priya was aghast at my behaviour and would ask me often why I had kept quiet, "Why don't you tell them that it was your wish? Or are you suddenly ashamed to accept that? I have never seen someone who is more selfish than you."

It irritated me, partly because what she said was true. I decided to don the garb of the elder one and told her that she would not understand if I explained. She did not challenge me, may be she concluded it was not worth it, which was good, because if she had, I would have had nothing to say in my defence, as there really was nothing. The period of officially being engaged gave us new concessions.

Pattabi told me, "You cannot ride the cycle, but you can ring the bell." We could write to each other openly. Maria had started frequenting my house regularly and she and my mother took to each other quickly. Maria was interested in finding out the way of being a Hindu and my mother was not a very demanding lady. To my delight, my parents accepted her easily and for Priya it was just a transformation of a good friendship into a firmer relationship. The danger of putting women together lies in their basically garrulous nature. My mother, for reasons unknown, decided to be frank with her and Maria was soon in possession of all the details about me, including the graphics on the book cover. She pulled my leg so badly in her next letter that I sulked for two weeks and did not reply to her. Why my mother could not have been as good an editor that I had always been?

The seasons of Bombay were flitting by and the marriage day was surprisingly close. I had been performing well in my new job and by any stretch of definition, it could be said that I had settled well in the city and was capable of handling my family, which is Maria and I. My parents never asked and it never occurred to me. What is more, I had not sent any money to them from my earnings. That they did not send me money any more was considered enough for me. I was not good in saving and I almost spent all the money I earned and it was a shock to me that I had nothing substantial with me when I left home for my wedding.

I reached home with my mood downcast. Even the prospect of meeting Maria could not cheer me up. The ever vigilant eyes of my mother spotted the trouble and she responded in the only way she knew. Point blank!

I was consumed with shame and told her about my careless ways of spending all my earnings, and no saving whatsoever. She replied by saying that the marriage was the responsibility of the parents and there was no need for me to worry about; but she politely told me that she hoped that I would start living with more responsibility after my wedding. I lived on a very short vision. Once my immediate concerns were addressed, I had nothing to worry about. Tackle the future when we reach there, I told myself.

My marriage was different on many counts in my family – mine was the first wedding outside the community. I also was the only one to go through the marriage ritual twice with the same bride. To keep both the families happy, we completed our three-day affair of a Hindu wedding and followed it with one at the church. Pattabi came to the wedding, Mukund could not, but he sent his wishes after I informed him. Pattabi dropped something in my coat pocket with a conspiratorial wink and it turned out to be a pack of Durex, a well-known condom brand. A pack of three! How thoughtless!! I said to myself as I had made a decision that I would not have intercourse with Maria on the stupid 'first night' that happened after the wedding. We had things to discuss – her life with me, life at Bombay, the crazy bunch that passed as my relatives (my biased view, as usual), her wishes, mine and a thousand other things.

The compromise I had made in converting to non-vegetarian food had not been told yet. I wanted to break that suspense in Delhi Durbar at Grant Road, Bombay. The finest mutton biryani in India is available there. She needed to be handled gently. Though we had known each other for years, there had been a marked absence of physical intimacy. We would both behave like mature individuals, stepping into their life together with clear vision and understanding. We would not reduce our holy matrimony into an act of urgent copulation at the first opportunity. I did not tell any of this to Pattabi but these were the thoughts that coursed through my mind when I fingered the pack containing three condoms. It was as good that I did not tell him anything, as I used up all the three condoms on that night.

There was only so much one could talk when closeted with someone like Maria in a room filled with the seducing scent of jasmine. The proximity and the fact that she was mine officially increased my longing to a point beyond possible restriction and my first act of copulation proved to be a bigger pleasure than I imagined it to be. I could fulfil a part of my promise. I decided to stay up all night and talk; at least I stayed up all night. To waste time on going to sleep with someone like Maria in your arms seemed blasphemous.

The unbelievably complicated task of getting ready to leave for Bombay began. I had never before travelled with so much luggage. Maria's mother accompanied us and I still do not know why? It was a prevalent practice, then, to send an elder in helping the newly wed settle down. It was a contradiction. The newly wed only wanted to be left alone. As my mother was still a working woman, the honour went to my mother-in-law. I had nothing against her in principle, but could never forgive her for daring to intrude into our initial days of intimacy. Of course, I was thinking only about Maria; in our bedroom, on the kitchen table, in the bathroom, on the living room carpet; the few places I had fantasised had to be shelved, all except one, due to the presence of her mother. That her presence was a great help to Maria in a new place, a place as indifferent as Bombay, never occurred to me.

Maria had better sense in financial planning and she took over the task of distributing my salary into necessary expenditures, allowable extravagance (isn't this a perfect oxymoron) and savings. I would soon realise that the bank balance started to grow regularly, without any noticeable drop in my style of living. Impulsive purchasing was booted out and any spending had to be planned. This was an act I was not good at and I happily handed over the finance ministry to Maria, one of the few wiser things I had done in my life. Maria's mother was an exceptionally quiet woman and I was not a natural conversationalist. This combination led to a total of about thirty words in exchange between us, and very soon a period, that seemed appropriate to her mother, passed and she wanted to return. I was glad, but would not show it, and registered a formal protest, imploring her to stay back a little longer. This interaction alone used up about ten words *out of that thirty*. Maria was genuinely pleased at my request, taking it for real, which reconfirmed my opinion that women could be impossibly naïve while I was worried about the possibility of my mother-in-law agreeing to the absurd proposal.

She was smart or she longed for the comfort of her hometown. She decided that she should go. Bombay could be difficult for someone who did not know Hindi, and my mother-in-law, like everyone else from South, did not know anything about that language. Maria knew Hindi. I had no idea where she had learnt, and I would brush up her spoken Hindi in the initial years.

I had planned the day well in advance. We would go to see my mother-in-law off at the railway station and after a stroll on the Marine Drive, I would take her to Delhi Durbar. Neither Maria, nor her mother, said anything about non-vegetarian food in the time that her mother stayed with us, and I took this for the general decency that they displayed. I planned it all wrong. I did not expect Maria to be so sentimental. She was crying at the station which I considered normal, after all, this would be the first time for her to stay away from her parents, completely. She was not hardened by the experiences I had, and had spent her entire life till then with her family. She was crying when we went to the hotel. This I considered slightly abnormal. She was not her usual curious self and did not enquire about our destination. This however, suited me fine, as I wanted to spring that as a surprise on her. Though it was a great restaurant, it could have done better with its location. One had to cross the well-known brothel to reach the restaurant. It looked odd to me to cross those lanes accompanied by my wife when only months before I had used the same road with gay abandon, and at times even ogled shamelessly at some of the well-endowed prostitutes, who stood in every door and window. She was so preoccupied that she did not even notice these women, and I felt relieved.

Maria was still crying, silently of course, when we positioned ourselves at a table, which I found ridiculous. I asked her to take hold of herself lest the waiter thought that I had raped her, after abducting her. This was in poor taste and did not go well with her. She asked for the menu and I delivered my practiced laugh of derision. I told her that people did not ask for the menu at Delhi Durbar. Everyone came here for only one thing and we would go ahead and order the best they had to offer. She flinched when I said that the best in question was their famous mutton preparation. This could happen only in some stupid movies with cross-religious marriage as the central theme – the hero and the heroine trying to outwit each other with meaningless sacrifices. She told me, very casually, that she had stopped eating non-vegetarian food the day she accepted my proposal. She knew we would marry and she wanted to fit into my household and this was her first change in the lifestyle. I was angry. All my plans and surprises had evaporated. Almost as an afterthought, she asked me about my consumption of meat. I could not help being sarcastic and told her that I also could be considerate and accommodative. I told her that I started eating meat for the same reason that she found it necessary to stop, and remained sullen.

The dinner was a disaster. She was not ready to budge from her resolution and I did not want to have the famed preparation all alone. That must have been the only day, in his entire lifetime, that a waiter delivered vegetarian fare at a table. I could be difficult, which Maria learnt that day. It was not fair. She had as much right as I did in readjusting personal choices and was equally entitled to keep it away from me, much in the same way I had mine from her. In all probability she planned a similar situation to spring the surprise on me. Between the two, she chose a better option (PETA was taking shape and vegetarianism was catching up) but I was too self-centred to realise or appreciate. I could have chosen another day to display my erratic behaviour.

The departure of her mother coupled with my sullenness was too much for her, and she continued with her silent crying. This silent crying could get on your nerves. It was quite uneasy to spend time together without conversation, but to spot a continuous stream of tears could do two things to a human being – make him mellow or drive him to frenzy. On me, it did the latter. I told her that she should have gone with her mother, if the parting was so painful. I waited for five years, so a few more months would not have mattered. I actually said that also. I never stayed behind to complete an argument, because I usually ran out of logic and sense, as most of my arguments were anyway over trivial matters, or on the wrong grounds. I left her looking dazed and went to the bedroom and for good measure slammed the door shut.

Only someone, as heartless as I, could actually go to sleep after such a performance. I was capable and so I did. I woke up around four in the morning and was baffled to see I was alone in the bed. I got up, slipped my feet into the slippers and noticed a light beneath the closed bedroom door. I panicked and opened the door. What I saw in the living room would stay with me forever. Maria sat in the chair where I had left her the previous night, still silently crying. It was heart wrenching. How long had it been? What must have passed through her mind in those hours when I slept like a log without a care in the world? I had never felt so miserable in my life. It was instinctive. I sat besides her on the floor, hugged her legs and said something I have never said before in my life.

"Sorry" I said and started to cry. This startled her even more. Her staying there was not a punishment for me, but plain grief and clear shock. My reaction to her state of helplessness melted her like wax. We were soon a jumble of arms wiping each others' tears and consoling each other. The physical proximity, the pressure of the last twelve hours, and this sudden comfort and understanding in each other, led to two things – to the completion of one of my fantasies, having sex with my wife on the living room carpet. Like father, like son. I was conceived, against all odds, on a rare night of depression. My child was conceived that early morning, when we made love to each other, with tear-streaked faces.

The confirmation that she was pregnant with our first child came about twenty days later. She had missed a cycle and when the delay was more than what could be considered normal, we went to a doctor for a check-up. We were not prepared for the news. We did not know how to react. We knew it was sudden and we did not plan it this early, but an emotional union in the early hours normally does not wait and look for contraceptives to be employed. We accepted it, as we had no other choice. We would have very much liked to have spent at least two years before having our first child, but we did not implement it properly. Maria insisted on calling home to inform the news. Only women could be so casual about these things; men could be hypocrites. To my horror, she called my mother and told her the news, while it would have appeared normal if she had called her own mother. I did some mental calculation to see whether my first child would be born in time to celebrate my first wedding anniversary. It might just miss it. Somehow that looked like a relief.

Women either go through their pregnancy in a fairly normal way or suffer every day with nausea. Maria suffered. This meant another visit by my mother-in-law to look after her and they both left in the eighth month of the pregnancy. My pleas that Maria could deliver the child at Bombay were rubbished immediately, and I came to the same conclusion that it would be better if Maria went back home. After they had left, I felt devastated. I had never felt lonely before. Years with my aunt, life in a hostel and the few years on my own before my wedding had taught me to enjoy solitude. Maria in the last eleven months had taken such a strong hold of my life that I felt orphaned by her absence.

I had cancelled my original application of leave and rescheduled it to match with the child's arrival. We informed the doctors that we were not interested in knowing whether it was a boy or a girl. I reached home and immediately left to see Maria, who was at her mother's place. She never looked more beautiful than she did that night. We kept talking late into the night, and within two hours of having slept, Maria nudged me awake, with her face grimaced in pain. We rushed her to the hospital and my radical view of staying in the delivery room along with my wife was negated by a fairly conservative doctor – a bespectacled, short, overweight, sixty-odd lady, and I was confined to the corridor outside. My mother took a day off and stayed with me while both our fathers were conspicuous by their absence. My father was not around when I was born and it was not fair to expect him and I had no idea about Mr Antony. Then a nurse came out and said the three sweetest words I had heard till then, "It's a daughter!" I then did something which I used to do regularly when I was a child, but not in recent memory. I hugged my mother.

That vacation of mine flitted by and before I could realise, it was time to return. I wanted to take Maria and Neelam (that's what we named her) with me when I returned. My daughter was not even a month old and even Maria did not agree to the proposal. The whole family went nuts over the new addition and my father, who was never comfortable with children, barring the initial days of mine, admired her from a distance most of the times.

Priya was in her college and she continued to remain a mystery. There was no exuberance in her and she was an exceptionally quiet girl. All her acts were methodical and it was impossible to find fault with her. She was not beautiful in the classical sense, but very pleasing to look at. She was never conscious about her looks and if she ever appealed to anybody, it would be because she appeared impossibly clean and fresh. She was exceptional in her studies and was all set to land a good job at the end of her college. My father would retire in two years and my mother, two years after my father. My father did not have someone like Maria to guide his finances and his savings were very near zero. He had acquired no properties either. With children around the house all the time and a never-ending stream of responsibilities, he managed life on a day-to-day basis. With the prospects of my parents accompanying my family ruled out, the honour went to my taciturn mother-in-law again. I found it strange that Maria was more comfortable with my mother than hers. Priya became Neelam's godmother, a concept not strange to my family (Bhaskar was already my godfather) but one proposed by me as if I invented it with my half-baked knowledge on Western culture and Maria with her Christian roots.

I had noticed something different about Priya but could not locate what it was, and I told Maria about my observation. "She is smiling!" Maria replied. It was so natural an act that I failed to notice it and it was indeed the first time I had seen her smiling. Priya was very comfortable with Neelam and she took the title of 'godmother' a little seriously. Maria gave me an impossible list of things to be done, goods to be procured and arrangements to be made before mother and daughter reached Bombay. I was beginning to feel the responsibilities of a married life. A wife, a daughter and in a few years' time my parents would join me too. I never questioned that. They had to, as I was their only son and here I would face a few surprises. They delayed it as much as possible. and might never have joined me but for the persistence of Maria. May be things would have remained better, if they had stayed where they were.

I did not know that it would be possible to have someone other than Maria to occupy my mind most of the time. I had spent the last seven years thinking about Maria, that it looked impossible for someone to share or dislodge her place. But it happened. It was the incredibly delicate fingers of my daughter that I missed, when I left for Bombay. Inside the house, in the last few minutes before my departure, I bent down and kissed my daughter goodbye, and was almost at the doorstep when I realised that I had *not kissed* my wife. I stopped and turned and Maria looked at me knowingly with a smile that dimpled her cheeks that had the capability of making me delirious. I went back and placed my lips on hers and whispered, "I love you" to her, all the time looking at my daughter.

The day I reached Bombay I circled the date of their arrival and started my countdown.

31

Good...Bad...Ugly

I lost track of days once they arrived. If I had slept almost twenty hours a day, when my father was operated, I now hardly slept. The girl of mine, who could be such an angel, proved adept in being a demon when she chose to. She slept the whole day, when I was in the office, and was fresh by the time I returned. I crammed my house with toys that she would not be able to use for another three years. Affection for me had to be overt and materialistic. Subtle love was something I never grasped and I smothered my daughter with things in which she had no interest. My evenings were heavenly and I talked with my daughter. I refused to make silly sounds and always held a conversation with her, a thing I copied from Ishwaran; there was not much that was original in me, any way. Of course, I did not know that this trait was something that Ishwaran *himself* had copied, from the father of one Mr William Lowell Kane, from the novel Kane & Abel by Jeffrey Archer. Her responses were usually a dollop of drool on my nose or a slap in my face. We used to retire to our bedroom early and I insisted on seeing my daughter being breast-fed by Maria. She did not like the idea and when she failed to give me an answer that would convince me to look the other way, she gave up.

"I am not looking at something new," I would tease her when she initially was against it.

"That is a very insensitive and crass thing to say," she replied with an edge I had not detected before in her tone.

Neelam would finish what was apparently her dinner and start making sounds that only a child could. She would be fresh and active. She would crawl all over us and any intimate moments I was dreaming of with my beloved, would evaporate. She would tug my hair, try to eat my nose, deposit saliva all over me, put a finger in my ear and urinate on my chest. The volume of urine a child discharges is unbelievable. I used to marvel at the energy reserves and patience of Maria. She would clean the child, change the nappy and put the child back in the bed as many times as the child decided to soil the bed and its occupants. She would wrinkle her nose when I just lay there without even changing my inner garment. Everything dried fast in Bombay's heat and any way, she would piss on my new dress soon as I changed into something fresh. The urine of a child, still being breastfed, did not have an odour. This would continue at regular intervals. Neelam chose her place of discharge at random, but, for some strange reasons, I was the recipient on maximum occasions. Maria's routine, at getting Neelam cleaned and ready, would remain constant, whether it was at ten in the night, or at four in the morning. We lapsed from a semi-comatose state to an absolute slumber only towards the morning, and that too only for a few hours. The duration of this peace was dictated by Neelam, who could be whimsical. We slept little. I forgot the last time I made love to my wife. But we were happy.

There used to be regular phone calls, from a public telephone booth, near my home, to my mother. Maria and my mother exchanged information about Neelam and I noticed an absence of any mention of my name, or news about my welfare. The focus in their conversations had shifted from me to my daughter, while my focus remained firmly on the ticking meter above the telephone, displaying the amount being spent on that call. I would tell Maria that if she had prepared well what she needed to speak, and cut down on useless routine exchange of pleasantries, the call charges could come down by half. She would reply with a look that one normally reserved for the stinking carcass of a rat in the gutter. Money was not an issue with my decent earnings coupled with Maria's prudence. I could be a pest on petty issues and despite its apparent stupidity, persisted with my agenda.

I started everything with great enthusiasm, but could sustain none for long. The journal I maintained on Neelam was meticulous for the first three months, but it petered out with time and altogether stopped by the time she was a-year old. Even the schedule of vaccination suffered the same fate. I insisted on methods and systems in every day-to-day activity, a fallout of my professional side and could never accept the fact that Maria could remember the date for the next vaccination without referring to anything written. I would insist on her maintaining a written record, which I started, but did not pursue.

She was casual and prompt, while I was diligent and erratic.

We were left on our own when Maria's mother left after a period of time she considered appropriate. Though the responsibility was scary, life was enjoyable. Neelam resembled her mother and I was thankful for that for I was sure she would grow up into an attractive girl. We had a surprise that year as Priya came to Bombay to spend some time with her goddaughter. She had just finished her graduation and has been accepted in one of the nationalised banks with her initial posting in my hometown. She had time on her hand and could not think of any other place. I insisted on taking her around Bombay but she was not interested. There was not much that interested her anyway. She started resembling a normal girl only after the arrival of Neelam. Neelam remained the same despite passing months. She slept the whole day and remained active most of the night. The scene of Maria and I walking around in our society building, with Neelam cradled in our arms in the middle of the night, sometimes even as late as four in the morning, was quite regular. The night watchman, that every society building in Bombay employed, would have found this strange, if he had remained awake. The night watchmen in every building slept the whole night, as it was an additional job for most of them and I used to wonder why we ever employed them. I was earning enough and our expenses were minimal. Further, thanks to Maria, the balance in the bank was fairly decent. Life was good without any complications. One can trust one's wife to throw the spanner into such an arrangement. This is what Maria did.

She got this crazy idea that we should own an apartment. In Bombay! When I had no interest in a matter, I generally ignored it. The scheme was crazy. Bombay's accommodation prices were outrageous, and why now, when my father did not own an apartment in his entire life, and he was close to his retirement? I was not interested. My lack of interest and Maria's determination to pursue the idea to its end, were equal. Maria qualified to be a monomaniac. She could organise her defence and assault on any set agenda with military-like precision. Every topic I started in the ensuing days ended with the purchase of a house we could call our own. It made no sense to me. It demanded commitment, something I abhorred as a concept. Unable to fend it off any longer, I acquiesced to do a back-of-the-envelope calculation, to assess our affordability. This I agreed to as I saw the proposal impossible to execute. It was alright to dream, but reality demanded cash and not some promises.

My initial exercise destroyed her hope, as it was clear that though we could afford the initial down payment, there was no way we could survive on what was left of my salary, once the payment of monthly instalments began. It was an open and shut case. Though it was pathetic to see Maria so downcast, I was elated after winning the battle so easily. I had sense to contain my elation. I commiserated with her and there was only one way I knew to celebrate, or mourn, when Neelam slept that night for a change, to allow me to perform my act.

It was a premature celebration as Maria renewed her battle with new strategies. We had not considered the tax sops, the jewels that could be sold, the rent we would save and any help we could demand from our parents. The open and shut case was opened again and with no fight left in me, the battle was over before long and I threw in the towel. I managed to buy my own house, no – my home, without any help from our parents; something that my father never managed in his whole life. That I did not have eight dependents or scores of other responsibilities were not reminded as I did not verbally boast of my achievement. Our life became difficult, no doubt, but to sleep under a roof that you could call your own was a great feeling.

With passing years, the burden became manageable and ceased to be a problem to address. We made compromises and minor changes in our lifestyle, but nothing that was impossible. My father had retired two months after our housewarming ceremony. Maria started renewing her plea for my parents to come over and stay with us, though I never understood, why. I did not miss them and I saw their arrival as an additional responsibility and an invasion on our privacy. My parents were not still mentally prepared to make a shift to Bombay and the invitation was kept on hold on two very valid reasons – my mother was still working and because of Priya. Though the first of the reasons would evaporate in another two years, the question of Priya was open-ended. Maria kept stressing that an invitation from me would look more appropriate and was wondering why I was not showing any initiative. I was never comfortable with straight questions and Maria did not ask any other type. I evaded with my usual craftiness, as I did not want to end up as a stonehearted man in her esteem. I breathed easy knowing at least two more years would pass without a need to contemplate this. Maria never allowed me to rest for longer durations. Within six months of achieving the enormous task of possessing our home, I was made a partner in search of Neelam's school. I had gone to school when I was six-years old.

This need, when my daughter was hardly three-years old, did not make sense to me. We scouted the neighbourhood and finalised on a pre-nursery to put our daughter in. The sum in question towards her first year in school outstripped my expenses at the engineering college, hostel included, and all four years'. My mother retired soon and Maria's pleas were renewed. The fact was that my father was into his routine of dividing time equally between his two passions. He had cut down on his drinking, whether due to the prevailing of sense, albeit delayed, or reasons financial, was not known. My mother had reached a stage where she was thankful for every minor mercy. Priya continued to be a puzzle. Her inclination to remain single was not questioned initially, but efforts were put into action, once she started her job. She remained steadfast in her resolution. Family meant my parents and my family to her. This single-woman status gave my father an excuse not to shift base. In the absence of Priya and the implied responsibility, it would be impossible to resist the advances of Maria. Whenever Maria told me to take an active role in convincing Priya to get married, I refused, citing honouring one's privacy as the basic decency, though the real reason was that her independence meant bringing my parents to my home. I was all for financial support, if needed, as I still did not send any money to them, but to have them around full time was not appealing. I had never liked my father and my mother's failed efforts in scuttling my union with Maria and a few things remained fresh with me. It was alright for them to be cozy together now, but the fact was that my mother had tried her best to stop the marriage. I never forgot and rarely forgave. The spinsterhood, which Priya selected for her, suited me fine.

Maria was explicitly cheerful when she called me on the phone at my office. She said she had good news and wanted to tell me personally, so would I be home on time? It made no sense to me. If she wanted to tell me in person, why waste a phone call to tell me that? I had a premonition that this good news was not going to be good for both of us. She was wild and incoherent in her enthusiasm. The gist of what she said in forty minutes was this:

Priya had got a transfer.

She would move to Delhi.

My parents were coming over.

For good.

By Christmas.

For the first time she noticed that I was not really excited and asked me what the problem was, with real concern. I did not voice all my inhibitions and changed my worry into a concern over how would the two of them adjust to Bombay and some such nonsense. Her knitted brows straightened at once and she laughed away my worries that everything would be alright. I prepared myself for the inevitable. Any other son would have been joyous at the prospect of uniting with one's parents after nearly fifteen years.

Neelam must have been a reincarnation of the Lady, as she and my mother just did not get along well. Neelam found something amiss in everything that my mother did. My parents were not used to 'freedom and children' together as a concept, and while my father knew how and when to keep quiet, my mother had to don the role of enforcing discipline in Neelam. We practiced non-interventionism in our approach, the result of child psychologists and the convenience it offered. Neelam found it difficult to get on with my mother, who took part in everything. Neelam considered the demonstration of affection as an intrusion of privacy, and many an evening, I would return home to a tear-streaked daughter and an indignant mother. Maria tried to be a bridge but failed miserably. My mother was still very fond of Maria, but in her opinion we did not know how to rear children properly. My father soon found ways of keeping himself occupied, and not knowing Hindi, never came in the way of finding the bigger and more attractive race course, though his days of playing cards were clearly over. They were still financially independent of me as their collective pension and their severance pay was substantial. So I never interfered with what my father did with his money. I would advice my daughter to keep her interaction with my mother to a minimum to avoid these conflicts and thereby incurred the wrath of Maria.

"Is this an advice a father gives to his daughter? You also should notice that she is adamant sometimes. Your mother is saying only what is good for her. After all she should know better. She had brought up more children than we ever would. You are spoiling her in the name of affection."

I would think of Ishwaran and his elder brother and their gory end, as an example of my mother's track record in bringing up children, but kept quiet. I knew what her reaction would be. My approach to a problem had always been to find ways of circumventing and here I and Maria did not match. The home which looked big enough now appeared small, and as expected, my intimacy with Maria had to be kept inside the bedroom. If there was one thing that had not changed over the years was my obsession with her. I still loved her as much, or should I say, I still longed for her flesh.

Neelam started complaining about nausea and would often stay quiet, longer, with a face twisted in grimace. After allowing the usual stupid period of time to pass, when we tried all explanations and medicines, Maria decided to approach our paediatrician when we spotted a slight trace of blood in her urine. This, we kept away from my parents, as my mother's tendency to slip into hysteria was known. Our doctor concluded on a possible urinary tract infection, which was normal in girls, particularly in monsoon, and asked us to contact him if it persisted. The traces of blood went away, only to return again stronger, accompanied by more instances of uneasiness. We went to the doctor again and this time he took it a little more seriously, and ordered a battery of tests. The matter could not be kept away from my parents any more, and we briefed them, actually Maria briefed them, and my mother's diagnosis was immediate. According to her, the child did not eat properly and slept late and less. If she corrected these two habits, she would be a sprightly young lady. I wished life were that simple, but did not say anything. Unknown to us, my mother would commit offerings to many temples for the welfare of her granddaughter. The dreaded day of finding what ailed our daughter arrived.

"About one person out of every 750 is born with a single kidney, a condition called renal agenesis. It is more common in males, and often it is the left kidney that is likely to be missing. If you have a single kidney, you are unlikely to have any problems. In such congenital cases, the single kidney works harder and achieves 75 per cent, instead of the expected 50 per cent," the doctor said, as though reading from a text, though there was no visible sign of any such text. I did not understand the need for a lecture of some hypothetical condition, statistically proven to afflict one in seven hundred fifty and the sheer terror I saw on Maria's face drove the point home – the doctor was talking about our daughter. I was glad that Neelam stayed at home and did not accompany us. It would not be fair, or practical, to withhold the information from her forever, but she was anyway too young to understand this. How old was she? Not even seven. I stopped listening to what the doctor was saying.

But he droned on, "Many are known to have lived their life with a single kidney with no noticeable complications (the catch is in 'noticeable' I thought to myself) and we do have treatments to assist the single kidney perform effectively, and in the case of a donor being available, well, the problem is over. Of course, we will have to look for some one with the matching blood group, as it's not as simple as an eye transplant. It is possible. But we do not have to worry about it right now. She is young and all young ones are fundamentally healthy. Ensure she drinks enough water and give her lot of fruits."

I was inconsolable. It did not look fair. Maria had to become mentally stronger after looking at how hopeless I was. The atmosphere in my home was like a funeral that evening, and we told my parents that we would discuss after Neelam had gone to sleep. The grave look, combined with a hint at a discussion in the absence of Neelam, was enough to drive my mother mad and she started throwing abuses at most of her gods, thankfully not very loudly.

I was in no condition to speak and it was once again left to Maria to explain everything that the doctor said to my parents, including his assessment that the situation could still be labelled as under control with the distant possibility of a donor being found. She then called up her mother and parted with the news. It was decided that the matter would be kept under wraps and there was no need to tell everyone. The problem within a family is that everyone tells only one person, and soon the matter becomes a common knowledge amongst everyone.

I became withdrawn and quiet and Maria was now worried more about me than my daughter. I had been planning a second child in our household, as I had missed a brother or a sister as a lonely child, but this news destroyed my confidence. I was confused. I did not have the courage to go through the prospect of a second child with some other complications. I had finally made up my mind and convinced Maria that we would not go ahead with our second child. That was the least of her problems. The family became a group of individuals driven by guilt. For reasons unknown, it is a common practice for elders in the family to hold themselves responsible for any ailments that the children suffered. We were no different. Maria was more practical and she carried on with the certainty that there was no grave danger immediately, and her faith in finding a future donor was laudable.

A future problem can occupy one's mind only that longer with constancy, and over a period of time, slowly fades into the background. The threat it poses is always there, though shadowed by the assurance of the quiet, before the threat becomes a reality. Anyhow the family learnt to limp back to normalcy.

It was a warm and sultry Saturday evening when my father announced that he had been to the doctor, and carried out a few tests to confirm that he could donate his kidney to Neelam, and would like to do it. He had already completed the paperwork that was necessary, and as there was no urgency, the actual transplant could take place when Neelam was old enough or after he died, whichever was earlier. He said it without any emotion or drama. The silence of my mother meant that she knew. We left it at that and did not discuss it further. Maria had tears in her eyes.

"Wasn't that wonderful? What Dad said?" Maria asked me in the bedroom.

She never said "your Dad", it was always just Dad; I could never be that comfortable with her parents. Those were exactly my feelings too. I could never be appreciative of my Dad, and despite what he said, I did not want to agree with Maria wholeheartedly. I had to look as indifferent as I always managed to look. Why? I had no idea. I had to say something smart and curt. It was a compulsion. "If it comes to that, I hope the kidney in question is capable of processing blood without traces of alcohol," I replied.

When two people are lying besides each other on their back, it is difficult to slap another one. Maria managed it and turned away to cry. The slap was feeble and the act hurt, while the actual slap did not. May be I deserved it. I did not make any attempt to console Maria. I knew she would not listen to anything that I would say that night. I was also confused. Why did I say what I just said? Did I actually mean it? Would I ever say this to my father on his face? Then why did I say that to my wife? Was she right in slapping me, even symbolically? The famous soliloquising of Amar had begun. It would go on with no real conclusion till I slept. I knew myself well, so I surrendered to the relief that only sleep could bring.

Maria would not forgive me and I had to apologise to her for what I said, to get her back to normal, though in reality I did not care. It was almost a month before she became normal. In my memory that was the longest that she stayed that way in our married life.

Rewind.

Anand could not believe what he had heard. The apartments of Bombay are built with maximum space utilisation and terms like carpet area, built up and super built up ensured that the walls were thin. Sound carried easily from one room to another. His son was not trying to be quiet and Anand wanted to believe what he heard was just a joke, though in poor taste. Jodhi was fast asleep next to him, removing kidneys of Shiva, Vishnu and Lakshmi with a trident, without anaesthesia, in her dreams. The sound of what appeared to be a mild slap and silent crying followed. He remained there, unable to bear the fact that his son meant what he had said. He was not good in soliloquy. He had learnt to bury his sufferings. Only this time he repeated what he was well known for when he was a child; he cried – silently, without waking up his wife.

The tremors in his right hand started that night.

32
Parkinson's Disease

The affliction was not noticed in the initial stages due to the fact that my father remained outdoors most part of the day. The slight tremors he noticed were ignored as a result of lack of sleep, the strain of recent events, the scorching sun, sapping humidity or a combination of some of these, or, all. The evenings were not dwelt on mutual scrutiny, as each was lost in their own world of miseries and hopes. Neelam spotted it first as she was fond of my father, may be due to her incompatibility with my mother.

"Stop drumming on my leg," she told my father one evening and possibly that was the first time my father also noticed the involuntary movements of his fingers. He made an effort to contain it, but failed, and so he concealed his hand with the other, like a boy caught with his hand in the cookie jar. All of us paid attention to the transaction and the efforts my father was making. There is a general inanity that elders are capable of looking after themselves; and it is only children who are taken to a doctor when an anomaly is spotted. If there was something wrong, my father was old enough to spot and organise a visit to the doctor. Or so we thought. It never occurred to us that those symptoms unfamiliar, or never heard, or encountered before, could lull you into a catastrophic complacency.

My mother stopped disciplining Neelam after her medical reports, and while one could not say they became the best of buddies, a noticeable absence of animosity was easy to spot. All grown ups must have some imperfection. The desire to become a perfect torturing mother-in-law was the case with the Lady, the obsession of gambling with my father, an absence of pure unconditional love in me and a compulsive drive to correct children was with my mother. I was still too consumed with my blinding passion to spot anything amiss with Maria, or may be she was perfect.

With passing days, the martinet in my mother surfaced again and it was wartime once again between them. Maria balanced the job of a good daughter-in-law and a loving mother with consummate ease. I addressed it the only way I knew – I paid no attention and made no efforts. Neelam would often rush to me in the early days with complaints on what she perceived as unfair. I feigned a headache, remembered an urgent errand or buried myself deep in an office file. Children are very observant and soon she realised that I was avoiding the issue and she stopped embarrassing me. It did not mean that the problem ended; it just shifted its court of arbitration.

On those rare evenings that my parents went for a walk, rare because my father was not available most of the times, he would tell my mother to go a little easy as times had changed. "I am sure today's children have a greater sense of responsibility due to the freedom they are granted. They are more intelligent and their easy approach need not be confused with, or, as a lack of respect," he would reason with my mother. Either she had her mindset on what was correct, or she was not used to this much conversation from her husband. She had decided on a course of action and nothing dislodged her course easily. My mother became an expert in finding fault with everything that my daughter did. The soiled school uniform, the dog-eared books, the stray puppy that she befriended and housed in the society, the way she walked, the friends of hers, the time she returned home in the evenings; it was a fact that Neelam could have benefitted from this disciplining. She was caught in between two extremes – the parents who believed and allowed her to be free; and one grandparent, who also believed her, but wanted a modicum of restraint. She had inherited some of my genes, Neelam, I mean, because she became an expert in handling the problem her grandmother posed; she ignored her. She was never insulting in her manner or posture, I was thankful as I did not want another dimension to the domestic chaos, but could be irritatingly stoic.

This classic paradox of an irresistible force meeting an immovable object was put on overt demonstration virtually every day. History was repeating itself. My daughter started disliking my mother in much the same way as I disliked my father. If someone were ever to ask me as to what I disliked in my father, I would have returned a blank sheet. Imagined prejudices and unresolved differences proved to be vital and final in both instances.

Maria was caught in the crossfire. She respected my mother and loved my daughter and was distraught because she could not bridge the gap, the two allowed to grow between them. Once in a while, she would start discussing this predicament with me. Discussion was not the correct word here, as the word indicated an active participation of at least two individuals. I remained silent on all these attempts. When asked why I was not venturing any opinion, leave alone a solution, my answer would be a cryptic, "What can I say?"

Whether this was a good answer or not I never knew, but this made continuation of the discussion impossible. Maria knew when a cause was lost and she did not pursue this for long. She resigned herself to this imbroglio and involved herself only in damage control. The free time my father had at his disposal helped him draw closer to his daughter-in-law. His sisters left him only boys, and he had only a son. Barring Priya, he never had an opportunity of living with a daughter. When Priya was growing up, he spent so little time at home and now for the first time he was enjoying the comfort that only a daughter could offer. His demands were little and Maria was consideration personified and the two of them hit off very well. She was surprised to find a sense of humour in my father and this she found very appealing. *I did not know he had one.* This proximity of Maria and my father brought to the attention, the continuation of the tremors, which were now fairly permanent. His fingers would tremble on their own volition like that of a flautist mentally practicing various tunes. This was now accompanied by an involuntary curling of his toes inward whenever he was seated. Neither of these was noticeable when he was on the move. Maria first asked my father about this. He confided he noticed it recently, and though slightly odd, it was not coming in the way of any of his activities. Not yet. In fact he knew the exact date when the tremors began, but was not in a position to tell her. My mother knew only one cause for all her problems.

According to her he was not eating well and sleeping less; he has abused his body beyond its limit when he was younger and what was the point now in mulling over it – this she would confide to Maria when my father was out of earshot. Maria knew me well enough not to approach me for my comments. She decided to take the initiative, as it was anyway becoming regular in my home of late. She took my father to a doctor. The usual routine of a doctor ignoring any major illness and dispensing with harmless medication, took a back seat for a change. This guy happened to be smart and was smart enough to realise that the ailment was beyond his specialisation, and referred them to a specialist. This needed an appointment and they managed one for three days later.

Maria was sharing her worries with me and I exercised a great restraint from delivering a wisecrack. The last occasion was still fresh in my mind. She thought it would be better if I accompanied 'our' father to the specialist. She had no answer when I asked why that would be. In fact she was sensing a rift deepening between my father and me and wanted to play the matchmaker. I was not interested and of late, the interaction between father and son had reached a stage of gestures and nods. My mother considered the entire exercise a waste of time, but did not want to discourage Maria. She also spotted the state of non-communication between her husband and son, but did not know how to go about addressing the issue. Maria and my father went to the specialist for an elaborate test and returned.

About a week later, Maria came to my office after meeting the doctor and collecting the results. This was most unusual. One look at her face told me something was seriously wrong. I wound up whatever I was doing and we sat in a restaurant down by the road. She was in a state of shock and I could not be patient, for I feared the worst with Neelam. I asked her what was wrong and she said one word, "Parkinson."

I did not know she had gone to the doctor about my Dad, nor did I know anything or anyone called 'Parkinson'. Given her Christian origin, such name was not completely out of place. But two things did not fit in; the Christian names from south had a character of their own, and Parkinson did not qualify as a south Indian Christian name; the second was the look of pure sadness that engulfed her face. The story unfolded over two cups of coffee. The fancy name was what was ailing my father. She was sad because the doctor told her that there was no cure for the malady. It could be contained at best with regular medication and the disease was progressive, whatever that meant. She explained that the problem would gradually grow and the rate of deterioration was unpredictable. Honestly, it did not affect me one bit.

If I showed that, I could kiss my wife goodbye. I put on a serious countenance and made all the proper sounds at the correct intervals. She would have seen through my charade on any other day, but that day she was consumed with grief, and did not. Why all these tragedies should befall our family, she lamented. Regarding Neelam, I had no idea; but in the case of my father, I was certain. He had it coming to him. I just heard the name of the disease for the first time, but I was sure it was caused by everything that my father had done, that he should not have done. This covered a vast ground and again I had the sense to keep the diagnosis to myself. Unlike in the case of Neelam, there was no point in holding the fact back from my father and she insisted on accompanying me back home, where the two of us would break the news to our father. My lame excuses would not work and I did not make any attempts. I just dropped in my office on the way back, converted the one-hour break into a half-day leave and accompanied my wife back home.

My mother was alarmed at seeing me back earlier than usual and the sad face that I practiced and perfected led her to conclude that something was wrong with me and started fussing over me. The comedy was that my father was not home. Half a day of my leave wasted and to still make good of the leave, I went off to sleep after telling my mother I was alright, and hoping that Maria would tell her everything. It was later that evening that we broke the news to my father.

"We" is used here in a loose sense because it was Maria as usual. The impact of the news on my parents was zero, as what you did not know, did not hurt you. The description of the disease was easy in English but there were not many equivalent terms in Tamil to explain it lucidly. May be there were, but we did not know. Maria managed to convey the gist; the problem in question was a neurological disorder with no immediate cure (she improvised a little to dilute the seriousness). Continuous medication and the recovery demanded a cut down on outside activities (the last remedy was invented by my wife on the spot, as she did not want my father to be out in this foreign city on his own with this Parkinson's stuff). It was slightly anti-climatic.

If the problem had been identified as cancer, or tuberculosis, the identification and reaction would have been on the predicted line. A new disease that carried the name of a gentleman did not scare anyone easily. Maria would read all there was to read about the illness and started briefing me about some famous personalities who were affected. Mohammed Ali, the greatest, was one and it was understood that the incessant blows he received in his boxing days were one of the reasons. It was a little ironic as I was the one who received the blows and my father just delivered them. If anyone qualified, it was I and not him. This time I could not hold myself back and shared this observation of mine. Maria looked at me curiously and asked, "I cannot be sure whether you are serious or joking most of the times. It is our (again 'our' and not 'your') father we are discussing and you are trying to be funny. I am serious and am worried. It says that the disease is progressive. Will it mean he will deteriorate slowly? I am used to seeing our father active and lively and I do not want to see him confined to a chair."

The womenfolk of Tamil Nadu were greatly influenced by the thespian actor Shivaji Ganesan, who portrayed many roles in which he died due to all known diseases that are catalogued. He had a vast repertoire of films and was able to cover the entire spectrum of maladies known to mankind. I was not sure whether it included Parkinson's. This melodramatic actor was invariably confined to a wheelchair in his dying moments, irrespective of whether he suffered from leukaemia, or leprosy. It was quite natural for the women to imagine a dying man, a slowly dying man at that, in a wheelchair and Maria was no exception. I had become an expert in knowing what to share and what to keep to myself.

The regular medication began. The medicines were to be taken every day at the appointed time. Like all medicines, these also had side effects and the doctors insisted on never missing a dose. A missed dose or an overdose would have negative effects and he was advised to stick to a regular suggested pattern.

Inderal

Pacitane

Syndopa Plus

I learnt to remember them by heart without referring to a prescription. Not difficult, when you end up buying these tablets on the first day of every month. On some occasions, the shopkeeper did not even ask me and packed the stuff when I stood at the counter. It was as regular as buying grocery for the house. Maria became the Florence Nightingale of the family. Though my mother was ready to take the responsibility, it was Maria who administered the medicine at the allotted time, seven days a week, every week. In my opinion if we had allowed him to move around as he used to be, the progressive nature of the disease would have met with some resistance.

The progressive nature of the disease became exponential in a docile, stationary patient that my father slowly became. I was alarmed to see the instability that was settling in. He was withering away in front of our own eyes. The lack of motor control was now accompanied by a slur in his speech, and a once proud man was now being reduced to a sad caricature. My mother, who did not take the malady seriously at first, was driven to despair at the speed with which the monster was consuming my father, and she renewed her association with all her Gods. This gave a respite to Neelam as she was spared from the constant scrutiny of her self-appointed mentor, tutor and guardian, all rolled in one.

I, being the narrator of this story, have the freedom to adjust facts and paint a picture of a repenting son, who made up for lost time with angelic behaviour towards his father. That would not be true. I did nothing of that sort. In fact I did not change at all. While paying for the medicine at the beginning of every month, I would put on a face to convince the shopkeeper the burden that was being borne. The fact was my parents still needed no money from me. Why should the shopkeeper know this? Two old people confined to the house needed virtually no spending at all. The confinement of my father to the house meant that he had no avenues to spend. They had no extravagant tastes. Going out on a dinner also dried up, given my father's condition. It was pathetic to watch him consume his food, with his hands so violently shaking. He refused assistance and ended up taking twice the time that he would normally need. This led to his loss of interest in food. Never an avid food enthusiast, this drove him farther away. All their earnings, their pensions, went to the bank and my daughter and Priya were the beneficiaries. Priya came when she heard the predicament and I was surprised to see the camaraderie that she still shared with my father.

My only concern was whether the kidney would remain healthy when it was time for him to die as my daughter's future depended on that. I would try cursing myself for being so selfish and heartless and try practicing to be more considerate. If a performance was necessary to convince someone that I cared for my father and that my heart bled for him, I would have succeeded. I could not fool myself. I did not feel anything for my father and while the physical deterioration of his was painful to see, there was no emotional attachment in my perception. In fact, what I felt could be more correctly categorised as disgust than concern.

The doctor who gave a lecture on the malady and the nature told us that Parkinson's disease had a way of destroying the whole family and not just the patient. I treated that as a case of exaggeration that all the doctors were capable of. He was true. Parkinson's deprived my father of his faculties; my mother of her smile; Maria of happiness. Neelam was young and was not affected except for her genuine sympathy for her favourite grandparent's condition. It affected me because it affected my family. I could not be natural in the house any more. If I enjoyed a cricket match on TV, I was perceived as heartless. I could not listen to music that I liked. It looked pointless to curtail all my natural instincts just because my father was not well. He had done enough to screw up my childhood and now he was completing his mission, destroying my independent life also. That was my perception of course!

Priya asked me whether there was any misunderstanding between me and my father and I was terrified for a moment, thinking that may be my father had said something to her. I still wanted my dual role to go on as before. To the family I should appear to be a concerned loving son. I told her that I look subdued due to his present state. I was not able to digest his plight. I talked less for the fear of breaking down in front of him. I could lie through my teeth. Fortunately Maria was not around as she would have despised me as nothing hurt her more than hypocrisy. It was a tightrope walk for me. I could not afford to let my guard down for a minute. I was not sure whether my answers convinced Priya as they looked thin even to me. The family was falling apart.

With travel for my father ruled out, most of my relatives ended up at my place at regular intervals. Gopal came to see his brother and was inconsolable. I had to tell his wife to control him as his breaking down, in front of my father, would emotionally upset him more. Many of the surviving children that he had brought up, came out of affection and gratitude. These two emotions were alien to me. Privacy in my house was long forgotten. I failed to recall when the last time the home had only the five of us. Maria became a classic example of so near yet so far, as far as I was concerned. It was still not possible for me, after all these years, to look at Maria and not immediately think of rolling in bed. The visiting relatives were not expected to spend the entire time sitting with a forlorn look at my father's feet and the weekends were occupied by taking them around. I must have seen the same show at the Nehru planetarium seven times in less than two months, when I had managed never to even visit the complex in close to ten years. I mentioned to Maria that I had all the qualifications that a tourist guide needed. She was not amused.

This was another new twist. Nothing amused Maria any more. While she participated in all the discussions and shared all her gossip with me, she was a compulsive talker; she needed to tell everything in all its details to me, yet the spark was missing. She was sorry to see my father in this condition and the fate of Neelam, when she grew up, also traumatised her. While she did not ever say this openly to me, my indifferent attitude was not acceptable to her. While I felt the reason for his faster deterioration was in being confined to the house, she was certain that I was part of the reason. She believed in providence and stupid proverbs like 'as you sow, so shall you reap'. She expected me to change my approach but did not have the heart to tell me openly for that meant facing the truth; and she was scared to know what the truth was. She was still considering my indifference at a level of absence of demonstration and did not possess the courage to find out whether the love was really absent. The swarm of relatives also could not continue for ever, and excepting Priya, the visits by the rest slowly dried up – a small relief. I first agreed with the doctor when he said Parkinson's disease affected the whole family; I was wrong. It was an understatement.

33

Continued Indifference

The trip to Europe was what I needed. The home front was becoming stifling; even the ever desirable Maria could not hold all my frustrations down. The presence of my father, in what appeared to be an accelerated path of depreciation; the morose mother and Maria without her trademark twinkle in the eyes were getting on my nerves. Neelam was in a world of her own, and contrary to my accepted belief that daughters were close to their fathers, was close to neither me nor Maria. Strangely, may be it was Nature's way of compensating – she was very intimate with my father; even more so, after he was stricken down with Parkinson's. I would often see them closeted together and discussing. Neelam would talk animatedly and there would be a constant smile on my father's face, almost atavistic.

Organisations have many methods of rewards and motivation. One of the reasonably expensive common means was to send a deserving executive on an overseas business trip. The company declared the expense as educative and research, and got some tax sops. The underpaid, slogged to death executive is suddenly free for a week, and achieves what he will never do with his hard-earned money;

he goes abroad. Usually these 'business trips' achieve nothing. You are normally sent as a formality on a business tie up, already concluded. You are lulled into a make believe that your visit, and the discussions, are crucial to the culmination of the partnership. You know it is a lie, but you believe it. An executive in the fifth rung of the hierarchy gets to meet someone as lowly placed in the other organisation, and comes back with a sense of achievement, that exists only in the combined imagination of the two hapless employees. You return with brochures, meaningless minutes of nonsensical interactions, and even proposals for future tie ups. All that you bring, and hand over to your boss, who graciously accepts them and even starts going through in your presence, is usually dumped into the dustbin even before you complete the process of closing his door behind you. Everyone knows about such trips and everyone plays the charade. To the individual what actually matters is a trip to a foreign soil and the sightseeing that he has to plan in one weekend – that was always built into the itinerary.

The atmosphere in the house was electric. Neelam started making the list of things that she wanted. One look at her unfinished list made me dizzy, as there was no way her list could be completed, with the pittance I got as my daily allowance. Mere acquaintances became friends with the prospect of a Marlboro or a Chivas Regal becoming a reality. Maria and Neelam came to the airport and my father stayed back for obvious reasons and my mother too. My mother was wondering about my food as I was a vegetarian, according to her, for that was the picture I led her to believe, and I convinced her that I would manage. Maria almost exposed me with a chuckle.

"Papa, please ensure my list of things. Do not forget Barbie," from my daughter. She already had seventeen Barbies and it made no sense to me how one more could add any value.

"Take care. I am told that the women there are very beautiful, and more daring. Do not try to become a Casanova. No adventures. Come back safe. I will be waiting." Maria had never before been this blunt about the subject. Her last statement, "I will be waiting," accompanied by a discreet press of hand gave me a hard on.

The executive in the fifth rung of hierarchy is slated to travel economy. The Boeing 747 had ten seats in a row, and I, like all the fools who travel first time, opted for the window seat. The plane took off at almost three in the morning, and all I could see out of my window, was the wing of the plane faintly lit by a flashing bulb. As I travelled West, the journey kept slipping back into early hours and sunlight was seen only when I was about to land. The seats were uncomfortable; there was a constant fight for elbow room on one armrest, which I and the one seated next to me shared. The food was plastic and I had to mumble apologies and step on toes every time I made a trip to the bathroom. Conditions half bad would have invited my wrath, if I had been travelling in a bus or a train in India, but here I was going to Germany for the first time and everything looked perfect. All my body parts and joints were aching when I left the plane, and the time difference made me a little wobbly on my feet.

The first two days I spent little, and ate almost nothing, as I was constantly converting everything into Indian currency. I was also worried at the prospect of running out of cash before I returned. The food was another nightmare. The non-vegetarian fare that I saw was not what I was used to. The meat looked as if it had been stripped fresh, and I was certain, that I would find the remnants of the carcass, if I looked. The ones that looked edible tasted bland. I learnt to live on breakfast, and though there were few restaurants that served Indian food, what they charged was, almost, obscene. One dinner would take care of half the provisions at my home, for a month.

In the shops, which closed at six in the evening, I was the perfect Indian shopper. A walk through the entire shop, sometimes all three floors, regular inspection of articles, a sneak look at the price tag, a quick conversion in mind to Indian currency, and the return of the product to its place with an alacrity of a frog jumping out of the snake's dart. I ended up buying nothing and decided I would buy something on the last day at the airport; and photographed everything. To a normal Indian, every building in Europe was photogenic and I ended up taking photos of a residential building, a supermarket, an array of fruits in a shop, a market square, an ice-cream shop and even a mobile lavatory. Passersby were often amused to take a photograph of mine with many of these ordinary places serving as a background. My pride, in my assumed mastery over the Queen's language, also suffered a huge blow. It appeared that between India and England, no other country spoke English. The days of playing dumb charade, when I was in my college, returned to bail me out. The much anticipated weekend arrived and I left for the city of lights, Paris.

The train journey was as memorable and enjoyable as the plane journey was deplorable. The availability of space and the comforts of a European train have a major impact on an Indian. The inevitable comparison of the daily torture of travelling in local trains, packed like sardines, make it appear even better than it actually is. A journey of some five hundred kilometres was completed in just over three hours and Paris exceeded my expectations. It was a pity that I had only two days to see what the city had to offer when you needed, at least, a fortnight.

The Louvre alone needed more than two days. It looked like a sin if I spent time on regular activities like eating. I had little time and did not want to waste any of that on meaningless activity. I learnt to live on a heavy breakfast and finish off with a light dinner. I was my own guide and charted out my own route of exploration. The first day was simple as I had only the Louvre on my agenda. I had lost myself in its vast offering, and my appreciation went towards the ostentatious and enormous edifices. I had no appreciation of fine art and the paintings of great masters could not hold me for long. I was more impressed with the marble statues. The fact that most of them were nubile nude nymphets also helped. The famous pyramid with its 666 glass panes looked a wasted effort, to me, and it appeared just to be an enormous waste for an entrance. The famous 'Mona Lisa' was another anti-climax. The actual size of the painting disappointed me and however hard I tried, I could not find anything enigmatic about the smile. The garden was more relaxing and the pyramid did look beautiful with lights, but I ran out of my film roll to take more photographs.

The second day I went to the church of Notre Dame followed by a visit to Arc De Triomphe and finished it off with an evening at the most acclaimed spot in Paris, the Eiffel Tower. Either because of my engineering background, or due to its sheer magnificence, the Eiffel Tower appealed to me enormously. The symbolic representation of an erect phallus did not escape me and I stayed on longer than I intended taking in the architectural brilliance, the view from the top and the unbelievable symmetry of the Trocadero. I stayed late into the night, mesmerised by the light show.

The remaining part of my stay, the business part, did not interest me and I was already longing to get back to India. I bought the Barbie that my daughter wanted, and a few more items from her impossible list, a pair of Swarovski earrings for Maria, and the customary carton of cigarettes. While returning, I was smart enough to ask for an aisle seat, and thereby suffered less. It was while returning home, that I realised I had bought nothing for my parents. It was too late, but to reach home with nothing for them, looked odd. I was more worried about Maria getting upset than my parents' reaction. A willing and waiting Maria would be a better lay than an upset one. A week of abstinence had suddenly made her more desirable.

'Poonam Novelties' caught my eye and I stopped my taxi and rushed into the shop. The first thing that caught my attention was a walking stick which looked appropriate for my father. I could not locate anything for my mother, so I gave up the idea of buying her anything. Did not she say that she would be glad with my safe return? While I respectfully doled out crisp dollar bills at the duty free shop, I bargained hard for the walking stick. I returned to my taxi and headed home with a clear conscience. It was close. I was saved by some timely thinking, thank God for that.

Neelam was ecstatic, though none of what I bought for her, would hold her attention by the fourth day. I gave the walking stick to my father with a grandiose gesture. He accepted it with great humility. It reminded him of his state and I thought I should have chosen something more subtle. With a Bombay taxi waiting, with its meter running; your choices were bound to be limited. He had a closer look, turned it around in an obvious look of admiration, and held it by the neck and did not let it go. He refused to even submit it to the scrutiny of Maria or my mother. That I bought nothing for my mother was thankfully forgotten as both my mother and Maria were genuinely surprised at my thoughtfulness.

The evening went by quickly and we retired to our rooms for the night after my mother deposited her offerings at the nearby temple, the bribe she had promised on my safe return. Neelam was very fresh, to my great irritation, and she was brimming with questions about all the places I visited. Thankfully those were the days when I did not own a digital camera and I convinced her that an explanation with the photographs would be more appealing, and told her to go to sleep for the thirtieth time. Maria was amused at my desperation and did not come to my rescue. It appeared as if only I was starving for her warmth. Enthusiastic questions, when constantly met with insipid answers, lose their steam and Neelam also lost her interest in the face of my lack of interest. How could a father tell his daughter that the warmth of his wife was occupying his entire faculty? Her inquisitiveness died gradually and I was never happier to see my daughter go to sleep than that night.

With a slight rearrangement I nestled close to Maria, and breathed in her scent with a glee, that only someone, as famished I was, could be capable of. I had rehearsed this scene all the way back. I whipped the Swarovski earrings with a sleight of hand, which would have put a conjurer to shame. The pure delight on her face added fuel to the situation. Thankfully she did not say much and at the end of a long hour of vigorous love making, the earrings were all that she was wearing, and I, not even that. I made love to her again that night and there were moments that caught us stopping dead in the act, when Neelam turned in her sleep, or talked to Barbie in her dreams.

In the other room, my father remained awake, waiting for my mother to be completely asleep. My mother slept quickly and in her dreams, she saw me shopping at Wal-Mart. She knew very few foreign names and places and spending close to a fortune on a walking stick for her husband made her smile in her sleep. Getting up and moving around now required more effort for Anand and he was aware of that. Still he had to complete the task in the night as continued scrutiny would reveal the faux pas. He was certain and was determined not to allow the sorry spectacle to come to light. He picked up the walking stick and applied his saliva, and the trembling fingers, to the task. What would have been a simple task, if he had asked Neelam to carry out, took him close to ten minutes. But no one else could be entrusted the job. With great care, and with his eyes screwed up in concentration, in the dim light that engulfed his room, he pried out the sticker that said 'Poonam Novelties, Dadar' from the neck of the walking stick, the place where he was holding it throughout the day, at the precise moment his son and daughter-in-law reached their orgasm in the next room. He went to the toilet and flushed it down; staying long enough to ensure that it was successfully flushed out. Light flimsy stuff sometimes floated and refused to be flushed out, so he had to be sure. There was an immense sadness in his chuckle as he crept back into the bed.

The euphoria of the sojourn died quickly, and after thumping through the photo album a few times, the general interest in the family also petered out. I found it impossible to describe the grandeur of the edifices I had seen, in mere words. There was also a tendency to exaggerate anything that was not Indian and it became repetitive after a period. Overuse of superlatives, in continuous succession, ended up with a negative impact. The monsoon followed immediately and my natural reaction to a dirty city, after having been exposed to the cleanliness of Western Europe, appeared to be a show off. After my return I had noticed that my father had become quieter; and it mattered more to Neelam than to me. Life was getting back to its predictable routine. Even a generous organisation could not be expected to send you on attractive trips quite often and I was suddenly looking for some change, a release from my daily routine, and a boring life. Every plan I thought of was vetoed by Maria with one reason – my father. There was no way we could go on a holiday as Father would not be able to withstand the strains of a journey. Who had spoken about taking my father along, I wondered!

Forget going on a holiday, Maria was not even willing to travel anywhere within Bombay either. It would not look proper, was her only answer to every proposal of mine, and I soon gave up attempting to convince her. I realised that I had not been able to lead a normal life ever since my parents had moved in with me. A wasted knowledge, as I could share it with none. I started longing for my freedom days, as I dubbed them, when family meant only Maria, Neelam and I. An arrival of someone from the family made us realise that we actually spoke very little at home. Only Neelam and my father continued their association although even that was slightly subdued. My mother became more reticent and was engulfed in her silent prayers and many dreams. In her last dream, she dipped Mr Parkinson in a vat, bubbling with hot oil.

Priya offered me the relief I was looking for, when she came during Diwali. She came prepared to take my parents to Delhi, as she wanted their comfort and felt they also needed a change of atmosphere. Her decision to remain unmarried had been accepted by the family and no one discussed it any more. She came prepared with her agenda. Flight tickets, coupled with her unadulterated love, swayed even the staunch Maria from her determination. I was overjoyed, but had the sense to keep my joy to myself and tried to look disinterested, as if the whole circus did not affect me at all. My parents were not warming up to the idea and tried to dissuade Priya. They needed the change, there was no doubt about that, but the burden that they would be on Priya was making them unsure about their decision. I was getting nervous and I decided to step in. I had to convert the plan, into a firm journey, without being too obvious. I knew the way the minds of my parents worked and I was going to capitalise on that.

"Forget it Priya! Why do you want to trouble them if they are not really particular?" I waited for some reaction, and when nothing came, dealt my next card, "I am sure the cancellation charges would not amount to much."

Money only meant one thing to my mother – that it could not be wasted. She fell into the trap I laid, and started enquiring with Priya about the amount that she would have to forego, if she cancelled the trip. Priya was not comfortable with the direction the situation had taken, and blurted the amount as she was incapable of lying, at least not to my parents. That settled it. There was no way the airlines would get that money and the journey became a reality. Maria became a nurse again and spent the next two days instructing Priya about the needs of my father, the doses of medicine, the emergency number to contact the doctor, just in case, God forbid, she crossed herself – one act that would not go away despite years of marriage to a non-Christian, and repeated everything to my mother, as a back-up. They were lectured endlessly not to strain themselves, and Priya was told not to ignore any failing signs of health. She (Maria) would call my mother every day. I immediately converted the calls into money and raised my brow and Priya should not hesitate to call on us if anything was amiss. Her concern was so genuine that it bordered on the comical.

"You looked very determined to ensure that parents left with me," Priya cornered me with a day to go. "I am glad they are coming, for I dearly miss them, but I think you have changed. I have a feeling that you are happy to see them go. I have known you for a long time, and I can surely say that you have changed." Priya had this habit of addressing everything straight – the one approach I was never comfortable with, and had this excellent control of delivering all her statements without any trace of emotion. Her voice and tone would have remained the same if she was telling me about the weather update for the week.

There was no way this could be sidestepped. I had to invent on the spot, "You are partly right. I played that money angle to ensure that parents would leave with you. However, there is nothing beyond that. I feel that you deserve their company as much as I do, and I just wanted to do a favour. We are not young any more. The strains of a family life could be telling on me. Do not let your imagination fly." I could have stopped there, and may be she would have believed the bullshit, I just delivered. My whole life had been like this only. I had to stretch and spoil. "You are lucky, you do not know the strains of a family." I bit my tongue even before the last word was fully out. It was no use. The missile hit the target, alright.

She looked at me, with incredulity written all over her face. Her eyes welled but she retained her tears with monumental restraint. I knew my charade was over. She was able to see through me, as if I was transparent. She did not speak another word till their departure. She avoided coming to my house after that and the next time she came was after my father died.

The daily updates from Maria kept me posted about their life in Delhi. They had fulfilled few of their desires. Priya had taken them to Varanasi, one holy city that all Brahmins must visit in their lifespan, the practicing ones that is, and to Badrinath, Kedarnath and some such holy places. I am not very sure, as I was not really listening. Maybe they visited some other places, as I learnt some of these places could involve some arduous journey, which my parents were not capable of undergoing. I was happy once again. There was no need to escape, as home was home once more and I was discovering how charming my wife could be, once again. Maria wanted to know the masculine word for a nymphomaniac, as she wanted to call me that. I murmured 'Amar' and bit her earlobe.

The phone call came on a Friday evening when I was alone at home. It was Priya. She hesitated when she heard my voice and I waited. She said that parents were not comfortable with the winter of Delhi and wanted to return to Bombay. She was putting them on a Sunday morning flight. It would be easy for me to collect them. I was calculating. How long had they been away? Just six weeks.

"Shit," I said after keeping the phone down. Or so I thought; Priya was frozen, with her hand gripping the receiver, when she heard my exclamation, in a rare moment of excellent connectivity, bereft of any static.

34
The Decison

It was a perfect paradox – the digits that had a mind of their own and moved without instructions, and the rigidity that set in. This made the spectacle appear worse than what it actually was. Try shaking your fingers when they are held loose, and try the same thing when you stiffen them, as if ready for a karate chop, and you will understand what I mean. The rigidity and stiffness accentuated the tremors. The rigidity spread like cancer. He started spending a ridiculously long time in stepping into his slippers. His face was screwed in concentration, as he inched his unwilling, disobedient toes into the slippers. The toes curled inward and all his efforts to loosen them or straighten them proved futile. To an outsider it looked as if keeping your fingers and toes stiff needed an effort. To the patients suffering from Parkinson's, it was exactly the reverse. They kept trying endlessly and often fruitlessly to loosen up their joints and failed constantly. The whole period of staying awake was a survival test, a constant battle against the disobedient joints and muscles. When you lose control over fundamentally simple things, like everyday movements, it affects your psyche very badly. The inferiority complex sets in and takes very firm roots. Emotional vulnerability follows unfailingly. The once proud human is reduced to a joke, in his mind certainly, if not in the eyes of the others.

I was never certain about one thing – whether he became dependent because the walking stick was available, or the walking stick arrived when he needed it? The walking stick and he became inseparable soon. He started using it regularly and in my opinion it was more an impediment, than assistance. His strides became shorter and gradually he started walking lesser, and lesser. The sight of him, confined to the chair, with the newspaper clutched in his hand, waving like dry leaves in an autumn wind, was becoming common. The newspaper and the mindless soap operas, which played on the television, occupied his entire time. It was strange – the hold, that these soaps had on the elderly.

The episodes started at seven in the evening and lasted till eleven in the night. There were additional women-centric episodes, which played between eleven in the morning and two in the afternoon. The elderly become a common gender with passage of time. He sat glued to all those meaningless soaps, and soon the discussions that my parents held concerned the lives of the actors and actresses, and their on-screen persona. Listening to them, one would not believe the discussion revolved around fictitious characters. The serials were all so similar, and so predictable, that it never made sense to me on what retained their interests. The new addiction brought in another twist that I could have done without. The timing of a popular serial, almost all the serials they watched, belonged to the popular category, clashing with Scooby Doo or Power Puff Girls. I was brought up when television was not around, and like all men of my age, when it finally caught up, I watched only sports – football and cricket for the game; and women tennis for the shapely legs and wonderful cleavages. Serena and Venus would arrive a few years later and destroy the main reason for watching tennis. Cartoon for me had been a teaser, of a Tom and Jerry, before a full-length movie at select theatres. I could never readjust myself to Addam's family, or the above-mentioned shows, as cartoons. They were as deplorable as the soaps that my parents were addicted to. The remote control of the TV became the most prized possession on some evenings with my daughter and my mother both wanting undisputed rights on what they wanted to see. There was no way this could be settled. I refused to step in for any arbitration and Maria dispensed justice in favour of my parents which made Neelam sulkier.

On the rare evenings when there was a three-way battle, and I was pitching in my claims, my parents withdrew their bids. I was left to watch the games that held my interest, and they were happy just to swap channels during the commercial breaks, to catch up with the death of another character, the swindling of ancestral property, the scheming of the super vamp or any such calamities that regularly befell all the families, in those soaps. Neelam would run to Maria, asking why her grandmother would not show her the same consideration which she was showing to me. Her arch-enemy had been her grandmother, and she never complained about my father, though they were both equal partners in depriving her hours of cartoons. An answer to such questions did not exist, and Maria did what every mother did, "Stop comparing yourself with your father. Learn to respect elders. I do not want to hear such rubbish again from you."

These statements could have been patented. They were from a standard instruction manual, for helpless parents. All the three statements carried prejudices and a child could never be expected to accept them, or believe them. Neelam would slip away quietly, or convert the conversation, first into an argument, and then in to a fight. In the latter scenario, I would step in and utter something authoritative and unfair, which would invariably drive her into a crying session.

The outcomes of such evenings were not the same. The game would continue on television with a sole viewer; my parents would discreetly retire to their room, giving up on their sneaks at the distraught families in commercial breaks; Maria would try and fail to convince Neelam.

In the second scenario, I would change channels to those playing the soaps and immerse myself in some meaningless office files, which needed no attention at all. My parents would feel guilty and change the channel to the one playing the cartoon, but Neelam would refuse to watch.

The third scenario would be that I would switch off the television and march off to the bedroom – my preferred, grand, closing act. The third had the most devastating effect, as it normally left a television and a remote at the disposition of two rival groups, who could put it to use, but did not. The whole thing might appear funny when viewed in isolation or in retrospect, but in real time, it really mattered.

No one paid any attention that Maria never watched anything of her choice. While one would think, that the television would remain switched off during the days, immediately after such an event, had no idea about the functioning of a household or human mind. The parents returned to their solace, as soon as they could and Neelam could be seen, lost, in her fairy world of Power Puff Girls. Tranquillity lasted till the same combination of events played again, unfailingly.

Sometimes an apparently ordinary event takes control of our life and turns it on its head. This happened when I was gifted a bottle of scotch, when one of the guys reciprocated the visit from Germany. I should have gifted it to one of the scores of my subordinates. This would have brought in a temporary loyalty. There was the danger of that guy boasting about acquiring the famous scotch, and while temporary loyalty from one could be assured, a longer acrimony from others was also a certain possibility. It was not worth it. I could have given it to someone outside my office circle, but I did not make friends easily. It had been years since I made any contact with even, Pattabi or Mukund. I brought it home, stashed it in my cupboard and forgot about it.

A few weeks later, Maria told me one night, that the next day was my father's birthday. She wanted a quiet celebration and at the same time wanted to gift my father something. She was weighing various alternatives; a gold chain (at least Rs 8000), a Ray Ban goggles (minimum Rs 2000; and would he not look like Stevie Wonder), a shawl (that was affordable, but Bombay did not have a winter. Winter in Bombay, arrived and departed, in the span of one night, unnoticed, when the city slept), a ring (at least Rs 5000, and it would take you a better part of an hour, just to align the ring with the finger) or something meaningful. What could add value to the existence, that my father called life, I wondered. Maria suffered from the same syndrome of all women. Gifts meant either jewellery or something fashionable, irrespective of its utility. Men on the other hand, are capable of depriving any sense of pleasure and appreciation in the name of utility. None of this appealed to me and the only item I thought worth spending on was a shawl, but it did not fit into Bombay weather. Maria was waiting for an answer, and even a hint of a discussion, on what was there to celebrate, or money involved was bound to be calamitous.

The solution, when it occurred to me, looked so obvious that I kicked myself for not thinking about it when the discussions started. I give my mystic smile. "Leave the gift to me. I have a wonderful gift which your father will very much appreciate tomorrow."

She was prepared for a long battle. The quicker than anticipated capitulation of mine stunned her and in the euphoria that engulfed her, she even failed to notice that I mentioned 'your father' when referring to Anand.

Believe me! I really had good intentions of making my father happy, though the driving force was, spotting an opportunity, not to spend any money. Maria was disappointed when I reached home emptyhanded. She had made it a point not to wish my father during the day, and forbade Neelam from doing the same. The cake, eggless, would be delivered at seven in the evening. She wanted the whole arrangement to be a surprise. My father never remembered any birthdays, or anniversaries, and this included his own. My mother knew, but was not certain how to point out the omission to her son and daughter-in-law without causing any hurt. She decided to wait till dinner. Her plan was to ask Neelam to wish her grandfather a happy birthday over dinner, thereby accomplishing the act of wishing him, if others continued the act of not remembering. For this reason she also did not wish him formally. Maria kept asking to see the gift and I was preaching patience. All in good time was my only reassurance. After the third daughter-in-law of the house executed a complex and devious scheme of tarnishing the reputation of the first daughter-in-law of the family, the serial ended, for the day of course, with a close up shot of the matriarch, naturally a widow, with her forehead creased like Gene Hackman.

Maria timed it perfectly well and the sublime joy that I had seen on my father's face, as the trolley with the cake was rolled in, was something that I had not seen before. He was touched. The ever-enthusiastic Neelam shouted the birthday song. The quicker it was over the better, as no one could be more impatient than a child in front of a cake. My mother was moved to tears. She was thankful that she decided to wait till dinner time, and silently cursed herself for thinking that no one remembered. She was almost correct in her assumption as it was only Maria who remembered. After the cake was cut and consumed, Maria raised one of her eyebrows, an act that drove me mad for I could never do that, in an infinitesimal movement; the universal sign language of a question mark.

I gave her a small nod and went to the bedroom. Neither my father, nor my mother, noticed my disappearance. I returned with the bottle of Glen Livet. Maria was not certain that the 'gift' was in good taste, but she held back her counsel. My mother was clearly unhappy. Everyone in my family knew about the drinking days of my father, but he never drank at home. My father was visibly excited. He had not had a drop in close to a year, and had learnt to forget what alcohol tasted like. That I was not drinking, gave me the courage, to offer it to my Dad. At the unexpected turn of the events, the ladies retired, and I poured a good measure to my father. I stood near the fridge, enquiring whether he would have ice and water, or ice and soda. I turned around when I received no reply. He had finished his first drink. He did not even spend the time that I took in pouring the drink. Two more generous measures were gulped in the same manner and my mother stepped in, calling an end and signalling dinner time. My father took a fourth drink with him to the dining table, and if I had seen him happy in the evening, now he was delirious. I was patting my back on a job well executed. The purse did not become any lighter and the old man was happily drunk.

On seeing how happy my father looked, even Maria started to accept that the 'gift' was not all that bad. I sincerely hoped that another bottle of scotch would find its way, before the next birthday, as this could well be considered a precedent. If I were to buy a good scotch, I was aware of the size of the hole it would burn in my pocket. He did not give me that embarrassment, as he did not live to see his next birthday. After dinner, I told Maria that my mother could look forward to a good night's sleep, as my father would sleep like a log, after downing four large measures of a good scotch.

My mother did not sleep that night. My father had an attack of diarrohea and was dehydrated by morning. My mother was not certain when to ring the alarm bell. When she noticed that my father looked visibly pale, and did not have the strength to complete the short distance between the cot and the bathroom, she panicked. We were woken up at five in the morning by a distraught mother and she was incoherent with tears. The last time I remembered her anywhere in a similar plight was when Ishwaran had slit his wrists, ironically at around the same time in the morning. I rushed to get the doctor, who lived nearby, and Maria started making oral rehydration salt solutions. She always knew how to do the correct thing. He was in an advanced stage of dehydration, by the time the doctor arrived, and the doctor insisted on transferring him to the hospital.

The next four days were a continuous nightmare. His recovery, which could have been faster, was hampered by Parkinson's. He was out of danger very quickly. His complete recovery, still, took four days. It also made my mother hysterical beyond her accepted norms.

For a change, she had a different diagnosis. She discovered a new link between diarrhoea and scotch. My mother was a strange woman. By any stretch of imagination she should have blamed me; but she directed all her pent up ire on my father.

"If your son offers you a drink, you should have the sense to decline. Are we living in America? (anything depraved belonged to USA) Even if you have to accept to keep him happy (!), don't you know the condition of your health? Did you have to gulp so much?"

Her famed monomania came into play again. A few times my father thought about intervening, but had neither the strength, nor the inclination to the task. She would go on endlessly. I was certain that my father would never touch the stuff again. I could have intervened and stopped my mother, accepting the blame partly, if not completely. It might have satisfied my father, even if it had failed to stop my mother's harangue. Of course, I did no such thing. On the second day, when I returned from the hospital, I smashed the bottle of scotch in the bathroom in my only act of violence. I did it out of a directionless frustration. Maria misunderstood that as an act of repentance and never spoke about it.

My father returned home but was never the same again. He had seen bitter days in his life and some better days. The last few years had been very unkind and he was not resilient any more. If continued indifference of his son was silently killing him, the recent outburst from his wife, who had never spoken more than ten words at a stretch to him, knocked him out cold. That the outburst of my mother was but an exhibition of her concern was lost on him. Though she spoke to my father, she wanted me to understand but that was lost on both of us. That there could be a limit, even to the patience of someone as docile, unfortunate and helpless as Jodhi, was also missed. He had become quieter, if such a state was possible.

I felt guilty about the whole episode and did not speak much either. The only difference was I stopped any communication with my mother also. The remaining members of the family made all efforts to keep him in good spirits. Neelam no longer fought for the remote, but ironically he had lost his interest in the trials and tribulations of the television families. He still spent his allotted time scanning the newspaper, but it was not clear whether he grasped any news, or registered any events. He was simply going through the motions that day-to-day living demanded. My mother became the normal mother, which all of us knew, but Anand was not able to forget the outburst. He suddenly looked lost. He did not know whether he had been a good son to the Lady; a responsible uncle to his nephews; a good husband to Jodhi; a model father. He was not sure of anything any more. All that he knew was that his desire to live had been extinguished. This conclusion was the culmination of a process, which many would label as his life, but he had come to a conclusion, and for once he was clear about the next step.

35

The Final Chapter

It was difficult to say who was appearing for the exams. Neelam was in her sixth standard and her final exams were around the corner. Maria's blood pressure shot up as the days to the exams neared. Neelam was as casual as Maria was distraught. Neelam was never very particular about percentages and marks, and she cleared all her papers without being a topper, either in individual subjects, or, collectively. The daughter of an engineering graduate was expected to perform well even though there was no evidence to support this desire. The poor girl had to suffer, and fulfil the unreasonable expectations of the family, or, carry on without paying any attention. Neelam chose the latter. This gave her a reputation of being casual and living without responsibility.

Responsibility is not a word you should attach to the life of a twelve-year old, but the expectations of parents and grandparents often border on the unrealistic. The children are expected to meet all your achievements and fulfil all your unfulfilled dreams.

In a Tamil Brahmin family, like mine, academics rated very high and the purpose of a living was directed only towards academic excellence. Anything less than a topper was labelled as a failure. 'Centum' was a unique word that everyone from my community understood and used, irrespective of their literacy; it meant one hundred per cent. Etymologists may fail in tracing its root and meaning, but it existed in the use of all families, and was the main cause of most of the children's nightmares. If you had scored less than hundred (on hundred, obviously) in mathematics, you were labelled a failure. Subsequent reforms, which made distribution of marks more generous, transformed this nightmare, which was restricted to only mathematics and allowed it to spread its tentacles to science and civics also, and eventually the ultimate unthinkable, even in languages. This was too much on an easygoing young child like Neelam. Forget getting hundred in one subject, she often did not manage that even in two subjects combined. Maria believed persistence and practice would compensate a natural lack of desire to excel well in exams, and was not willing to accept the present outcome. Neelam just ensured that she passed and did not bother to put in extra effort. The girl was not stupid but she did not befit the description of intelligence by conventional norms.

The dilution of my family's Brahmin fixation on academics, by a dose of Catholicism did not help either, as Catholics were as bad in their obsession with formal education and excellence – a double whammy on an ordinary child. My mother would not stop comparing her performance with mine, or when the situation demanded, with that of the impossible Ishwaran. My mother was quite liberal in exaggerating and often inflated my actual performances to have a greater impact. The misconceived notion that engineers are good at mathematics made me the tutor for her in that subject, while Maria handled all other subjects.

I was a bad teacher. My first assignment at *teaching someone had a vested interest*, and I embraced that mission with all my heart and inventiveness. The system of teaching also had changed. I had no patience. I was not comfortable or patient when my daughter spent an inordinately long time to arrive at the result of seventeen times fourteen, wrongly at that. I would ask her to memorise the tables first before we stepped any further, and Maria would argue with me that I was wasting her time in teaching her the fundamentals, with the exam just seven days away. I agreed to it in principle but could not find a way of teaching her how to score marks which was what interested Maria, not any real knowledge, and the sessions had a predictable run.

A convivial start, false hopes, an acid remark at the impossible stupidity on display, brave and sincere attempts, constant lapses, consistent errors, raised voices, silent sobbing, my prediction that she would amount to nothing and her inevitable final act of complete resignation and incessant tears. The order of the above events might change, few parts could be missing, but the general scheme of things remained the same.

Grandparents are an unpredictable lot. My mother, who would make her life miserable with constant and meaningless comparisons, and impossible goals to be achieved, would become her guardian angel, when I became harsh and she started crying. There was no point in continuing this exercise any longer and I became a part-time consultant, from a full time tutor. Over the years, Maria arrived at the span of time that I could hold my patience, and entrusted Neelam and her doubts for durations less than the magical figure. It was difficult to say who was more relieved, when the exams finally ended – mother or daughter.

The desire of a mother and the wants of a daughter are always mired in conflict. If Maria wanted her daughter to attend dance classes, Neelam was interested in swimming lessons. A compilation of such a list could easily fill a lot of space. Sometimes I felt my daughter deliberately avoided doing what my wife wanted. We were, of course, the parents of the new generation and gave in to all that my daughter wanted. This would set my mother on another nostalgic trip, and comparisons between then and now. Neelam would roll her eyes and vacate the place the moment my mother started any statement with "In our days…."

In the absence of Neelam to listen, she would turn her lecturing on Maria about how we were failing in bringing up our daughter. We were spoiling her. If we gave her what she wanted, we were committing the crime of not allowing the child to understand the meaning of the word 'no', once in a while, and affordability. If we refused her something, we were being insensitive and money-minded. I was not certain what her reaction would be to a given situation, and soon did not bother any more to find out. I was sure of one thing – whatever I did, was wrong.

The end of the exams heralded a period of calm that all of us needed. Planning vacations was a forgotten enterprise with my father's immobility. My mother would often insist that the three of us should proceed on a vacation, if only for a change, and Maria would have none of it. Most of my contemporaries had a problem of a rebellious wife, who would not mingle with the parents-in-law, as their main grouse. My problem was an understanding and a submissive wife. Her affection and dedication was not faked, and I admired her sincerity, which I never was in possession of. To be honest, I was increasingly getting concerned about my affection towards Maria, as passing years would surely erode her attractiveness. Maria told me that my father was not getting any better and even his consumption of food had gone down. I had given up hopes of any improvement, and for me an absence of any deterioration, or further complications, was good enough.

If you spend the whole day at home, doing nothing, how much could you possibly eat? Reading newspaper was not an exceptionally calorie-consuming exercise. Of course, these were my thoughts and I was not a fool to share them with my wife. After the scotch incident, I had pointedly avoided any active interactions. If the status quo continued, without the wheelchair confinement, that my wife prophesied, it was as good as it could get.

Gopal and his wife came that summer. It was a surprise to all of us as they had not informed in advance. The popularity that Gopal had amongst the children continued in his old age also. Neelam was always very comfortable with both Gopal and his wife. Gopal was in good health despite being elder to my father. Looking at them together, it would be difficult to believe that Gopal was the elder one. He had a general joie de vivre towards life and managed to remain cheerful, irrespective of what life decided to throw at him. He was a living confirmation to me that people, who laughed more, remained healthy. He was not part of any stupid-looking laughter club. He just managed to laugh most of the time and at most things.

The laughter club, which woke us up every morning, had this gathering in our society premises, and would often make me smile, looking at them uproarious in their forced laughter. The traces of laughter would vanish the moment the group disbanded. There was no laughter in their eyes. I learnt from Gopal that the true laughter could be detected from the eyes, which laughed along with the lips. I learnt but could never practice. I rarely laughed. The maximum I could do was smile. I had perfected restraint in all my actions, except with Maria. Gopal's wife and my mother still shared the same camaraderie that existed in their initial years. There was more life in the house suddenly without any extra activity. The attraction of a big joint family was becoming evident to me. I looked with envy the closeness my father and Gopal shared; the comfort my mother and Gopal's wife relished in their proximity; the unselfish interaction of an innocent Neelam with all.

I was wondering who I would have when I grew old one day. Excepting Maria, I could not think of one relative, friend or even an acquaintance. Did I miss out on the larger picture, in my single-minded pursuit of what I wanted, to keep me happy? Did I ignore the signs and insulted others? Did I alienate everyone in the name of non-intervention? Did I successfully insulate myself from all the problems that my family threw at me, and at the same time, lost the warmth that togetherness could have provided? It was suddenly looking scary. I did not dwell on any subject that was unpleasant for long. I buried the nauseating process of catharsis and went about addressing the immediate act of day-to-day living.

Anand was acting strangely. He was looking at his bank balance frequently. He rounded up all the passbooks and spent considerable time and energy in transferring all the money to a single account we held in Bombay. He replied to my mother that it would be easy to keep track of the money if it was all in one place.

"As if we own millions!" my mother would scorn derisively.

I sometimes felt that the money he was spending on those phone calls was more than what he ended up transferring. An exaggeration, of course! It was my basic compulsion to find fault with anything that he did. He frequently spoke with Bhaskar and Priya. The urge to look at my wristwatch, or at the wall clock, while he was on the phone was almost obsessive. There is a book by name Magic by William Goldman, in which the main character of the book, Corky, who is a ventriloquist, is so addicted to the role of his alter ego, portrayed by the ventriloquist's doll, that in the end the doll controls him, instead of he the doll. My urge to do things that hurt other people bordered very close to this.

The month had just begun. We normally have a very active month end to boost up the sales, and an equally active first week to finish the paper work and project figures at the office. It was like any other day. I returned home, and after the routine of small talk with Gopal and his wife, the evening news and dinner, was ready to retire. I left the medicines with my mother, and was going towards my bedroom, when my father said,"Goodnight."

I looked back, and yes, he was addressing me. It was impossible to read emotions on a face, which was constantly contorted in pain. I tried to recall whether he had ever wished me before.

Nope.

For that matter neither did I. Only Maria had the habit of such inanities, throughout the year, though she never received much reply. I nodded, slightly bemused.

My father died in his sleep that night. He never woke up. He was lucky in my opinion. He had his whole family next to him on his last living day. Priya arrived, as soon as she could, when she was informed. The crying of Priya was heart wrenching. Priya, who did not cry when her parents died in front of her own eyes, was inconsolable. Her pain and misery was evident; her grief, genuine. It made me uncomfortable, as honestly, the only feeling I was able to feel was relief.

Love Tadka@Wedding

By Deepali Nandwani

Price	:	Rs. 125
Pages	:	150
Size	:	5.0 × 7.75 inches
Binding	:	Paperback
Language	:	English
Subject	:	Fiction/Romance
ISBN	:	9788183520935

About the book:

Dr Radheesha completed her MBBS and meets her Prince Charming at her cousin's wedding in Punjab. As luck would have it, she meets not one, but several guys who try to woo her but it is only Abhinav, a handsome hunk who holds the strings to her heart, despite the fact that both are always at loggerheads with each other. Amidst the wedding preparations and different ceremonies providing the backdrop to their tiffs and quarrels, would the two ever realise their love for each other or will Radhessha be left broken hearted? Read on.

About the author:

Dr Deepali Nandwani, hailing from Punjab but now living in Mumbai, is a dentist by profession and fond of reading romantic novels while writing too. Her articles and stories have been published in popular magazines. Her hobby is to dance to popular tunes, old and new.

Love in the Reality

By Hardik Dhamija

Price : Rs. 125
Pages : 189
Size : 5.0 × 7.75 inches
Binding : Paperback
Language : English
Subject : Fiction/Romance
ISBN : 9788183520850

About the book :

The word drishya in the name Drishya Roy means the sight to see a relationship develop and as per the meaning, he did try to strike a friendship with each and every girl he came in contact, but could not build a lasting bond with any of them as he could not forget his past, when he had been sexually abused. So what did he do to get rid of his past and free himself from the guilt of having harmed his loved ones? Did he have the right to fall in love and if yes, would the world allow him to continue? Did he deserve to lead a happy life? What provoked him to build a business empire? This is a story which shows how Drishya Roys story affects Adityas life and makes him realise that love actually means rejection of the practical and adoption of the reality. Will Aditya be able to recover from his screwed life? Despite losing his best friend in an accident and his girlfriend subsequently, with whom he had been in a relationship for at least five years, was he able to find the way to happiness? Read on to find more